SPIN ME RIGHT ROUND

SPIN ME RIGHT ROUND

DAVID VALDES

BLOOMSBURY

LONDON OXFORD NEW YORK NEW DELHI SYDNEY

BLOOMSBURY YA
Bloomsbury Publishing Plc
50 Bedford Square, London WC1B 3DP, UK
29 Earlsfort Terrace, Dublin 2, Ireland

BLOOMSBURY, BLOOMSBURY YA and the Diana logo are trademarks
of Bloomsbury Publishing Plc

First published in the United States of America in 2021 by Bloomsbury YA
First published in Great Britain in 2022 by Bloomsbury Publishing Plc

A catalogue record for this book is available from the British Library

ISBN: PB: 978-1-5266-4219-6; eBook: 978-1-5266-4218-9

2 4 6 8 10 9 7 5 3 1

Book design by John Candell
Typeset by Westchester Publishing Services

Printed and bound in Great Britain by CPI Group (UK) Ltd, Croydon CR0 4YY

MIX
Paper from
responsible sources
FSC® C171272

To find out more about our authors and books visit www.bloomsbury.com
and sign up for our newsletters

To Mikey, the sister I lucked into

Under the Rainbow

THERE IS NO POINT to senior year if it's not all about you.

Let's review: Freshman year is for *children* who have no idea what they're getting into as they spend months afraid of upperclassmen and cowed by teachers bearing homework; sophomore year is when the cis boys spend every waking minute impressing each other by doing the stupidest things while everyone else wishes they'd be escorted off to an island somewhere far away; junior year is for actual academic effort in order to look worth admitting to some school that will bankrupt your parents. But senior year? That's when you rule.

I like to think I rule Antic Springs Academy. Before you get all *oh my god, a prep school narrator* and throw up in your mouth, let me be clear: ASA isn't that kind of academy. It's a boarding school with only about 200 kids, but it's hanging on to life by a thread. You can work off part of your tuition with on-campus jobs and almost everyone does, so forget your notions of rich kids and scions of industry. There are a few silver spoons and a few kids from the opposite end of the spectrum here on scholarship, but mostly we're in-betweens.

I like to *look* like money without *being* money. As in, I had the velvet Vans before everyone else because I started noticing YouTubers in LA wearing them; but mine were factory seconds from an outlet mall. When all the '80s stuff started popping up on TV, I was at TJMaxx snapping up high-waisted acid wash (from the women's section, because, who cares?) while everyone was still rocking their dark denim. I'm always leading the pack even on my budget, which is like hosting a dinner party on SNAP.

Today, I am wearing a silk bowling shirt emblazoned with ironic '50s pin-ups, tucked into massive cargo pants that are cinched perfectly at my waist by a faux-ammo belt. My best friend Nix says I look like an influencer sponsored by a brand of questionable taste, which is, like, perfect. My boyfriend Cheng on the other hand—well, he tries to be chill when he sees me in the parking lot. And by chill, I mean he says something like, "Um . . . that's a look," instead of "Bae, I cannot be seen with you in that." (He dresses better since we started going out, but he still never met a hoodie he didn't like.) We have our morning kiss before we enter the admin building, where all senior classes take place.

2

We can't kiss *inside* the school, even a nominal peck, because it is apparently 1950 beyond those glass doors. Did I mention that for a century ASA used to be First Church of God Secondary School? (Go ahead: try to make that an acronym.) In its heyday—when my mom went here—it had 500 kids who came from all over the US for a good old-fashioned Christian education. But, what do you know? Demand dropped and the school rebranded itself with a new, mostly secular mission to be an "Accessible Academy for All."

It's not as conservative as when my mom attended, but Antic Springs is the land that time forgot when it comes to gender stuff. Not only is there no Gay Straight Alliance, there are still dress codes about boys not wearing makeup and girls not showing cleavage. (God help you if you're Nix and blow past the binary altogether.) But I think dress codes are meant to be broken and I do a lot of the breaking. Right this minute, I have on glitter foundation and my eyebrows took a solid half hour to perfect. No teacher is hauling me off to the bathroom to wash it off, like they did in my mom's day, because even they know that'd be stupid. But more than one teacher has encouraged me to do so myself because boys wearing makeup is not in keeping with "the spirit of things." Please: I *am* the school spirit.

"Luis! LUIIIIIIIS!"

Some unwritten law decrees that there should be only two kinds of high school principals: the ones who like kids and Try Hard to be cool but will never be, and the Demonic Spawn who think of each incoming class as target practice for humiliation and shame. Mrs. Malee Somboon-Fox is a Try Hard, which is sweet but can be incredibly taxing for anyone on the receiving end. It is also useful, if you know what you're doing. If you want her to soften a policy or fund your organization (I, for one, created Student Fashion Club, Mall of America trip, and Green Cafeteria Tuesday), you just tap into her eternal quest for youth. If you're really smart—and I am—you snap up the campus job as Principal's Secretary, which I did my sophomore year. I'm like her personal assistant, hype man, and confidant all in one. I excel at all three, but, seriously, there are only so many ways to answer "Why don't the kids like me more?"

She is making a beeline for me from across the lobby, nearly knocking over the kids taking down last week's banner announcing Senior Day at Darien Lakes Park. "Luis! You look so *FUNKY!*" Mrs. Somboon-Fox literally has the wrong word for every situation. "Don't forget we have Prom Council today! I've already told Ms. Silverthorn you'll miss the end of English."

I flash her my biggest smile. "I'm on it. You know me!"

Mrs. Somboon-Fox smiles back, a wattage to rival my own. "What am I going to do when you're gone?" And then she's off, probably to bring food to the new science teacher, since Mrs. Somboon-Fox is sure the woman hates her, which means the poor teacher is a campaign to be won.

Cheng watches her stride away and then slides his hand next to mine briefly. Seriously, we're not even allowed to hold hands. Everyone (and I mean everyone, teachers to janitors) knows who's gay at this school, but once we walk through the doors, it's all straighten-up-and-fly-right. Unlike in my mom's day, when kids could be kicked out for stuff they did off campus, our private lives are now our own, but our *school* lives are held hostage by a code of conduct written with a quill pen by Puritans. You have to sign the code to go here, but it's kind of a formality (like your parents signing that they won't hold the school responsible if you snap your neck playing soccer, a promise they would never keep). Even my Christian classmates play pretty fast and loose with the pledge to "respect authority as ordained by God." I mean, we're teenagers.

Sliding his hand back into his own pocket, Cheng fixes his brown eyes on mine. "Are you sure about this?" I know he means Prom Council and my Big Ask, so I give him a look that says, "For real?" This shouldn't be in question. Surety is my calling card.

In four years, I have sweet-talked Mrs. Somboon-Fox and the school board into adding an expressive movement elective for PE, un-banning leggings, having dances for the underclassmen, hiring an outside DJ for those dances, and making sure the required reading list is not just full of white people who were already dead when my mom went here.

Not all my quests have been totally successful. Last fall, I tried to get Mrs. Somboon-Fox to require student pronouns on all the class rosters, so people would have no excuse for their misgenderings. To my surprise, Nix thought *requiring* pronouns was problematic, because not every pronoun stays fixed forever. I pointed out that if it was optional, 90 percent of the teachers wouldn't do it, and we'd be right back to the old way of making assumptions on sight, but if it was a rule, teachers would have to comply, and kids could change their pronouns whenever they wanted. It didn't matter in the end: Mrs. Somboon-Fox barely let me finish my pitch before reminding me ASA isn't "that kind of school."

Naturally, as I am not one to accept defeat, I didn't so much change my tune as modulate the key. Under the gun, I can adjust really, really quickly to my circumstances, so I asked if it could be *allowed*. Mrs. Somboon-Fox said she hardly had time to go room-to-room policing class lists, so, in a way, it already was. She wasn't going to promote it, but I took it upon myself to nudge every teacher I thought might go along. I only got two takers, the school's oldest and youngest: Ms. Silverthorn (an early adopter by nature, despite being, like, sixty) and Mr. Kuranchabi (who is such a millennial he brings his avocado toast from home). That's two more teachers than, probably, ever, so it goes on my list of minor victories (though Nix likes to remind me that optional pronouns was their idea all along).

Today is going to be my biggest move yet. I'm going to remove the line on the prom ticket that says your date has to be the opposite sex.

I *know*. We're two decades into the twenty-first century and some schools are still buggin' over a pair of boys wanting to dance together. I mean, we have gay World Cup winners and pop stars and governors now. Gay dads doing corny dances with their kids is a staple of TikTok. And there was even a trans hero on *Supergirl*. Can you really get more mainstream than that? So you're asking yourself where the hell I live—is it the Deep South, maybe that town that staged a decoy prom to keep the lesbians away from the real one? Or some former Soviet Republic that sends police to crack down on Pride? No. Antic Springs is in upstate New York. The supposedly liberal northeast. Which only proves what every queer person already knows: prejudice, like fire, can live anywhere there's oxygen.

This is farm country, so maybe prolonged exposure to, I don't know, *silos*, makes people fearful of the gays. The towns here (including mine) are pretty small but always have room for at least three churches, and everyone's in everyone's business. There's no public high school in Antic Springs—if you want that, you have to go to Schuylerhook Regional, which is like a half hour away, with kids from six other towns. We only have the Academy and that cringeworthy code of conduct. So, farm country + old-school rules = no gays at prom. I'm about to change that.

This isn't just for me and Cheng. There are two more not-exactly-secret queer couples and a few more students who would bring same-sex dates if they could. And even in a small school, we have four kids beyond Nix who use them/they pronouns, so this policy doesn't just ban them—it ignores they exist. This is about justice! This is about equity! This is about—

Okay, fine: I want to be prom king.

Before you judge me, *everybody* wants to be prom king. Even, maybe especially, those who say they don't. Why wouldn't you want to know that your classmates picked *you*? Who wouldn't want that glorious yearbook spread and the car ride in the Memorial Day parade and, obvi, eternal bragging rights?

I want the real American dream, age-seventeen version: to dance with my boyfriend at prom, take silly pictures in a photo booth, make out during a slow dance, so intently that our classmates say *"Get a room!"* as we laugh and know they secretly wish they had what Cheng and I have. So yes, maybe it is all about me.

"Just be prepared, in case . . ." Cheng trails off, but I know what he's saying. He's so chill, he could be a greyhound. He's not even criticizing me, really, so much as preparing me in case my plan doesn't work. I get it: he's trying to watch out for me, but it's a little irritating, too. Like I'm not always prepared?

I face him, not saying anything, just quietly playing with the strings on his Quidditch Cup hoodie and giving him my best "Seriously?" face until he laughs. Shaking his head, he wheels off to join some of the other lacrosse guys crowded around a phone. Whatever they're looking at, it's got to be less interesting than me, but it also gets me out of defending my strategy.

We don't have the same first period, so I'm off to Earth in the Balance, the hilariously named enviro class. To get there, I have to walk down Picture Hall, which is lined with a solid eighty years of class photos. The walls are so crowded that it feels like being trapped in a museum. My mom's class of '85 is two-thirds of the way down the hall and it's huge (120 kids) compared to mine (a mere 50). It's still easy to pick her out: for one thing, there weren't a ton of Latinx kids then (still aren't, tbh), but her shortness combined with the tallness of her bangs makes quite an impression. The photographer has her down in front, so everyone can see the full splendor of the shoulder pads on the oversized shirt she wears belted over pegged white jeans. Two years ago, I was like, *omg Mom, what were you wearing?*, but now I kind of want the outfit.

My dad is less easy to recognize. For one thing, he had hair then. When Gordo—yes, I call him by his first name—left us eleven years ago, he had a perfectly gleaming bald head that he kept ultrasmooth as a point of pride. In his senior photo, he sports dark hair in a tight fade with three lines carved out on the left temple. He smiles a sarcastic smile beneath eyes that look troubled, at least to someone who knows how they can darken into anger. He wears a plain black suit with a wide tie that his spread collar barely contains. I have looked at this photo a thousand times trying to imagine why Mom picked *this* guy.

"You're obsessed with that picture." Nix dispels my reverie with a familiar complaint. (They're right, though—I can't pass this hall without at least a quick check-in with Mom and Gordo. There's probably a future therapy session in this.)

"And *you're* going to be late to AP Latin." I know Nix hates Latin—that's a language only a parent would choose—and I get why they ditch so often. Language Hall is just about as far from here as you can get without leaving the building. They'll never make it.

"Maybe I will, but your class is this way and I'm looking for you." Nix is chewing their lip, which means I'm about to get a little speech. Oh god, that's why they took the hall pass. I know what's coming before they say it.

"You have to get rid of prom king and queen." Nix knows I was expecting this and that I will try to duck out of it and they don't care; we've been friends since before I had pubes and they pretty much never hold their tongue around me. "It's so old school—not just an erasure of kids like me but like *aggressive*—Boys! Girls! Pair Off and Be Crowned!"

They step back, hands on hips that hide beneath the enormous T-shirt of the day, covered with anime figures I will *never* know, worn with boxy track shorts and tube socks. (Nix's undying worship of Billie Eilish dates back to, like, that spider in the mouth video, and shows no sign of ending.) We've been through this.

"As if allowing same-sex couples isn't *already* enough to get by Silverthorn? Let me leap that hurdle first."

"The hurdle that matters to *you*." Mostly, I love that Nix can read me for filth like nobody else, but right this second, I could do without it. (Cheng has already used up this morning's "Doubt Luis" pass, thanks.)

I do my best aggrieved voice. "It matters to *all* of us. I'm getting you in the door!"

Can an eyeroll make noise? I swear Nix's does. "The ticket policy isn't keeping *me* out. You know what? I think—"

"Okay, I hear you!" The look they give me clearly says *if you heard me you wouldn't be talking over me*, but I plunge ahead anyway, because I have like twenty seconds before the bell. "Let me get through today's meeting and we'll talk."

"I think you'll be hot for changing the royalty thing *after* you've been prom king."

Best friends are the worst. Because they *know.*

Once Nix sees in my eyes that they have me dead to rights, their job is done. They grin, a champion without a prize belt. "Go on, you selfish bastard. Whatever happens, I'll pretend to be all excited about it when everyone else is."

I know that's a real promise: Nix always has my back. I want to hug them but they hate hugs and, you know, bodily autonomy is a THING, so I blow a kiss instead, and they're off.

Comfort and the Cutting Edge

THE MORNING FLIES BY, and it's already time for Ms. Silverthorn's Senior Lit, the one class Nix, Cheng, and I all have together. Our essays on *A Connecticut Yankee in King Arthur's Court* are due. If no one ever made you read it, this guy Hank from *New* England gets bonked on the head and ends up in *Old* England (though I don't really know why). It's a little slow at first and then all battle scenes later on, so I'm not a huge fan, even though I *love* time travel stuff. (Before you get carried away, I'm not a huge geek: I like my sci-fi confined to this world, which means no aliens and hard pass on any series beginning with the word "star.") I'd bet money that most of the class wrote on expected (read: *boring*) themes like chivalry and the use of technology. Naturally, I wrote about the white male fragility of Hank, who blows things up or shoots people when he feels threatened. Ms. Silverthorn will eat it up.

She got a new weave over the weekend, and it's really working. Her hair game is fantastic and ever-changing, which is especially impressive because few people in a town this white would even know a box braid from a lace front, and I have to give credit where it's due. "That look is *everything*," I say, and she just shakes her head.

"Go on now," she says. She always waves off my compliments—tells me to focus on the *real* things—but I'm sure she likes it. Cheng, already seated, is using his bookbag to claim the desk next to him for me so that Douchebag McDouchebag (real name: Brad McDougal) won't sit there and flirt with him in that way only a super cocky het-bro can do.

Nix arrives last and claims the seat in front of me, swinging around to show me a TikTok on their phone of three kids doing the new On Blast dance challenge on top of a tower somewhere. "This could work, right?"

We're trying to come up with something memorable for the drama club banquet. Nix is emceeing and I'm presenting the first award, and there is *no* chance I'm going to just walk up and read "First-Year Rising Star" off a notecard. The On Blast dance has possibility, but it has this twerky bit three-quarters of the way through that I'm not sure Nix is built for. On the other hand, I know the other drama geeks will eat it up— they'll be on their feet in seconds. I show it to Cheng to get his opinion.

"Language." That's all he says as he passes the phone back to Nix. It's hip-hop, and the lyrics are kind of heavy on blow jobs, which isn't our fault. Nobody thinks they mean anything anyway. But the drama banquet is held on campus, so Mrs. Somboon-Fox (who is sure to show up and just gush about what great kids we are) could invoke the code of conduct. And honestly, even Ms. Silverthorn would complain. She's the most liberal teacher we have (though Kuranchabi is gunning for the title), but she has her limits.

Nix is not easily deterred. "I can find a song with the same time signature in two seconds flat. It's even better: we switch it up and people won't know what to expect. When we bust out On Blast moves, kids are gonna lose their minds. We'll kill it."

Now we're talking. "Not just *on*-trend but *beyond* trend. I like it." The vision is taking shape, twerk and all. It has to be good because drama club made me who I am; as Snoopy, in my first show freshman year, I wiped the floor with Charlie Brown, and people really ate it up (everyone except the kid playing Charlie Brown). That was enough celebrity to make me a class officer my sophomore year and now Student Body President two years running, and to make sure my crusades always have an audience. If I'm ever *famous* famous, I'm *so* going to be one of those kids who thanks their drama teacher.

Cheng sees the gleam in my eyes and just shakes his head, grinning, in a way that means he realizes it's a done deal. Mostly, he likes that I'm a big personality, which means he doesn't have to be. We're a good fit. His lacrosse buddies think I'm hilarious, and the drama club kids find him totally unthreatening for a jock. My mom loves him (though she jokes way too often that he would be easier to live with than I am), and his folks . . . well, they never pictured a boyfriend of any kind, so they're still working on how they feel about his first being as me as I am. But they've never interfered, either; they're very "let Cheng be Cheng."

Ms. Silverthorn finishes recording attendance and makes announcements, one of which is that Saratoga Remembers is hiring for the summer. *Please.* She can't really believe anyone wants to spend their last summer before college in a musty local history museum. Mr. Gale, the curator or whatever, is an old student of hers and sometimes comes to the drama club shows; she always lets him into the green room to say "break a leg." *Every single time*, she makes a joke of telling him to watch his step, so I finally asked my mom what *that* was about, and apparently, he was a klutz of epic proportions back in the day. He's seemingly managed to evolve into mild awkwardness now, but I'm not especially eager to spend a whole summer with the guy.

Yet when Ms. Silverthorn asks who wants an application, Cheng raises his hand.

"Seriously, babe?" I keep it a whisper but pointed.

He shrugs. "Easy money. Nobody goes there—I'll be watching YouTube all day."

He means it? My whisper gets less whispery. "And if someone comes in?"

He does what I'm guessing he thinks is a tour guide voice. "Look over here: Pictures of a horse. Look over there: That's an old hat."

"If you want to throw away a perfectly good summer—"

Ms. Silverthorn clears her throat. "You boys seem to think this is the lunchroom, but it's not." She waits for us to look appropriately remorseful. She has a soft spot for me, for all the drama kids really, but that doesn't mean I get a free pass; none of us do. Her classroom, our respect. That's the deal.

When the book discussion starts, it's worse than I thought. It's not about the good stuff—how Hank got there, how he used his knowledge of the future—but about feudal systems. Ugh. It's already been impossible to focus on homework since spring break because I've mentally already moved on to college. Every single hour is some kind of medieval torture, a fresh cut each time the bell rings. I can't even.

Fortunately, I am a pro at secretly checking my phone. A text bubbles onto my screen.

Ten minutes. Don't let Bryce get there first.

Shreya, my co-conspirator on Prom Council, has a special loathing for Bryce, who is inoffensively bland most of the time but stubbornly old school about prom. She wants us in Mrs. Somboon-Fox's office first so we can get her good and buttered up.

The class discussion has switched gears to time travel. A debate has erupted over why Hank doesn't go back to his own time, considering he's so critical of the sixth century. One camp argues that he *can't*; he didn't plan his arrival there, so there's no way to plan a return. The other camp argues that he never wants to go back because he's made himself a legend

16

with his "inventions" (which are really just DIY versions of things from his day).

"How many of you would stay in a past time if you had more knowledge than everyone else?"

Only two hands go up. Ms. Silverthorn can't be surprised at our response: there's no chance a generation raised watching HD movies on our phones is going to sign up for using torches for light or whatever.

Five minutes.

Shreya is relentless. I admire that. Maybe I should very discreetly text back—

"Would you like to add something, Luis?" Ms. Silverthorn stops me before I can type a syllable. I'm busted, but I fake it as if I'm engaged with this riveting discussion.

"I think Twain is being lazy. He didn't even have a logic for time travel—it was just a device to get Hank somewhere he could shock everyone with trains and gunpowder."

"Interesting," she murmurs, which is teacher speak for *wrong* and I know where she's going to go. We've already discussed every time travel movie ever made and she has a *deep* well of theories, so I know how to get her going. "*Connecticut Yankee* was the first novel to use a device now called a 'time slip,' a time travel method harder to control than either the portals or time machines of later fiction."

Two minutes.

I almost leap from my seat. I'll never beat Bryce. I eyeball the door and, without breaking cadence, Ms. Silverthorn nods that I can go. Cheng gives me a look that counts as a kiss for luck, and Nix gives me a look that says, "Don't leave me here." I race out, sure to be late, bound by the actual laws of time and space.

Through Mrs. Somboon-Fox's open door, I see I'm the last to arrive. (One must never be *last* last, only fashionably late.) I'm on Prom Council because I'm Student Body President. It's kind of a drag because I love people and I love parties, but I *hate* meetings. But you can't be President without attending a few along the way, so I make them more fun for the other officers by doing a group chat with everyone calling from their own rooms. Half of Prom Council, unfortunately, is composed of our Senior Class Co-Presidents Yasmin and Bryce; they're both believers in conducting business by Robert's Rules of Order, and neither would join a group chat unless it offered SAT prep. Yasmin, as always, is dressed like a forty-year-old real estate agent and has her day planner in hand; Bryce, as always, is wearing a blue checked shirt, khakis, and loafers and looks grim because prom is his least favorite duty: no one ever got into Yale by planning prom. Thank god for Shreya. The only elected Prom Council member, an election Shreya won by a landslide, she is also the Chair. The Beyoncé of ASA, she has a smile to die for and a magnetism that makes people do her bidding. She leaps up to give me a hug, occasioning a frown from Yasmin, who is not a hugger, and a wistful look from Bryce, who really needs one himself.

Once we're all assembled, Mrs. Somboon-Fox beams. "Look at this team! Aren't you just the FUTURE!" Mrs. Somboon-Fox is a big fan of diversity, and this room oversells by miles how diverse ASA is. There are definitely more kids of color here than there used to be. Still, it tells you something that me and Shreya and Yasmin have all been featured in campus ads, calendars, and handbooks *every single year* since we were freshmen, and three out of four times, Ms. Silverthorn was casually placed in the background. Ms. Somboon-Fox is Thai American married to a lefty white dude and says "inclusion" is her passion, which somehow means announcing it every time more than one of us is in a room together.

Shreya leaps on Mrs. Somboon-Fox's excitement. "We have the results from the prom theme poll, and the winner is: 'Under the Rainbow.'" Bryce's jaw clenches. He wanted Fireworks (the third-highest vote-getter) because anything red, white, and blue makes him cream himself. Yasmin is a little disappointed, too. Her pick, "Sophisticated," came in second. Nobody, not even the farm kids, voted for "Barn Dance," and only a handful voted for "A Night in the Stars"—but that's why Shreya and I proposed both. We knew they'd fail, and this would make it harder for Yasmin and Bryce to complain when "Under the Rainbow"—also our suggestion—destroyed the competition. We made sure to hype everyone up in advance, promising *Wizard of Oz* vibes to the conservative kids and true inclusion to the progressive ones. Comfort *and* cutting edge— who could resist? Not many; it got 80 percent of the votes.

Mrs. Somboon-Fox looks as if she won the lottery. Our theme fits her narrative of what the school is like now; the pictures will be pretty, and there's nothing sexy about it. Easy win. She claps—actually *claps her hands*—at this news and declares that this will be the best prom ever. Principals have to say "best [blank] ever" a lot, but while she's wrapped up in her enthusiasm, I pounce.

I slide the mock-up of the ticket Shreya and I whipped up across Mrs. Somboon-Fox's desk. It has the theme in big letters, smaller letters for date and place, the price (made less scary by being in a cute font), a box for the number of tickets, and a border of rainbow arches. In tiny tiny print, it states that guests must be between the ages of sixteen and nineteen.

"This looks dandy." Mrs. Somboon-Fox loves the rainbows. I knew it.

Shreya reaches for the form to reclaim it, smoothly moving on. "Now we have to talk about the buses, because last year's were—"

"OH!"

Mrs. Somboon-Fox has not yet released the paper. Her face reddens noticeably. She doesn't look at Shreya or Yasmin or Bryce. She looks only at me.

"I think you've forgotten a line."

One does not "forget" a line like *"ticket holder affirms he or she may bring one guest of the opposite gender."* It's been on the ticket template for years—no one seems to know when it started. I just made a new template, simple as that.

The room is quiet and for once I don't have the perfect retort, because I can see a lot of things on her face.

Right now, Mrs. Somboon-Fox is aware that I am trying to change school policy on the sly. She is also aware that Shreya is in on it. She is considering what it means that I think I can do this without asking. And now she is wondering if she has been trusting me a little too much for a little too long. How quickly can you reexamine three years of friendly banter and support? How fast can you decide some cocky kid with glitter—GLITTER—on his cheeks thinks he is smarter than you? Apparently, this takes about forty-five seconds.

She gives us a look. "I will ASSUME that you all know that you do not make school policy by fiat. That I alone ALSO do not make school policy. That we have a school board and that this school board would FIRE me and CANCEL prom if your little stunt worked." (Note: Whenever an adult uses the adjective "little," there is a deep reservoir of anger just beneath the surface sarcasm.)

Yasmin's mouth is a perfect O of surprise. Bryce's face is the color of the school's brick facade. He snatches the paper and scans it. When he looks at me—he kind of hates to look at me in general, tbh—his eyes are full of what can only be called righteousness. "What? You had to make prom gay, too?"

Shreya's eyes are blazing. "Inclusive means including people."

"Thanks a lot, Gandhi." Bryce is smart-ish, but he can still only name one Indian besides Shreya, so his insult catalog is

21

pretty shallow. He turns to Yasmin. "Did you know about this?"

"No!" Yasmin is trapped. Surface popularity is very important to her, and this requires seeming agreeable to everyone. She is unfailingly polite to me and Cheng, and really everyone, but every smile is kind of pinched, as if the effort hurts a little. She is torn at this moment between her love of order and the social storm she can imagine me whipping up. That Shreya and I cooked this up without the Co-Presidents is an offense against protocol, so she is vibrating from the disrespect. Still, she's a politician at heart and isn't going to personalize this.

She keeps her face neutral. "It's a moot point. Mrs. Somboon-Fox is the principal, and she says no."

"As I made clear, *I* did not say anything. I don't have that power. If YOU want to go before the board and ask for them to approve this change, you may."

Mrs. Somboon-Fox knows that *we* know: A) that the board will never agree to an emergency early meeting before its annual session after graduation; and B) that I would be laughed out of the room by those people. (You won't be at all surprised to learn that the board is eleven dudes and two women, and all thirteen look as if they just stepped off the *Mayflower*.)

I can't help myself. "So it's ASA—progress for *some*!"

She doesn't take the bait. "If you think this is the particular hill you want to die on, to make things better for EVERYONE, prepare your case for the June board meeting and win a victory for the future. You have to MAKE progress, and making it takes time. Perhaps you should have started this campaign sooner . . . and openly."

"We'll do it." Shreya is nodding. "Tell the board we want to be on the agenda. Right, Luis?"

I am blinking furiously now, because I am not going to let Yasmin and Bryce see me cry. What can I say? "Yeah," I barely squeeze out, then clear my throat and try again. "*Yes.*"

Mrs. Somboon-Fox softens, sounding more like herself. "Everyone is still welcome. Everyone is still included. You, Cheng, everyone—all you have to do is buy a ticket and come celebrate with your friends."

"And if we dance together?" She says nothing, but her eyes are sad.

I'm on my feet. "So we're *welcome* to be spectators at the biggest night of the year. *Welcome* to watch everyone else have prom while we, what? Drink Gatorade? Admire their clothes?"

"You signed the code of conduct with your own hand. You know where you go to school." I'm about to fire back, but Mrs. Somboon-Fox wants to puncture the balloon of my moral superiority, and dammit, she knows just how. "I'm sure you'll still be prom king."

My god, is it that obvious? I start to say that isn't the point, but Bryce seizes the moment. "You and *Gandhi* will make a perfect couple."

"Bryce!" Mrs. Somboon-Fox is now differently unhappy than she was moments ago. "That is NOT appropriate."

The bell for next period rings so loudly that we all jump.

Bryce bolts for the door like a convict released from death

row. Shreya squeezes my hand and tells me with her eyes that we'll talk later.

Yasmin waits a moment and says that I should have come to her first. For a microsecond, I think she's an ally, but no dice. "I could've told you the answer would've been 'no' and spared you all this." She really thinks this sounds sympathetic. I want to shred her day planner with my bare hands.

"Luis."

I can barely look at Mrs. Somboon-Fox. I'm hurt that the woman all about diversity has shut me down so fast and so thoroughly. And, okay, maybe I'm embarrassed that she can read me so clearly.

Her expression has softened. "If you really thought this would fly, you wouldn't have tried to sneak it past me."

"I—"

"Stop. Listen to me," she says, her voice firm but not unkind. "You know where you live and where you go to school. Antic Springs isn't the city, and ASA isn't *High School Musical*."

I get it. There have been a couple of minor incidents in my time here, like a sophomore who kept calling me Fancy Nancy my freshman year and the kid who wrote "gay" on my junior year election posters. And there was the time the baseball team mocked this one freshman constantly for his lisp, which is like caveman-level trolling. But I mean, please—if prom attendance was determined by who escaped teasing, nobody would get in.

And yes, I know terrible things still happen in other places. (Keyword: other.) But I'm not going to prom anywhere else. If you took a poll right now—gays at prom or not—we'd win by a landslide. Why can't the school keep up? I'm only a senior once.

"If there is any lesson life will teach you, it should be this . . ." She pauses dramatically, and I wait for whatever not-profound thing she is about to say. "You don't always get the outcome you want."

There's no point in arguing that, until about ten minutes ago, I pretty much did.

The Chaz Wilson Card

I NEED TO GET off campus and as far away from the humiliation of that meeting as I can. Nix sees me bolting and follows me into the parking lot. "What happened?"

A tiny part of me wants to say, "The school isn't ready for *me,* much less *you,*" but instead, I shrug them off and mutter, "Nothing," because I am not ready to admit defeat. Honestly, I'm not ready to deal with humans period right this minute, so I keep walking out of the lot and away from school. Nix lets me go. I mean, they know my moods—sometimes, I'm best left alone.

I live less than a mile away from school in the Wormwood Apartments (which have to be named for a dead person, because why else would you pick "Wormwood"?). Let me be clear: this does not make me a Townie. A Townie is a local who does *not* go to ASA, and no one would want to be lumped in with them. ASA is mostly a boarding school and the on-campus kids have always seen Townies as being roughly equivalent to cavepeople. I, however, am simply a "day student," which means I enjoy the privilege of living off campus and having more freedom than most—best of all worlds, which is just how I like it.

Most days, I eat lunch in the cafeteria, even though the food is comically bad, so I can engage in stealthy hand-holding with Cheng under the table and gossip with Nix and our friends. But sometimes I take advantage of my off campus privilege by heading home, which I do today because I am too angry to be around anyone. I need to come up with my next move, and I can't strategize while keeping on my sunny face and making nice. The only risk is that I will wake Mom, and she will ask why I'm home and trust me, that is *not* a conversation I am up for.

I slide my key into the apartment door quietly and tiptoe in. The door to her room is shut, and the place is quiet, so I think I'm safe. There's a printed picture of a sleeping kitty hung on the knob with a ribbon; if the picture is turned around to show the cat leaping at a toy, it means she's awake. She works the 11 p.m. to 7 a.m. shift as a charge nurse at a nursing home. She should be out cold till around three or so, and I'll be long gone by then.

Inside the fridge is my secret stash of Lime Frost Gatorade.

It is *so* not on-brand for me, I would never drink it at school, but I got hooked in fourth grade when I went through a two-year soccer phase. Mom thinks the electrolytes piece is okay but says the dye is bad, and whatever, but her paranoid list of things that could kill you is a mile long.

where are you?

Cheng has snapped me a meme of a dog looking around after its ball has been snatched away.

I snap back a GIF of a UFO sucking up a body.

😄 How'd it go

So Shreya hasn't told him. I owe her a smoothie.

I text Shreya first.

SAY NOTHING

Then Cheng.

I'm on it.

Neutral enough, right? I have barely hit send before he replies.

so . . . not good? lol

28

Cheng looks like a jock in his hoodies and sweats, but he's smart and emotionally on point. Sometimes it would be easier to date an airhead like Chris, who looks like a model but talks like a squeaky toy. Cheng may be chill, but he also doesn't miss a thing.

I snap Cheng a clip of Lizzo holding up a hand as if to ward off paparazzi and then put my phone down.

"Luisito?"

"Jeez, Mami! I almost spilled on my shirt!"

I had no idea she was behind me, standing in the bathroom door in the robe I got her at Nordstrom Rack on a trip last year. (I have a homing device for outlets and discounts.) It's so much softer than the ratty old thing she used to wear, which she got before I was born. She has a serious hold-on-too-long thing going on. Her hairbrush is three times my age. She has shoes that went in and out, back in, and back out of style. Even her job: In high school, she lived off campus too, and had a candy striper job at the same nursing home she works at now; when she became an RN, she didn't apply anywhere else. Abuelo had already abandoned the farm and moved to Florida (where there were actual other Cubans around), but she has lived in Antic Springs ever since. Like decades. My job is to sneak The New into her life whenever possible.

"Why are you home?"

She is rubbing the moisturizer I got her onto her cheeks, but her green eyes are focused on me. She worries *all* the time. "Born for a widow's walk" is what her best friend CeCe says. This makes her loving, diligent, serious, loyal . . . and exhausting. The gazillion ways she has fearfully pictured my sudden death—I could write a book.

The problem is, I try not to lie to her. She deserves someone to be true, which my dad, in the end, couldn't be. They were high school sweethearts who broke up just before graduation over something she vaguely describes as "trust issues." That should have been the end of it, except that one of Gordo's buddies became the gym teacher, Coach Vincent, fifteen years later and invited Gordo to visit their old stomping grounds. When he ran into Mom—well, Maria Elena, I guess, because they hadn't yet made me—they bonded over both being single (she worked too much, and he had moved too often) and agreeing that life seemed simpler back in their First Secondary days. He visited Antic Springs a lot after that weekend and didn't pretend it was to see Coach Vincent. When they got married, she thought he'd stay here forever.

I've given her plenty of crap about choosing my dad. If he wasn't a great boyfriend in high school, what made her think he would be different as a husband (or a father)? Her defense was that her doubts were always smaller than the potential she saw in him. She could rattle off his supposed virtues—strong, hard-working, protective, dedicated to whatever he loved—but I didn't buy it. I mean, none of those things held up in the end. He bailed on us and started a new life with a woman he met at Wegman's. Mom and I have this debate twice a year when we hear from him on my birthday and Christmas (that is when *she* does since I won't answer the phone), and every time she says it's harder to be a grown-up than to be a kid and maybe I'll understand someday. Fat chance.

She's still waiting for me to explain why I'm home with her instead of at school with my boyfriend, but I'm not in the mood to explain. It is *literally* impossible to be both seventeen and honest with a parent all the time. So I am the master of evasion, omission, and just plain running away from a conversation rather than lying to Mom. Today, I'll try a classic: incomplete truth.

"I needed lunch. You know I hate pizza day. They get it from Sal's, and it's cellulite on cardboard."

"And?"

"*And?*" Tactic two: deflection. "Why aren't you sleeping? You're going to be a mess tonight."

She isn't buying it. She passes me a tissue. "Your mascara."

Okay, so I sometimes do still wear makeup to school. Not a ton—a little for the lashes, a little highlighter, and some brow shaper, nothing that will be super obvious to teachers who sleep with the code of conduct under their pillows at night. It looks perfectly natural, as long as you think nature made me perfect, and I'm pretty safe as long as there's no, like, eye shadow or lip color. (The glitter is almost translucent, so it *barely* counts.) Cheng says I don't need any of it, but Cheng was born agreeable, and he says I look nice with it on, too. Sadly, my products are all from Walgreens, so they're not the best, and I save the good stuff for events. (Like, say, prom.) *Apparently*, she can tell I've been crying.

Fine. I'll tell her. It's kinda her fault anyway: if she isn't part of the solution, she's part of the problem.

"Mrs. Somboon-Fox said Cheng and I can't go to prom together."

She rubs my arm comfortingly, but I can hear the relief in her voice. "Pobrecito . . ." She really should stop there, but no. "You knew that was coming."

"Um, *no*, I did not. I'm like her favorite kid—I'm everyone's favorite kid. If they won't change for me, they'll never change."

She retreats into the bathroom, the door still open, pretending to fix her hair in the mirror. (Um, she wears it in a pony—she can do it without looking.) She doesn't face me as she defends Mrs. Somboon-Fox.

"Life is full of tradeoffs. This is a good school, a small one where they know you and like you. You're getting a great education and a safe one. You don't have the drug problem of Schuylerhook to worry about, and the word 'academy' will look good on your transcript." She's got her own bag of tricks, "count your blessings" being her favorite. "Just be grateful you're a legacy, so we get enough of a deal to afford it." I don't say a word, not one, so she switches to another classic tactic: shame. "Losing out on a dance isn't the biggest sacrifice ever."

"It's not 'a dance.' It's *prom*. Which matters to me, even if you didn't care about yours."

I catch her reflection in the mirror and see her wincing.

"I didn't make it to prom. But I never said I didn't care."

I am not taking that bait. "What matters is that *I do*—a lot.

32

It's not your school now and not your prom we're talking about. This is *my* senior year, and it's insane for them to *erase* me from my prom."

"Mrs. Somboon-Fox's not trying to erase you—"

"MOM!" For real?

This stops her mid-sentence, but she recovers. She turns to look at me, eyes full. "She's *protecting* you."

"Do. Not. Go there."

But she does. "You know what happened to Chaz Wilson."

Chaz Wilson is my ghost of gayness past. I mean, not literally—no skinny Black boy with violet eyes appears in my mirror or emerges from the shadows when no one else is looking. But he haunts my life like nobody's business, even so.

When I first came out, I got "I love you as you are . . ." and she meant it, but within minutes she was reminding me about Chaz Wilson. When I wanted to have the teeny tiniest rainbow flag tattooed on my bicep? "Sorry, honey—remember Chaz Wilson." When ASA turned down my proposal for an Allies Club (I mean, it didn't even have the word "gay" in the name!), instead of sympathy, what did I get? "Think about Chaz Wilson." It's like that kid died a thousand times instead of just once.

For all this "remember what happened" talk, nobody actually knows what *did* happen that night. Chaz was in Mom's class, but he missed prom, too. They found his body, still in his tux, at the base of the Ledges, an abandoned quarry deep in the woods across from the campus. There were no signs of

33

injury that couldn't be accounted for by the fall from such a height, and the school solemnly announced that it was a suicide. Among his classmates, it was whispered that he killed himself because he was gay. Mom wasn't so sure. From what she tells me—and, trust me, she has told this story a hundred zillion times—he never had a boyfriend or anything. He was just too pretty, too quirky, too unconcerned with how to "man up" to ever really fit in with the straight guys. And the girls were split about two to one between those who found him unsettling and those who wished more boys were like him.

Even though he wasn't actually out, a few of the guys had picked on him, including Gordo (she hated to admit). Still, she isn't convinced the teasing was the real problem; if he did kill himself, she thought Chaz was probably more concerned with his salvation than his classmates. (Though, jumping off a cliff does *not* seem like a way to solve that.)

Suicide wasn't the only theory. A rumor went around that Townies had attacked him. All bad things get blamed on outsiders, eventually. And there was no evidence to support this, but it wasn't impossible. Fights occasionally happened between academy kids and Townies, who had "raided" campus for a little petty vandalism once or twice during my mom's time at the school. She always favored this theory—not because it was less awful, but because she and Chaz were friends; it was unbearable to think of him feeling so terrible about himself that he'd end his own life.

Mom's lack of surety about *how* Chaz died didn't change the fact that he *did*. She can picture every possible scenario, and she doesn't want them to happen to me. I mean, I've never given her reason to think I'm a suicide risk, but I can see why she'd worry about gay-bashing. And as she likes to remind me, Chaz Wilson had a mom, too.

I asked her once if my dad left us because of me. I mean, please—from the time I discovered that toy stores had wands and tutus, they knew what kind of boy they had on their hands. She always says no, not at all, but I still think about Chaz and the fact that my own father was apparently a dick to him, and I have to wonder.

It doesn't matter. It shouldn't affect me now; Gordo is gone, and Chaz died three decades ago. Seriously, not in this century. Whatever really did happen, the outcome was tragic for sure, but Mom needs to treat it like what it was: a rare exception, not a rule. Instead, he's forever linked to the idea of gayness in her mind, the image she summons to determine the boundaries of who I can be.

"Chaz Wilson. Chaz Wilson. Chaz Wilson! I think you ought to care more about your own son's rights!"

She crosses her arms. (To be clear, this is *never* a good sign.) "How 'bout I care about my son's *life?* Which is my actual job?"

"Yeah, well, if your job is to be okay with my life counting for less than everyone else's, you're crushing it."

I leave the room so fast, she has no choice but to let me have the last word.

If You Can't Trust
Your Boyfriend

MY PHONE IS STARTING to light up like fireworks. I don't have to even swipe the first bubble to know that Bryce (it can only be Bryce) is telling people about how my prom coup backfired. Of course, that's exactly what happened, but at least the kids who text are all on my side. There's already talk of a protest and even a hashtag, #LETTHEMDANCE. I don't want any of it: the embarrassment of failing publicly or the prospect of people boycotting an event I've been living for. Between a crown and a picket line, you know which I want to be seen in.

Nix texts to say to meet on the green instead of going to sixth period. I'm pretty sure you can't improve over Nix as a best friend: without me saying it, they understand I can't yet face a class full of kids who know I blew this. And they also know my schedule well enough to know that I have Kurunch-abi for sixth, and any good sob story I drop on him later will get the absence excused.

It's Cheng I see first, though. I kiss him right on the green (which technically is the same as being at school) because I want to and because I am done playing by their rules. I am immedi-ately grounded by the warmth of his forehead against mine and the familiar scent of his shampoo. Feeling slightly less deranged, I launch into a litany of injustices: Mrs. Somboon-Fox is a hypocrite, my mom is holding me back, and neither are keep-ing up with the twenty-first century. He listens and nods and rubs my back. He doesn't say much, which isn't that unusual for him, but right this second it kind of bugs me. I need him to tell me I'm right.

"Aren't you going to say anything?"

He shrugs. That's not chill, that's evasive.

I take a step back and stare him down. It's never a good idea to put words in someone's mouth, especially in a fight, but, sis, I am in a mood. So I do. "You're going to say it's my fault, aren't you?" I don't even give him a chance to deny it. "Go ahead, say you told me so."

He hesitates. Oh my god, he's considering it! Only a fool would dare—

He goes for it. "I couldn't say that if it wasn't true . . ."

"So instead of comforting your boyfriend, who will be a school joke for the next few days and who you won't get to dance with at prom, you're blaming him for screwing it up? Nice, babe."

Even as I feel my face heating up, part of me knows Cheng will say something to defuse the situation and cool me down. It's a major perk of dating someone so chill.

Except that's not what he does. "Sometimes," he starts, voice soft. "I think you just don't listen to people."

"What?"

"You could have started a petition last fall instead of sneaking it through now and hoping the 'cult of Luis' would be enough to get by."

"The what now?"

I can't believe he's using one of my favorite terms—the cult of personality—against me. Worse, he's making me sound self-absorbed and shallow when I was doing this for us!

Cheng's cheeks are reddening. He may be as surprised as I am by what he just said. And he sure as hell can see that I'm volcanic. "I . . ." he starts and stops. It's pretty clear he's regretting heading down this path, so he switches gears. "I wanted to dance together at prom. And maybe we could have, if . . ." He can't finish the sentence because there is no end that won't spawn an eruption.

"If *I* had done things differently? What about you? Or Nix or anyone? At least I tried. I'm not just slouching along pretending that second-class treatment is enough. I'm a doer. You're—"

"Luis." He reaches for me.

"You're as bad as Mom!"

He tries to make it a joke. "Lucky me then, 'cause you love your mom."

"Are you *smiling*? Right now? You think I'm amused?" He reaches for me, and I slap his hands away. "Maybe it's a good thing Mrs. Somboon-Fox said no. You can go to prom alone."

I turn away, and he doesn't call out for me, which is fair but *maddening*, and now I don't want to see Nix either. I want to see Ms. Silverthorn. She'll know what to do—not about Cheng, but about the mess I've made.

It takes just under three dozen adults to keep ASA running: three administrators; thirteen faculty; one school nurse (daytime only); twelve staff in cafeteria, maintenance, and housekeeping; and a pair of deans for each dorm. For as long as I can remember, at least twenty-eight of those thirty-one people have been white. And not white Latinx but white-white. Even as the student body has gotten more diverse, the faculty pages of the *Intrepid*, our yearbook, remain a sea of clouds. Ms. Silverthorn has been an exception since my mom was here. This year, the only nonwhite staff are her, Mrs. Somboon-Fox, and Mr. Kurunchabi. Mr. Kurunchabi started last fall, just months after Mr. Ramirez retired as if some great constant prohibits the ratio from ever changing.

Ms. Silverthorn is a pretty great constant herself. All the kids of color flock to her because she *gets* it. So do the queer kids. She knows what it is to be the Other in the room. (You should hear her break down microaggressions—my god, it's amazing.) The drama kids also love her, as does the whole #Resist crowd, and really the only people who don't are the ones who hate English class in general. Her room is full after school, with kids getting support or just hanging out, and she has to shoo people away to get to the arts building for the drama club meetings. She writes, like, fifty recommendations a year.

I stan for Ms. Silverthorn because I'm a double-dipper: gay *and* Latinx. (Though she is first to remind me of the privilege of having light skin, especially when I'm on my high horse about something, which is, like, all the time.) I've spent so much time at her house with drama kids that I have a favorite mug there, and everyone knows my spot is the corner seat on the sectional. If I am going to get sympathy from anyone but Nix, it will be Silverthorn. After thirty-six years here, her outrage meter is probably long broken, but she continually pushes the school forward more than anyone else ever does, so a plan is forming in the back of my mind.

I know the board loves her, and they can't afford to fire her—they'd never hear the end of it. So all I have to do is get her on my side with the prom plan and have her push it with Mrs. Somboon-Fox. If she's for it, even more kids will be—and it won't take some ugly picket line. Maybe that'll give Kurunch-abi permission to stop being so coy about his sexuality—I mean, I read him *instantly*. And then what? It would be a bad look for the school that's been selling diversity for years now to shut down two of three faculty of color (and piss off all their loyal followers).

I'm almost running to the arts building now. Why on earth didn't I think of this sooner?

The double doors of the main entrance to the arts building are propped open, which means it's load-in for *Charlotte Sometimes: The Musical*. Ms. Silverthorn loves a big set, and Mrs. Somboon-Fox loves the woodshop kids to feel included, so no school play budget is ever too big. This year they're transforming the stage (big, airy, modern) into an old British school from 1918. Though the script only says it's set in a boarding school, which probably means wood and wallpaper, Ms. Silverthorn has decided to make it look more post–World War I industrial. So lots of black and white and shadow to capitalize on the art teacher being all about chiaroscuro this term.

She is onstage, her arms raised like someone in a flight crew directing an airplane to a gate. Backlit by stage lights, she is pure silhouette, and I see only the motion: *come this way*. She is not summoning me, but someone behind me. I turn, too late, to see who.

Four of the strongest kids in school struggle under the weight of a huge beam intended for the set. As they navigate the raked slope of the auditorium, their sweating hands cannot restrain the beam, which becomes kinetic. Their eyes widen in terror at the prospect not of dropping the beam but of launching it—onto me.

You know how I adjust really, really fast to my circumstances? This time my body betrays me. I freeze. Like the proverbial deer in headlights, I'm confused by the image of this enormous missile heading my way—my brain overloads with a million thoughts at once.

Is this really happening? Can I outrun it? Why am I not running?

This is going to hurt.

And then—

The Past/Future Tense

MY HEAD THROBS SO much I'm afraid to open my eyes, knowing the stage lights will be like an instant migraine delivery system.

A brass section is playing "Eye of the Tiger" with a rowdy percussion riff between verses. I cover my ears because the sound is making this headache worse, until a new thought pierces the fog. *We don't* have *a marching band*.

Gingerly opening first one eye and then the other, I discover something even more surprising: Sky. As in, above me, a beautiful blue sky, wide and clear of clouds almost to the horizon. The stage crew has knocked me clear outside.

Sitting up, I am stiff at first, as if I have lain here for days.

Vertigo seizes me. I can't see the arts building, so where am I? I don't remember anything after impact—what happened next when I left the building, or how I ended up here.

And then I realize something important: I don't actually know where *here* is.

Stretching before me are green fields that lead to a two-lane road. On the other side, forest kicks in. It's Antic Springs for sure, but I can't quite locate where I'm standing in relation to campus. It worries me that I've completely wandered away from school with a head injury, though with every moment, my mind clears, and the throb lessens.

I stand to look for landmarks and—

I throw up.

Oh my god, oh my god, oh my god.

I don't even want to say it. I can't. If I do, it'll be real.

The marching band, which I can see now, a phalanx of blue and gold marching on the grass next to a ball field, is making precise turns to cadences counted out by a very short majorette with very tall bangs. Beyond the band, my red brick campus glows in hot May light.

I sit down, so I don't *fall* down.

I can clearly see the ball field that was turned into a parking lot my freshman year; right now, it is lush and green and being marched upon by a band that no longer exists, led by my *mom*, who I left standing in a bathroom at home like twenty minutes ago.

I lay flat on my back and try to calm down.

So, I read a lot. I see a lot of movies. And I know instantly where I am and what has happened *and* that this is impossible in real life.

I have basically memorized all three *Back to the Future*s, even though only the first one is any good. I binge-watched *Outlander*, despite having figured out the big twist way early. I wrote a book report on *A Wrinkle in Time* in third grade (though, really, it was more like A Wrinkle in *Space*, but whatever). I was obsessed with *Hangin' Out with Cici*, this totally '70s book about a girl who has to go back to the '60s to appreciate her mother; it was my mom's original copy from when *she* was a kid. My favorite *X-Men* movie is the one with the Nazis and John F. Kennedy, and all the time-leaping that Cheng says is too confusing, but which I love. (Next to any of these, *Connecticut Yankee* is kind of a snooze, IMHO.)

Right this moment, two options present themselves: A) I have a traumatic head injury—oh my god, am I in a coma?— and my addled brain is imagining all this; B) time travel is real, and my semi-obsession with it made me ripe for the picking. Both options have serious drawbacks.

I know I'm being dramatic, but that's kind of my brand. And I've just been wiped out by a huge beam, so . . .

I close my eyes to block out the sunlight, which is killing me. I take in a slow, deep breath and then another. A vastly more likely scenario presents itself: I have a super basic concussion, and this is just the part where I'm passed out. I will wake up any second, and it won't be a big deal. Cheng has had *two* concussions, and they're no party but he's always fine in a week-ish.

Just thinking of him makes me hot with anger again: Could he have offered a worse response to my Prom Council fiasco? It makes my head hurt even more.

If I remember right, you're not really supposed to go to sleep right after a concussion—at least not till the doctor says what's what—but it's tempting right now. The sun is warm, and I can feel the afternoon breeze on my face, damp with sweat. It's kind of dreamy . . . except, again, I'm supposed to be inside the currently nonexistent arts building.

I open my eyes, and the world is as old school as the last time I looked. I sit up again and stare at my hands like that's going to tell me something. The imprint of grass that needs to be cut has made a cross-hatch pattern on my bare arms. If I *am* out cold, my subconscious has a killer way with details.

Okay, let's say this was more like a real-life crisis: a bad break-up or a huge test I didn't know was happening. I'd give myself like five minutes tops to freak out, then strategize about what I needed to do next. When Alex dumped me in eighth grade (do not ever speak to me of Alex), I sweet-talked the middle school registrar into switching my gym class, so I never had to see him in cute shorts again (my feelings about his legs were hard to hide if you know what I mean). And last year, when I mixed up the AP Bio and English test dates, I claimed a two-day migraine that got me out of both and really deserved an Emmy.

So what now? I've pretty much used up my freak-out five, and what I need to do is stay calm and assess my options if, in fact, this *isn't* a concussion. Obviously, I don't have a time machine—there's no DeLorean or energy-shooting orb in sight. So I guess there's always the time portal thing. But if there is some mystical rift between past and present at ASA, *someone* would have noticed. Especially if it's in the middle of the arts building, which I realize is not gone; it just hasn't been built yet.

As much as I hate to admit it, being knocked out *is* super common in time travel stories. In *Hangin' Out with Cici*, she gets bonked on the head (on a bus, which doesn't seem like a big place for head injuries, but no stranger than a school auditorium). The good news is that she wakes up back in her regular life at the end. Hopefully, I will, too.

Listen to me. My recently torpedoed head is already making room for this to be true. That's not adaptability; that's insanity.

"Off the lawn, Townie."

I scramble up to face the speaker. A backlit silhouette, like my last image of Ms. Silverthorn, fills my view. The afternoon sun outlines a massive brown torso, and it takes a moment for my eyes to adjust.

The first detail I can make out: three little hatch marks in a perfect fade.

Holy crap. It's Gordo. As in, my dad.

I really *have* time traveled to the '80s—and whoa, actually thinking the words makes me nauseous again. I'm shaking all over at the very idea, despite how much I used to love that stuff. *Used to?* I'm already past-tensing my own future life? Oh my god oh my god oh my god.

47

Breathe. Breathe.

"Did you hear me, ass wipe?" He sounds outraged that I have not immediately obeyed his command.

Now I know the exact year: 1985. Gordo only attended ASA during his senior year, after being kicked out of another boarding school, which he went to after being kicked out of the one before that. I can't help but think that 1985 means ASA is still a church school, and he could get busted for swearing and, for that matter, smoking, which his stinky shirt suggests he isn't great at hiding. If it's 1985, he and Mom have just started dating, which means that she was attracted to this smelly, hulking, rage monster. (And also that, regardless of what she says, he has *always* been the guy he was when he left us.) Gross.

He grabs my shirt collar—*um, hands off!*—which starts to give because it's silk and not really meant for wrestling. His aggression jolts me into clarity and I slap his meat paw away. He is so surprised that he actually takes a step back. His voice gets even lower and meaner. "You haven't heard what we do to Townies here?"

"You mean when you're done shaving each other's backs?"

"What did you say?" He knows this is an insult of some kind even if it doesn't quite make sense, and I see he is tensing up to punch my lights out. Trust me, I will lose this fight. I don't do so much as yoga, much less karate. I have to redirect.

"Yoo-hoo, Ms. Silverthorn!" Oh my god, even *I'm* not gay enough to say "yoo-hoo" but that's what comes out, and it works. He turns to see how close his English teacher is and, at that moment, I sprint for it.

Athletic, I am not, but speedy, I am. I have always had absurdly long legs, and fear makes me a jackrabbit. Gordo looks more muscular here than I remember him from growing up, but he's always been stocky and broad-chested. No one this bulky is going to be able to catch me. (I just now realize his name is funny—what Cuban would do that to their kid?)

I race uphill toward Faculty Row, where the teachers live in mirror-image split-level homes. When I hazard a glance backward, Gordo isn't following me. In fact, he's nowhere in sight. It occurs to me that he won this fight: I did just what he wanted. Instead of feeling relieved, I'm a little pissed that he got his way.

Flight no longer necessary, I double over, holding both knees to brace myself. This is not a concussion. This is something all at once much worse and, like, kind of *amazing*.

I know just what to do. The next-to-last last home on Faculty Row is Ms. Silverthorn's. If there is any door in all the world to knock on when you've come from the future, it's hers. Or, at least, I hope it is because I have no plan B.

Seriously, I'm kinda proud of myself. I've only been here for minutes, and I'm already working it. I don't know if that is a mental flaw or a testament to my fierceness. But there it is.

I'm here, I'm queer, it's 1985—get used to it.

Careful What You Wish For

MS. SILVERTHORN'S HOUSE, WHICH would be new to her in this time, is where we hold all the drama club cast parties. I have fallen asleep on her sectional more times than I can count, and I've even cooked in her kitchen (an ill-fated attempt at a big Cuban feast, for which I was, um, underprepared).

I feel better—until I knock on her door.

It swings open to an empty house. The layout is eerily familiar, but it is freshly painted and unoccupied. The fireplace where we made indoor s'mores is pristine, and the mantel above it begs for artwork. I could cry. Except, the view from her window is wrong. This isn't her house.

I step onto the lawn and count. One, two, three, four,

five—ohhh. In my time, there are seven houses on Faculty Row, but here are only six. Though Silverthorn's house is second-to-last in my time, it's the last one here, and when I knock at its door, she answers.

She has to be in her twenties if she's already teaching, but she could be somebody's kid sister. She looks that young. And different, too. Her hair is a *trip*. The sides are slicked back and held in place with plastic combs, but the top is a mass of curls that spill onto her forehead like bangs, and the back is doing the same thing in the other direction. There is more product in her hair than I have ever seen, each coil individually defined. I'm so startled I can't do anything but stare, which she does not love.

"Can I help you?" Her voice sounds exactly the same.

"Ms. Silverthorn!" I croak. I can't think how to follow up, because it's one thing to allow time travel into my own mind and another to say it out loud.

I recognize the look in her eyes: concern for me, even though I'm a stranger. Her empathetic nature means she's always ahead of most kids who come to her with a secret. There's no way she's ahead of *this* one, but she's figured out I am in distress.

"You're not one of my students, but I am Ms. Silverthorn. So . . ." She steps away from the door and ushers me in, and even though it's what I hoped for, I'm also like, whatever happened to stranger danger? I'm relieved when I see that not everything is different. She's years away from the sectional and the plasma screen TV, but her mother's rocking chair sits right where it should, and her framed lithograph of James Baldwin is already in place over the faux fireplace, though hung in a cheaper frame.

I need to figure out the fastest way to convince her I'm from the future without having her summon mental health professionals.

I should ask for today's date and then just google some historical thing that happens today and when it comes true—

My god. I can't.

There's. No. Internet.

I have to say something, though, and soon, because she is casually making her way to a phone the size of a toaster, which is, no joke, attached to the wall. Whether she's calling campus security or the police, I need to stop her.

"*Connecticut Yankee!*"

She pauses, one hand reaching toward the phone. "I'm sorry?"

"Um, you know how you said what happened to Clarence is a 'time slip'?"

Her brows rise. "Said to who? We haven't started it yet."

"Oh . . . uh . . ."

"How did you know I was going to end the semester with that?"

"You *always* do . . ."

"I what?"

"Er . . . or you will . . . like, forever." I have just dropped some real mind-bending news on her, and there's no way but forward now. "You will teach this book only to seniors, and you will tell us it's your idea of a treat, some light reading because you know we are already checked out, and you remember that feeling yourself."

The surprise on her face would be priceless if it wasn't mixed with a little fear, too. I'm nervous about where this might go.

Ms. Silverthorn looks me right in the eye. "I assume this means you're from the future."

I could kiss her. "Yes! YES!" I did say she was the original early adopter, right? She didn't even wait for me to announce it. "Wait—you believe me?"

Her laugh is warm and a little shaky. "I want to, for sure." She gestures at my clothes. "You know my name and where I live, but we've never met, and, trust me, I know every brown person in Antic Springs. You've somehow memorized my lesson planner, despite me not yet having filled it in. And there's that bizarre outfit—a classic man-out-of-time trope. So, yes, I want to believe you because otherwise, you're a stalker who knows way too much about my business."

I start to speak, but she presses ahead. "I teach the Twain because I *love* time travel. If it's in a book, I've read it. Movies, too." I want to tell her that I know this, and it's one reason I love her, but I don't want to interrupt. "I even had *The Two Worlds of Jenny Logan* on VHS until I accidentally taped over it during the Sarajevo games." I have no idea what she's talking about, but I don't ask because she's on a roll. "I've always believed it was just a matter of time before scientists proved time travel possible. I even wrote a paper on how Einstein's quantum physics might allow for *parallel* time."

"I thought you hated physics class!" She'd confessed her one high school C grade to me after I nearly failed my physics final.

This insider's access to her mind slows her up for a moment, and she shakes her shiny curls. "That's why my final project was on time travel—it was as close as I could get to making it fun." A wry laugh. "I can't believe I complain about that class to my students! Why am I revealing so much?"

She falls quiet. "I suppose that hardly matters. I should be more concerned that I'm buying this so quickly. As much as I want it to be real, now that it's here—now that *you're* here . . ." She falls silent a moment, mulling.

"Do a trick or something. Tell me what's going to happen or reveal a secret you can't possibly know. And make it a good one because now you have my hopes up."

I look around and . . . aha! *The chair.* "You are sitting in the same rocker where your mother nursed you, and in exchange for having it, you had to give your sister Cora your parents' wedding album. And *then* because you didn't trust her not to try and snag it back, you had your own name carved into the underside."

"Well, you're half right." Her eyes gleam with excitement. "Cora did fight me on this, and we settled on the wedding album swap, but I haven't carved my name into it. Yet. I told myself it was a silly idea . . . but I guess I change my mind, huh?" She is on her feet, electrified. "Though I'm still not sure I like how much Future Me talks about her private life to her students."

"Only the drama kids! We practically live at your house."

"So First Secondary doesn't cancel us?"

"Huh?"

"I just started Drama this year, and there are some parents who didn't like my musical choice."

This is a story I've never heard. "What was it?"

"*Godspell*. It's a religious allegory, so I thought it was a good way to ease the school in."

"It wasn't?"

"Too much allegory, not enough religion. The board wants to end the program, and some want to end me."

It's impossible to picture ASA without her or drama club. "Not gonna happen. You're the most popular teacher by miles. The board practically worships you!"

Now her eyes are really wide. "Just how far into the future are we talking?"

I hesitate. It occurs to me now that by my senior year, she will have been teaching for longer than she's been alive at this moment.

She waits for an answer. "*Now* you're shy?"

I do the math. "Uh . . . okay . . . would you believe thirty-six years?"

This lands just about as heavily as I expected. "I'm still teaching at First Secondary when I'm *sixty*?"

She goes to the window and gazes out at a setting she apparently didn't realize would be permanent.

I try to make it okay. "Um, you've won all these awards, and drama club is like the big moneymaker for the school . . . I think you still kinda love it."

"I hope so." Her voice is soft a moment and then she shakes it off. "How can I complain? It brought me a time traveler."

Turning to me with game face on, she says what she has said to me a thousand times in the future, in every emotional crisis I've made her bear witness to. "I think we need a hot chocolate." Regardless of season or time of day, she says hot chocolate solves everything, and though I can't prove this applies to quantum physics, I'm not saying no.

Gale Warning

THE PLAN IS TO pass me off as her nephew. "Sometimes, you have to put a blind spot to work for you." We are standing outside Frohmeyer's door, and Ms. Silverthorn says this so quietly that I am not sure whether she is reassuring herself or me. We worked it out over breakfast, which I wolfed down out of nerves, forgetting the intermittent fasting I do at home—which I now think of as a time, not a place.

"You think he'll buy it?" I try to keep my voice low. We look nothing alike: no overlap in skin tone, hair texture, or features. Mom's family, Cuban immigrants from the revolution, prize their comparative paleness; they marry only other light-skinned Cubans (or, in a pinch, white people, so that they can at least keep a fiction of their purity). But she went and married my dark-skinned dad, which pissed off her family and produced me, a midpoint on the color wheel.

"I think Mr. Frohmeyer doesn't know enough Black people—or Hispanics for that matter—to doubt it. And since he only employs *one*, I don't think he'll dare question me." (*Hispanics*? Whoa. This really is the '80s.)

His door swings inward, and he waves us in. Frohmeyer looks like Alfred Hitchcock with a mullet. The trail of snowy curls hanging to his collar is jarring in contrast to the shiny dome. His round cheeks seem permanently stuffed with something, which makes his small mouth look even smaller. "Tell me again what this clown's doing at a new school a month before graduation?"

Clown? I can't imagine Mrs. Somboon-Fox talking about a student that way and getting away with it, but I try to keep my face neutral. (Oh god, imagine if I hadn't wiped off the glitter.)

Ms. Silverthorn bites her lip. "Well, Ninevah . . ." She swallows and blinks to forestall tears. "You remember my sister, yes?"

Frohmeyer clearly does not and just as clearly has no plan to admit this. "Of course." He fills in the blanks. "What—is she sick or something?"

Ms. Silverthorn steers her wet eyes away from him and toward the framed portrait of the dead Mrs. Frohmeyer. She takes a breath and then can't continue. I am loving this. I don't think people said *you go, girl* in 1985, but I am screaming it on the inside. Ms. Silverthorn's performance is masterful. "I'm all she has . . ."

Frohmeyer shifts in his seat, rolling between his fingers a golf ball he has magically produced from his desk. I get the sense that he hates *feelings*. He starts tapping the ball on the desk, *ratatatatat*. Clearly, he'd rather speak for her than wait this out. "Which means you're all *he* has," he says, not clowning me this time.

He nods my way. "What's your name, son?"

"Luis . . ." I reach across the desk to shake his hand, playing along, then over-answer. "Luis Silverthorn."

This lands awkwardly. Duh. In using my teacher's last name, I have just made her sister an unwed mother, not a great detail in a school that's still so religious. A gently raised eyebrow on her part tells me she can't believe I said it.

Somehow my error does the trick. "Sounds like a hard road," he mumbles, by which he means "brown-skinned fatherless son of a woman too ill to care for him." How could he turn me away? But he can't be too soft, either, or it'll ruin his reputation.

"Luis, we have rules here. A lot of 'em. Ask your aunt." He makes the word rhyme with "haunt," which is the whitest thing ever. (And in real life, I only have tías.) "You're expected to abide by them. So read the handbook." He slides a heavy blue spiral-bound notebook across the desk.

"Anisha, you need to get me his records. He's not graduating without a transcript, and he still has to pass our classes." This must be his default principal mask: tough love face.

"Of course, Carl." Their use of first names makes them sound like a team and leaves me on the outside for a moment, a feeling which gets worse when she asks him, "Do you have a room for him?"

Wait. She's making me live in the dorm?

Bruce Hall is—was—famously dumpy. It looks like someone threw an enormous cement block at the hillside, and it got stuck there. The "first" floor is at ground level, but a steep slope makes that same floor the second story on the opposite side. It may be thirty years younger now than when it was razed the summer after my freshman year (replaced with a different ugly building that has better ventilation and a pool), but still.

"Can't I just be off campus?"

They both look at me like I have lost my mind. His expression reads *ungrateful brat*. Hers says *are you kidding me?*

"Do you live in this town?"

"Uh . . . no . . ."

"Are you planning to camp?"

"I meant—"

"Your aunt is an unmarried woman, so it's not like she can have some teenage boy living in her house." (Where does he think I spent last night?)

He says this as if it's so obvious that her (presumed) chastity trumps our (falsified) blood relations. She doesn't argue, so I swallow hard and play along. "Right. Um, thanks." And then to show contrition, I add, "Sir."

Frohmeyer looks at me a moment, trying to decide if I'm

sincere or trouble, then turns back to Ms. Silverthorn. "The dean will set him up for now. Ernie Gale could use a roommate."

As he says this, he chuckles, and I see her trying hard not to respond, as a distant alarm bell rings in my brain.

"Now get outta here." We all rise at once, and Ms. Silverthorn thanks him again before he shuts the door behind us.

We're in the hallway, which is beginning to fill with students in what I think of as vintage clothing, and, of course, they just think of it as clothes. Her first words are reassurances. "You'll be fine in the dorm." Having never lived with anyone but Mom, I'm not convinced, and my teacher can see this. "I hate to say it, but I agree—I met you less than twenty-four hours ago, no matter how well we know each other when I'm an old lady. I'm not ready to be your house mother."

She indicates my notebook. "You have the class schedule? And a map of the building?"

I nod, feeling lightheaded. *Try not to panic.* "You're my first period, right?"

"Yes. Seems like a good day to start *Connecticut Yankee.*" I think she wants to hug me. I know I want to hug her. But neither is going to happen, and the first bell rings. *Oh my god, oh my god.*

"Welcome to First Secondary," she says with a hopeful smile and leaves me to the '80s.

I know the floor plan of the school—I mean, it's *my school*—so I don't really need to stare at the map to find my way, but it's very calming to just focus on a piece of 8 ½" x 11" paper instead of, say, the enormity of my actual situation.

"Sorry!" A bellowing apology registers about a half-second before I am face-down on the floor. Pale hands are lifting me to my feet, and my thoughts are jumbled before a skinny white kid with red cheeks and a deeply concerned expression fill my view. "I didn't see you! I was in the ninth inning!" He thrusts at me what appears to be a calculator topped with a baseball diamond. I have no clue what he wants me to do with it, and I push it back roughly.

"Earth to clueless: you're actually in a hallway *where other people are walking*!" He looks shocked and, honestly, I kind of am, too, but it's been a stressful twenty-four hours. Poor kid kind of runs away before I can figure out why he seems familiar.

"Someone's got an attitude. I like it." The speaker—a girl, Persian maybe?—looks too cool for (this) school. Jet black hair cascades past a headband onto olive skin. One eye is covered by her locks completely, and the remaining eye is heavily outlined with kohl, beneath eyeshadow in the colors of a Caribbean beach party. I recognize her from Mom's yearbook, which I dug up last year just to gawk at the clothes. I don't remember her name, but her senior superlative was "Least Likely to Care About Your Opinion," which obvi makes an impression. When I asked Mom why she wasn't that cool, she'd laughed and said they were friends, which made her cool by proxy. I honestly can't see them as buds, and she never talked about her, so they can't have been close.

The girl's eyebrow is raised expectantly, and I can see she wants the scoop.

My offender has beaten a hasty retreat, and it's just me and this stranger I have to know. "He just surprised me, is all."

She drops a husky laugh. "Don't apologize. You didn't get a Gale warning, so you had no way to know what was coming."

Gale warning. Now I know why the name is familiar.

I almost spit. Gale, as in the museum nerd. Ernie Gale, as in *my new roommate.*

As if we're old friends, the stranger tells me Ernie's the biggest klutz in the school. "He's lost just about every on-campus job, not because he doesn't try, but because he's a continual disaster." Her eye sparkles as she rattles off the litany. "He set fire to the cafeteria, flooded the chapel, wrecked a tractor on the farm . . . Don't get me wrong: he's not a bad kid, just *spacey.*" She takes on the voice of a confidante. "Maybe it's a little mean, but kids say 'Gale warning' to warn people that's he coming."

And I'm going to live with him?

I can't think of what to say, which is okay because the second bell rings. I imagine it means the same thing here as in my time: we have sixty more seconds to get to class.

"First period English?" I don't even have to look at my schedule.

"Yes!"

She nods down the hall toward what was and is Ms. Silverthorn's room, but I pretend I don't already know this. "Lead the way!"

"Straight into trouble," she laughs, and I like her already.

I whisper my name, and she returns the favor, introducing herself as Leeza as she leads me to the very last row. Our still-teenage-looking teacher isn't surprised to see me sitting so far back because she doesn't know that someday Cheng and I will always, *always* claim the two seats nearest the door.

Other kids are noticing me now. I hold my breath a little, but Mom isn't in my class. Naturally, because I don't want him to be, Gordo is. (Note: There is no universe in which I'm calling him Dad.) He's whispering to some buddies about me, and it's everything I can do not to blow him a kiss, which is how I'd piss off cavemen types in my day (and, um, guys who didn't spawn me). Some of the others give me welcoming (if slightly confused) smiles, and this white girl in front of me turns around to introduce herself. Strawberry-blonde hair frames a face dotted with *amazing* freckles, the kind fashionistas were tattooing on in 2018. "You picked a perfect time to start First Secondary—it's almost over!"

Ms. Silverthorn does her thing, a move that is so familiar to me I become homesick for my real life. She always begins class with a clap clap, her hands somehow perfectly cupped to make the sound ring out. It is never one clap, never three. But it's always enough: even this young, she has a natural presence that makes you listen, paired with a warmth that makes you want to.

"Today, class, as you can see, we have a new arrival." Now, all heads turn, and I try to smile. (Too late, I realize, I am sitting with my legs crossed, which is *very* me but is true of no other boy in class.) She asks me to introduce myself, and I stick with the story I told Frohmeyer: I'm Luis Silverthorn, her nephew, and, um, my mom's sick. She shoots me a look that clearly means "don't say more than you need," but I can't help myself. I say I'm from *Connecticut*, just as a little in-joke for her and me. (I *love* an in-joke.)

Happily for me, she gets down to business right away, and even happier, this class is running about ten days behind *my* class, so I don't have to pay close attention. While other kids are writing stuff about Twain in their notebooks (like literal paper ones), I am making a list of things I will need. Last night, we ran to a JCPenney (it was huge and busy, which was, honestly, so confusing) for a couple of basics to get me through the rest of this week. *So* basic: I have three polo shirts, two pairs of jeans, and a pair of sneakers that the pimply clerk swore are made out of the same stuff as the nose of the space shuttle. My underwear resembles granny panties, which I guess are a thing, but not a *me* thing, and I feel weird having such ugliness close to my skin. (I am grateful only that this is a big era for mousse, so I can do my hair just how I like. My skin, on the other hand—let's not go there.)

The ring of the period two bell is jarring to me. And a reminder that I need to get a watch. Like one on my wrist, which is so not me. Those boys who flex their watches? Gross. But I'm going to have to tell time somehow, and my iPhone battery is gonna last, like, ten more seconds. (That realization sparks another: I should probably keep this twenty-first century marvel out of sight entirely.)

My mom is in my next class, and I want to cry. She's so young and so pretty, even with those crazy bangs. She wears blue eyeshadow and too much blush, and exudes a playfulness and joy that I'm not used to seeing. And her skin, my god. No wonder Gordo fell for her. Right now, he sits next to her, his leg heavily against hers. Based on the way both look in my direction, he's talking about me, and whatever he's saying, she's not having it.

She comes over and introduces herself. "Maria Elena. Most people here call me Laney, 'cuz it's easier."

"How about Ma Elena?"

That's what Abuelo and all the tías call my mom and it earns me a smile, but also a bit of puzzlement. "Is Ms. Silverthorn Spanish?"

"Oh, uh, no . . . I get it from my dad's side."

Unfortunately for me, this invites a stream of Spanish that I cannot keep up with, and I end up repeating "lo siento" over and over. She lets me off the hook. "It was worth a try." And then leans closer. "My boyfriend says he thought you were a Townie, and he's sorry."

"No he didn't." Up go her eyebrows. "I mean, the Townie part, yeah, but he's not the apologizing type." Dammit, I said that as fact (which it is), not a guess (which it should be).

"How much time did you spend with him?" She doesn't seem to mind that I insulted him; she's only curious about how I pegged him so fast.

"I mean . . . it doesn't take long to figure out a guy like that."

She colors. "I know how he looks, but you don't know his story. And my advice is, on your first day, don't invite people to judge books by their covers."

I'm pissing off my own mom. "I'm sorry. Really. He just scared me a little."

Her posture softens. "Don't you worry. As long as he's with me, he has to behave. If he doesn't, he can be replaced!" That line is so sassy, I would have said it, and it's hard to believe it came from her lips. While I try to process that, she goes back to her seat, and I hear her whispering my name. It wouldn't surprise me if she's now telling him that *I* apologized. She's always hated conflict—Switzerland with spray bangs.

Two more periods (chemistry, which I'm bad at in any decade, and gym, from which I'm excused because apparently, you need these hideous high waisted gym shorts and crew socks nearly to your knees), then it's lunch. I get my tray and hop in line: today's options are lukewarm hot dogs or wan chicken breasts wrapped in ham, accompanied by two mayonnaise-based side dishes: macaroni salad and potato salad. Only the macaroni salad is vegetarian (the potato salad is liberally studded with bacon), and there's no vegan option at all (Cheng would starve). Maybe vegans don't exist yet? You could probably do a paleo diet here, but keto is out for sure. In my day, this cafeteria would beg for a lawsuit. (*In my day? Like I'm eighty.*)

Now, where to sit. My roommate is at a long table with a lot of empty space between him and the two girls hunched over a copy of *Tiger Beat* at the other end. He is chewing with his mouth open, eyes fixed on that electronic game console. I *can't*.

Leeza saves me, dragging me to the table where she sits with a white girl wearing a Care Bears sweatshirt. "Look what I found wandering the halls this morning." She's about basic as possible, which seems an unlikely fit with Leeza. She seems to accept that if Leeza has invited me to their table, I'm worth knowing, and she introduces herself as Tawny. Her eyes are pale blue and untroubled as she burbles a stream of questions.

"Did you really get Galed before first period? Did Gordo beat you up last night? Are you Black or Spanish because I heard Ms. Silverthorn is your—"

"Tawny!" Leeza is laughing.

"I'm just asking!"

Leeza winks at me. "Ignore her."

"He doesn't mind!"

"Who says?" Tawny fixes me with a serious look. "*Do* you?"

Leeza intervenes. "You're going to make Weese regret sitting with us."

Weese? My name is only two syllables long, and still, it's too hard to say? *People.* Maybe she can tell what I'm thinking. "I love a nickname. That's okay, right?"

Could be worse. A boy at summer camp one year called me Luisa the whole time, and though I didn't care that much (no skin off my nose to be seen as girly), I hated the scorn in his voice as he dragged my name into three syllables to show his disgust.

And the nickname spread, till half the campers were doing it. Having an ally here will be a good thing.

"Seriously, Weese is fine."

A melodious voice beckons. "Hey, ladies, may I?"

A skinny Black kid, the width and suppleness of a willow switch, slides into a space on the other side of Leeza. His head is wrapped in a silk do-rag—a bold move considering the rest of the crowd in this hall—and he wears a tracksuit made of what looks like parachute cloth in midnight blue. Purple and yellow parallelograms slash across one leg. He leans past Leeza. "And who might you be?"

Tawny looks nervous—for him? For me? I try to be cool. "Luis. But my friends call me Weese." Leeza glows. Point scored.

He doesn't have to say his name. I already know. Chaz Wilson. I've traveled through time to dine with the doomed.

What's Your Damage?

I'M SURE THERE'S A simple explanation for violet eyes. But it must be some crazy confluence of factors, or it wouldn't be so rare. I mean, I can't name anyone but Elizabeth Taylor and that boy from Spain on YouTube, and until this moment, I had never seen anything like it in real life. I try not to stare. And fail.

"You're new, Weese, so I'll just get this out of the way: Yes, they're purple; yes, they're real; no, I'm not an alien."

Leeza breaks out a laugh. "You so are! I mean, look around you."

Chaz kisses her on the cheek. "And that is why I love you."

He sits back and sizes me up. "You've been here how long? This girl already has a bestie, so step off!" He says this completely without animosity, and it feels like an invitation to join them, but she punches his arm anyway, and he swats back. "I was about to say—"

"You're always saying something," she cuts in. Clearly, they have a routine, these two. I'm jealous. I find myself aching for Nix, who has had my back since the first day of middle school.

Chaz shakes his head at me. "See what I put up with? I guess it's good you're here—you can take some of her crap."

"What Chaz wanted to say—"

"You think you know? Do you?"

"You tell anyone who will listen!"

Tawny spoils it. "They're moving to the city together after graduation!"

I can't help it: I gasp. After graduation. Oh god.

Leeza is genuinely surprised at the look on my face. "We're not living in sin or anything. Just roommates . . ."

Quick recovery time. "Oh—no—I just . . . I always wanted to move to Manhattan."

Chaz likes that. "Doesn't everyone?"

Tawny blinks. "Not me. My mom says it's dangerous. There are gang fights in broad daylight!"

Leeza rolls her eyes. "She's going to college in Iowa."

"I got a scholarship. So did Chaz. I made him apply, but he turned it down even though it's way safer in Iowa, and cleaner, too. Where are *you* going?"

My real answer is Boston Conservatory, but only if I get back to my time, so what comes out is "Home, I hope." Immediately their faces darken. Leeza starts to explain, but Chaz shushes her, having already heard about me.

"I'm sorry about your mom. Will she—is she . . . ?"

He's at a loss for words, really wanting to know if she's dying or just sick, but how do you ask that of someone you just met? And how do I answer? Ms. Silverthorn and I never even picked a disease! I don't have to answer, as it turns out.

Gordo and Ma Elena are approaching our table. (This teenaged girl stuffed into tight jeans and wearing all that makeup is totally not a version of my mother I can call Mom.) Ma Elena hugs Leeza and greets Tawny politely, while Gordo just broods behind her, eyes scanning the cafeteria for people he likes better.

She asks me how I'm settling in, and it's hard for me to sound casual, considering who she is (or someday will be). "Good," I say. "Classes are easy so far, and I already met these guys."

"Perfect." Her smile is so natural and effortless. I don't think I've ever seen it so unfettered. She jabs Gordo, and he finally forces out his own tight smile, the antidote to hers.

"Sorry I gave you crap. Townies keep vandalizing stuff. I'm just doing my part for the school."

Chaz makes the world's softest possible "mm-hmm" of doubt, but not actually soft enough for Gordo to miss. Gordo grips Chaz by the shoulder, his meaty fingers forming a vise, but his voice remains cheerful as if he's telling a great joke. "You know what I have against homos, Chaz? MY HAND!" He busts out a hearty laugh at his own line, and Ma Elena is mortified.

"I'll take him away before he makes the whole school look bad. See you later, Leez?"

Leeza nods at her and looks at me. Tawny stares at her meal and Chaz has become an obelisk. His face is dead neutral, and his violet eyes are focused far beyond this room.

I'm the one who breaks the silence. "What an asshole!"

Released from the spell, Tawny begins a long list of grievances about Gordo. Leeza laughs and squeezes my hand, making it clear that she appreciates my response. Only Chaz remains silent.

Leeza explains, "First rule of First Secondary: You can't listen to Gordo. He's all bark. He lashes out at whatever he doesn't understand. Which is a lot."

Still nothing from Chaz. I'm dying. I want to help, so I lie. Write the future I wish for him.

"You'll get your revenge. Trust me. When you move to New York and make a fabulous life for yourself and age flawlessly and come back for your high school reunion with a total hunk on your arm and Gordo is all old and fat—"

Chaz flees. Like, *flees.* He's out of his seat so fast, leaving his tray behind, that I think I've missed something.

Tawny is doing a stunning deer-in-headlights impression, and Leeza looks furious.

73

"Why would you do that?"

"Do what?"

"Mock him like that!"

"Mock him?! I was trying to help!"

"'Fabulous' and 'flawless'?" Her imitation of my voice is cruel—I don't *think* I really sound that queeny, but maybe the bar for queeny is different in 1985. "You're as bad as Gordo."

"I—I was trying to be supportive—to let him know it's okay."

"At First Secondary?"

"Or anywhere?" This from Tawny. "He has a girlfriend, you know."

This is news to me.

Leeza murmurs, "Ignore him, Tawny."

The news only gets worse. Tawny scoops up her tray and Chaz's too. "We've been together since tenth grade!"

Damage control—I need some and fast. I try to pop the balloon of tension I've just made. "My gaydar sucks. Everyone says so . . . back home."

"Your what?"

"Gaydar . . . like radar for telling who's gay and who's straight."

Tawny relaxes a little, curious. "Why would anyone need that?" She sets down their trays.

"Where I'm from, there are more gay kids at school." Oh my god, their faces. "It's like normal to be nice to them."

Leeza looks intrigued. "In Connecticut?"

I have no idea what Connecticut was like in 1985, but I'm

guessing I've oversold it. "My school, I mean. It's . . . pretty progressive. Run by hippies." God, I think I'm screwing up decades.

Tawny's face has returned to its previously untroubled state. "That explains it. If you're around them a lot, you probably just imagine them everywhere." Her use of "them" is killing me, but I just nod. "We don't have any here. It's not allowed."

"It's in the handbook and everything," she adds. "But any boy who's not like Gordo—"

"A human meat locker?" This wins laughs from both, my good graces being restored.

"*Exactly!* If you're not like that, the other boys pick on you. Call you all sorts of things."

Leeza's voice is grim. "Chaz has taken a lot of heat." She closes her eyes like she's imagining the future. "But that's all about to end."

My head hurts. I can't even.

The bell rings for second lunch. I apologize to Tawny and ask her to make sure Chaz knows I didn't mean anything by it. She assures me that he'll understand, that he's the sweetest guy ever, and we'll all be great friends. I am so relieved when she leaves, I could cry.

Leeza takes my arm when they're gone. "At some point," she says, "We need to talk."

Time travel is *exhausting*. It's been like twenty-four hours (and thirty-six years) since I bonked my head in the arts building, and I'm so tired I could cry. Right now, I have a number of good reasons to just howl. I am in my new room, home of the future Mr. Gale.

He has (reluctantly) taken down some of the posters on what is now my side, but the ones he left up are baffling. Who has Farrah Fawcett in a red bikini *and The Sound of Music*? KISS *and* Ms. Pac Man? There's even an authentic "The Scream" poster but with no meme. It's like someone gave him a dorm manual that said "Hang up posters" but didn't specify why.

The bathroom we share with the next room is a disaster. I mean not to gender stereotype, but this is straight-boy-in-a-frat behavior. A damp forest green towel is wadded up on the floor, begging the universe for mildew. The toilet paper sits on the floor, too, and the roll contains one shredded ribbon that will help nobody; it is not immediately clear where the next roll hides. The shower has three slivers of soap, one of them mint green like a toothpaste, and it is clear that no one has ever considered actually scrubbing the walls down or replacing the curtain liner. Half of the few products—a hairspray, a deodorant, a cologne—are called Brut, which smells like alcohol, and I'm guessing is the Axe of its day.

But the real reason I'm so tired is that it's beginning to hit me that I have no idea when or how or *if* I'll get back to my time. I'm a problem solver by nature, and I always get what I want in the end, so I've spent the last day in Action Mode. I had three tasks: find Ms. Silverthorn, convince her that I'm from the future, and find a place to stay while I work it out. Done, done, and done—but now what? Am I really going to live with young Mr. Gale and go to school with my parents and watch the train wreck of Chaz's future unfold? How long is this supposed to last?

This is the part in a time travel story that I like least: when the traveler doesn't know how long they're stuck. It's a real virtue to have a time machine, even one that breaks down and must be repaired (they always break down and always get repaired), so too bad for me. I just have to remind myself that in 99 percent of these stories, it all works out in the end . . . except for *Connecticut Yankee*, which makes the guy live, like, a thousand years that way.

I can't stay still, letting this all race around in my head. I know I'm not supposed to leave campus at all, even for Faculty Row a block away, but I'm hoping my first day and my imagined family tragedy will buy me some latitude. I have to get out of this Brut factory right now. I head for Ms. Silverthorn's.

As I'm walking up Faculty Row, I see the curtains part at the first house. Right until my freshman year, that was the Buckmans' house. She taught math, and he taught shop; they were as old-school as that sounds, and they taught at the academy for forty years each. Helen Buckman was a famous gossip who somehow missed the juiciest bit of all: her husband was a perv. Their location at the Faculty Row entrance meant she had a front-row seat to all the comings and goings; it also meant he didn't have far to go when returning from a campus tryst. I can't see her (though I'm dying to know what she looks like young), but I know she's watching me now, so I blow a kiss in the direction of the curtains. They stop moving. *Ha.*

When I knock on her door, Ms. Silverthorn is cheerful. "Good. You made it. I wasn't sure Frohmeyer got word to the dean that I was going to pick you up."

I don't mention that I never waited for word (or permission), but I am happy to discover that we are headed to the mall. Until it occurs to me the debit card in my wallet is as useless as my phone. She sees both the rise and fall in my expression. "I got you. You can't go too wild; I'm a school-teacher, after all. But I've got enough for some more clothes, stuff for your room to hold you over. If we're lucky, you won't be here long."

In her car, a hilarious walnut-colored monstrosity with a too-long nose and the sassy name Vega, she explains that she's been gathering all the time travel books she could find in the school library. After she drops me off to shop, she's going to expand on this with a visit to the big library one town over. "Even the craziest fiction is based on the human experience," she says. "Sometimes fantastical plot points are really just metaphors for emotional truth, and sometimes they're based on wild, but incontrovertible fact. Where would the ideas come from otherwise? The human mind only knows itself." (She's *such* an English teacher.)

I'm not sure if I agree with her, but I listen. (One perk of this experience so far: Me listening *before* weighing in is like *growth*.)

"Before yesterday, I'd have reluctantly agreed that time travel falls into the metaphor camp. But here you are. Fantasy became fact. And why not? Why would this experience occur so often in literature if it had never happened? The truth that this *is* the truth was hiding in plain sight all along, just like I secretly hoped. It's easier to pretend otherwise, of course, because it's just so rare."

"Like violet eyes."

Ms. Silverthorn lets her gaze drift from the road to me. "You've met Chaz, I take it."

Not ready to go down that road, I ask what she's found in the books. I don't add that I've read some of these myself; it was all entertainment at the time, not life or death, so I wasn't exactly mining them for instruction. "Is there anything that can help us?"

"Working on that." I don't like her answer—in its brevity or its worried tone—but we're at Finger Lakes Mall, and she's handing me an envelope of cash. "Maybe buy a wallet first, so it doesn't look like you're a drug dealer."

Whoa.

I think of the '80s as the neon lights era, but this mall is all country village, with stores tucked into two-story "houses" painted in pastels; the vast cream ceiling is held up by red brick pillars that match the cobblestone floor that runs through a fake park, complete with trees. They've worked really hard to make an indoor mall look like an outdoor mall and I guess that's hot these days, because it is *crawling* with people.

There's the JCPenney, its window full of norm core, and a Kmart, which will be cheap, but then I see it: Chess King. Oh my god. I have literally shopped vintage Chess King on eBay and Depop. My favorite bomber jacket—butter yellow—is Chess King. I *have* to go in.

Oof. Some of this stuff is garbage. I mean, I can't even tell what the skinny ties are made of—it's like the intersection of sateen and plastic. But the zippered parachute pants are the same material parachute pants are always made of, and they'll be so cute with a black bomber that I know is not remotely leather but has red epaulets, and I'm thinking: *ensemble.*

I count the cash Ms. Silverthorn gave me and realize that this purchase will eat up a third of it. I ditch the pants and snag only the jacket; it has a point of view. I'll wear tees and polos and jeans for the rest of my sentence in 1985, but at least I'll have a signature item. It makes me feel more like myself just thinking about it.

An Asian girl with a braided headband rings me up. "STYLISH!" she says. I'm so happy to talk clothes that I tell her I already have this jacket in yellow, and she's amazed. They haven't even SEEN the yellow in this store—when did it come out?—and I'm off to the lying races about how my cousin lives in the city and they get everything first.

"You may be too cool for this mall," she says, winking and opening the drawer. "I don't think you've been in before. I'd remember *YOU* for sure!" She's taking an awfully long time to make change.

Is she flirting? I smile nervously. "Thanks . . . I—I'm from Connecticut."

"Really? I've heard it's pretty there! I'll have to go someday."

My god, she *is* flirting. I'm somewhere between blushing and fleeing. Is Gordo the only person in 1985 who knows a gay guy when he sees one?

When I have my change, I grab the bag and just about backflip out of the store. Written in pink ballpoint on the receipt: a seven-digit phone number, 555-2334. Wow. I've only lived in a time when you have to include the area code *and* local exchange, so this is like being handed a letter from a Civil War general. But it gets even crazier. Next to a big smiley face is her name: *Malee*.

I'm so focused on the realization that my principal lived in Antic Springs as a kid—Mom *so* never told me that—that I don't see Gordo until I actually bump into him.

"Watch it, ass wipe!" He does a double take when he sees it's me. And looks nervous. "What are you doing off campus?"

"I'm with Ms. Silverthorn!" (It's kind of true.) "What are *you* doing here?" I'm pretty sure I have him in a bind because even all these years later, boarding kids still need permission to leave the academy, and you have to sign out, even if you're just going to Faculty Row. It has always been my great privilege to come and go as I please, and it's also one reason I would never break up with Cheng: dating a fellow day student is like a get-out-of-jail-free card.

Ma Elena comes out of Tape Lab with a red bag—I am dying to see what she bought—and she frowns when she sees me here. "Already breaking the rules? It's the first day." Now she sounds like Mom. Or at least that's what I think before she grins. "I'm only teasing. I work for Frohmeyer, so I get to run a lot of errands, and he wouldn't love me bringing Gordo along, so we'll all just agree that neither of you is here! Rules beg to be bent." And she flashes that smile again. My god, it's bright. "I'm getting an Orange Julius before we head back. Anybody want one?"

I don't even know what that is, but I pass, and so does Gordo. Ma Elena shrugs and heads off toward what looks like a smoothie bar and hops in a not-unimpressive line. It occurs to me that if she works for Frohmeyer, she has the same campus job as I will. We're that alike?

Gordo lets her get out of earshot before asking me, in his lowest voice. "Why were you sitting with the fag?"

Not Leeza. Not Tawny. All his eyes could see was Chaz. And he really wants to know.

"He sat with us, and so what if he did?" I can't remember if *Heathers* is out in 1985 or not, but I do my best Veronica. "What's your damage?"

"My what?"

Mom has always said that shame of any kind, any hint of being mocked, was my dad's Achilles. His eyes darken, and his cheeks clench, a look I remember and don't miss. I should keep my mouth shut. I don't.

"Your *problem*—what has he ever done to you?"

"Done?" He sputters. It's like I asked why it's bad to stick a cat in a microwave. "It's—it's just not right. You can't *be* that way." It offends him that I don't inherently know this. "Where are you from again?"

"Somewhere cooler than this, obviously." His brows are so furrowed his forehead is going to collapse.

Ma Elena spots trouble from a distance and gets between us before it gets worse. "I got you, babe," she says, thrusting a frothy orange shake at Gordo.

"Your new friend thinks it's okay for Chaz to be—" But now, for some reason, he can't say it. Maybe it's the fire in my eyes. Maybe the fire in hers. "You know."

"Let it go. Chaz is not your problem." She shoots me a look to let me know she is dead sick of this and hopes I won't hold him against her.

"But he makes the school look bad!" Gordo's ire is fading, and he leaves it there.

"Only to you, babe." She offers me a sip of her Orange Julius, but I'm suspicious and wave it off. "We better get back. Frohmy loves me, but there are limits." (She calls him Frohmy? I'm dying.) "You have a ride, right? I have a car—perks of living off campus—but I don't think I can sneak you both in. Gordo has to lie on the floor of the back seat as it is."

I assure them that Ms. Silverthorn is right outside, and they're gone—Ma Elena poking Gordo hard in the arm as they walk away. I recognize her angry lecture face. If she already knew he was a jerk at eighteen, why let him come back in her thirties? It's hard to imagine. Marrying your high school sweetheart is unwise enough, and worse when he's an obvious ass.

Music starts thumping above me, and I look up. The lights have come on in the second-floor village windows, and shadows fly by. It takes me a moment to spot the sign: Interskate 90. Oh my god—a roller rink. Two couples enter in a row, doppelganger mulleted boys in ringer tees and girlfriends with teased perms. Even though I'm still mad at Cheng, I wish he were here. He loves to be in motion: swimming, skateboarding, whatever.

Like a moth drawn to a flame, I find myself heading upstairs. Ms. Silverthorn won't be back for a while, so why not try it out?

Once I've paid my two dollars and fifty cents (!) and strapped on my skates, I immediately fall down. Pulling myself up, I have to hold onto the wall when I take to the skate floor, little kids zipping by me like I'm ancient. Apparently, looking down at your feet just makes you tip forward. Pulling off to the side, I watch the decent skaters to figure out why I'm such a fail. I see that I need to shift from side to side and lean toward the toe of the skate to propel myself forward. A lot of skaters glide past with their arms out, palms down; they look like baby birds learning to fly, geeky but also adorable, and since they're rolling and I'm not, I try it.

Sis, it's kind of great. Unlike ice skating, it's not freezing in here—and who can resist swirling disco lights? The music is unironically retro, though, on second thought, I guess it *can't* be ironic because it won't actually be retro for another decade or two. Picking up speed, I realize I can also put my hips into it, and it feels like dancing. There are plenty of couples (all straight, natch) who have the pair-skating thing down, and I am jealous all over as they sail by holding hands, leaning into corners in unison, and it's kind of beautiful. I can imagine Cheng by my side, rounding those turns with me.

I'm guessing Chaz never has done pairs skating. Or if he has, it was with Tawny—her keeping up a stream of chatter, him eyeing boys he doesn't dare talk to. This image presents itself to me so clearly, I'm suddenly emotional. *Of course* he can't skate here with a boy—not in this place, not in this time, not with the Gordos of the world watching his every move. Instead, he must hold on to Tawny for dear life, which must be torture and salvation all at once. Maybe she knows it, too. And that's also sad. For her, for him.

There, in the neon-punctuated dark of Interskate 90, the strains of *Xanadu* floating in the air, I realize I have a mission.

In books and movies, there's always a reason for the time travel—some lesson to be learned, some tragedy to prevent. I doubt I'll be learning much from the '80s, but I've already met a tragedy-in-the-making and the thing he lacks—the ability to be comfortable in his own skin—is the one thing I still have in spades. Assuming I don't whisk back to my real life in the next minute or two, that boy is going to have a friend he can be out to *and* out with. I'll show him how to be confident in himself, how not to take crap from het-monsters, and help

85

him see that his future's so bright, he'll have to wear shades (pink, naturally, with crystal frames). We're gonna be rainbow besties, and I will personally see to it that he makes it to prom.

I get it now.

I'm here to save Chaz Wilson.

Mash Note from a
Mystery Man

THERE ARE CERTAIN ADVANTAGES to having Ernie
Gale as your roommate. For one thing, he's so glad to have
company that he's eager to please. Do I want one of his extra
ramen cups? (Yes. Ramen is time-travel-resistant.) Would
I like to pick the music on the radio? Do I want to look over his
chem notes?

He's also giving me the tea on the school social structure,
which he has mapped out intricately. Ma Elena and Gordo,
along with Gordo's cronies and their girlfriends, are at the top
of the strata: good grades, good looks, good relationships with
teachers. (*Gordo?*) By his own admission, Ernie Gale is closer
to the bottom, a rung he shares with a twenty-two-year-old

senior and a girl who wears her fat wallet on a heavy metal chain, kids who perpetually zig when everyone else zags.

Forget the messy bathroom and array of random posters for a minute. I'm human, and now I feel a little sympathy for the guy.

Ernie groups everyone else in clusters: band, choir, praise team (*praise team?!*), basketball (the school's only sport), ham radio club, and categories of his own designation like the Keeners (which I gather has something to do with grades), the Attitudes (self-explanatory), and the Others. By "Others," he means my lunch table: Leeza is not only not religious but unconcerned with school spirit or winning over anyone; she came here from Queens, not knowing a soul, and bonded with Chaz the moment she arrived. Now Chaz is with Tawny, pulling Tawny along into their unit through no fault of her own. Ernie says no one dislikes the Others, but no one quite gets them either. He actually envies them, says they have the *best* position: no pressure from being on top, no drama from being on the bottom. They're the neutrals, the no-man's-land. He makes it sound dreamy.

I mean, seriously, aspiring to be neutral? Like, you're in a box of crayons and aim for *tan.* Aspiring to the color people use for sand or ethnicities they can't place when you could be cerulean or purple mountains majesty. (Yes, that's a color. #38. Look it up.)

"Do you have . . . who are *your* friends?" I almost hold my breath.

He sounds surprised. "I get along with *everyone.* No one hates me." He says the two things as if they are equal, and I'm not about to disabuse him of the notion, but it's tragic. A *real* friend is not like passively okay about your presence; they're actively interested. Nix and I have been tight since back in the day when their folks still called them by their dead name, and they say I'm the only one who's known who they are all along. We've compared notes on cute boys, raged against injustices like juniors not being allowed to have their own prom, seen each other through bad breakups (though, seriously, Nix always dates the wrong person and can't see it till it's too late), and have in-jokes by the mile. (Reading Nix's signature in my year-books is like deciphering hieroglyphics.) Maybe even more than Cheng, Nix has made my years at ASA. Ernie needs a Nix.

It won't be me. You can't fake a real friendship, but I can make him feel at home in his own (Brut-scented) room. He asks if I want to make a radio handle and try out his CB. I can't possibly feign enough interest in the world to make that happen, but I tell him I'll just listen when he's on.

There's a sharp rap at the door, and Gordo opens it without waiting. "Dorm mail in ten, jackoffs." Then he's gone.

"What the hell was that?" Ernie Gale blushes, and I remember this is still a religious school. But I don't apologize because, by me, that is *mild* swearing.

"Dorm mail. We can send letters over to the girls' dorm. We write notes, and the RAs take them over at break and then bring back theirs. Cool, huh?"

By "break," he means 9 p.m., when the required nightly "study hall" takes place. You have to be in your own room for two hours first, and only then, after you have been sufficiently trapped into doing homework, do you get a break. After that, you can be in any other room in the dorm until lights out at ten. *Apparently,* I'm in a medium-security prison for youth who committed the crime of being alive in the '80s.

Ernie shows me the note he has written. "JJ—Good work on the biography. I liked it. I didn't know who Gertrude Stain even was! Haha. Ernz."

I don't know who JJ is, whether Ernie is being funny in misspelling Gertrude Stein, and whether anyone on earth actually calls him "Ernz," but his joy in writing this note makes me feel a little better for him. When he folds it elaborately into a little tight triangular packet, I'm intrigued. He explains that everyone folds their notes so RAs won't dare read them—he says some of them are just nosy. "If you need privacy, like for a mash note or a breakup, write the girl's name on the outside but not *your* name, so the RA can't see who sent it." ("Mash note!" I get it and love it instantly.)

I'm stuck on a detail. "Okay, this is all fascinating from a high school anthropology angle, but why did *Gordo* tell us, and shouldn't he wait for you to answer before popping into your room?"

"RAs only have to knock once. It's to make sure we don't do drugs or sneak a girl in. Big Tom tried that—she climbed up the drain spout, and they got caught before they were done. I'm not even kidding. And he had terrible acne!" The stream of ideas is a bit wonky for me, and he'd never guess the part I find most shocking.

"*Gordo's* an RA? He's the biggest jerk at ASA!"

"ASA?"

"Sorry, that's my old school . . . at First Secondary."

"You think so? He's not really that bad. Teachers love him because he's first in line to help fix something or do the dirty work. Like, when the sewer backed up, he helped clean up the mess when other people were grossed out. He's in band and basketball and a class officer, and he loves this school like nobody else." And then he delivers the kicker. "Maria Elena wouldn't date him if he was a jerk."

"But he talks trash *all* the time. I mean, have you heard him around Chaz? Gordo's a bully."

Ernie looks at me like I'm an idiot. "That's just guy stuff. He's rude and mouthy, sure, but he wouldn't hurt anyone. You need thick skin around him. Like he says: 'Don't be a cream puff . . .'" He trails off.

Wow. Ernie, a kid who comes with his own warning, is taking Gordo's side over another target's. I don't love this.

I have an idea. "Where do we take our letters?"

"*Dorm mail,*" he corrects me, "goes into the mailboxes in the lobby during the break." Right. I've seen the wooden set: an Outbox and Inbox, tagged with those bumpy plastic labels that I think are made by some kind of tape gun.

Chaz needs a mash note.

I busy myself writing two letters, one atop the other in case Ernie gets curious. (Which he does, in seconds, his entire being leaning toward my side of the room.) The first is to Leeza, just a kind of bonding thing.

> hey sis, thanks for making my first day suck
> less, sorry about Chaz.—

I can't figure out how to sign off. Do they use "TTYL" yet? Or is that a text thing? My god, I would *kill* to just text someone right now.

The other is to Chaz. It's simple, a little flirty (who doesn't like to be flirted with?) but not too much.

> Sorry I called you flawless. Don't hate me cuz
> I'm honest. Tomorrow I'll behave. 😜

I'm pretty sure I don't need to sign it.

To say that I fold this does not accurately describe what happens. I went to Arts Camp eight summers in a row. I could do origami while juggling *and* texting. He's getting a tiny heart, with impossibly rounded edges, the note hidden inside something like the fifth tuck. Leeza gets a big showy llama, mostly because it needs to be large enough to hide his, and so that Ernie thinks I just wrote to her, a fact I announce loudly.

"Going to the mailbox to drop my note to Leeza—want me to take yours?"

Ernie's face lights up like I have offered to do his homework for a month. "Sure!" His appreciation is so genuine, I feel a little guilty that I really only volunteered so he wouldn't ask to take mine. Note to self: Be nice to Ernie—the kid is starved for it. Plus, you know, having an ally could be useful.

The dorm lobby right now is like a locker room with everyone's clothes on—guys talking, some of them doing that push-each-other bro thing that has to go directly back to early primates, a couple more clustered around another hand-held game. (Wait till they grow up and discover smartphones.) I see the outbox, filling rapidly with paper (dorm mail clearly predates concern with saving trees), and the empty inbox next to it. My little plan has a problem. Drop the mystery man note to Chaz in that box, and it will sit there alone, a beacon blinking: Look at me! Look at me! It will be obvious to anyone it originated within the building.

Before I have solved my dilemma, I hear a voice. "You're the new guy, huh? Smart move coming so late—no time to hate the place."

The speaker introduces himself as Vinnie. My first thought is *if a weasel had a face*, but then, of course, weasels do have faces, so I guess it's more if a weasel walked upright on two legs and wore a Rambo T-shirt. There's something greedy in his grin, backed by a host of self-love and confidence that could only come from a guy this white. His hair is shiny and dark, in contrast to his pale skin, and it's parted in the middle, '70s style—he's so straight, he defies decade logic. I try to sound pleasant, but I'm acid. "Trust me, I can hate anything and fast . . ."

He thinks this answer is hilarious and slaps my back before launching into some story about a band that, of course, brings up girls, and I tune out. When he asks if I play anything, I say fluegelhorn to be funny, and he looks disappointed. "Too bad.

Our brass section is overstuffed already, and Robbie plays that. But I bet Mr. K would let you sit in."

I don't actually want to keep chatting with him, but he's not going anywhere. "What do you play?"

"*SEX*OPHONE!" Vin Weasel has *clearly* said this before. *Vom.* "Chicks dig it. We're the top of the food chain in band. And I do like to eat—"

"I get it." I cut him off before I have to hear more. "Sax lessons in my next life." (What life would that be? Chronologically, it would be my actual life . . .)

Just as I pray to the social gods for someone to intervene and release me from this conversation, the double doors to the lobby swing open, admitting a trio that it is safe to assume are the RAs from the girls' dorm. Tawny is one of them, but I don't know the others. Their arrival changes the temperature in the room: the boys who were wrestling seem to ramp up their display, and everyone else is clustered around them, a few doing that tease-whoever-you're-attracted-to thing and others just chatting normally.

Tawny, one hand cradling a big basket of dorm mail, waves me over, and I seize my opportunity. When she gives me a hug, I drop my hand into the basket, freeing both notes but doing a little mixing up at the same time. "This is where the mail goes, right?"

My newness has bought me a pass this time. "No, silly— these are the notes for the *boys*. You have to use your outbox and then we take them."

She pours their notes—a pile almost three times the size of

ours—into the inbox and then asks me to help her find mine. I tell her it's a llama, which she nabs easily, but then everyone wants to see it, and the other girls crowd around. I'm a mini-celebrity for more than just my newness, and for the first time since I got here, I'm in my element. One of her fellow RAs, a girl whose fierce sea glass eyes counteract the doll-like effect of her Shirley Temple ringlets, says I should take art the rest of the semester. To my surprise, even Gordo acknowledges the llama, muttering, "Cool, man."

A mustachioed man in a sweater vest set steps into the lobby and whistles. This is the dean, and we haven't even formally met since he was teaching Christian Entrepreneurship when I was moving in. "Time to break up the lovefest," he calls, and the girl RAs scoop up their trove to leave. As guys begin to fan out back to their respective halls, he calls me over. "Silverthorn," he starts, and for a moment, I look for my English teacher. Oh right. Me.

"Most of the good campus jobs are obviously taken since it's *May*, but you can do anything for a month, right? The two industries left are broom shop or cutlery."

I can't answer his question because the word *month* hits me. I have been rolling with the punches since I got here, but a month of playacting in this painfully retro-present? I don't know if I can. And what if it's more than a month? What if it's years? I feel dizzy.

"You with me, Silverthorn?"

"Yes, sir, . . . *dean*. I guess . . . cutlery?"

What in hell is a cutlery job?

95

"Good, good." He eyes me quizzically, trying to decide if I'm okay. "You hanging in there? This is a big adjustment and I hear you have a lot going on."

"Yeah . . . I'm just . . ."

He gives my shoulder a squeeze, having heard enough, and tells me he's *really glad* I'm here, a meaningless sentiment that is also his exit line. But as he walks away, he has one last thing to add: "Get to your room. Break's over."

From my bed, I can see the sky. The Big Dipper sits where it always does, scooping up a ladleful of universe. That helps a little.

I've heard that if you go to Australia or Fiji or whatever, somewhere upside down from you on the globe, it's really confusing to look at the sky for the first time because nothing is where it should be, and the patterns you do recognize are inverted. That could be a lie, but Nix and I think it's cool. Nix once made a sketchbook of what they thought constellations really looked like in our sky: Aquarius was a woman in a cocktail dress reaching out to snag a glass of champagne off a tray; Canis Major was a grumpy old man waving his newspaper at the kids on his lawn; Cassiopeia had witch boobs; and Cygnus was the celestial emoji for "I give up." Because we were thirteen at the time, Gemini was a penis.

Upside down, the same constellations became a potato on a string, someone stretching, a boring old M, and a squashed

tripod. (Gemini remained a penis.) I like their northern coun-
terparts better.

I can see the Big Dipper from here. But it's hanging in a
sky that isn't mine.

I miss Nix. I miss Cheng. I miss Mom.

I miss my whole constellation.

A Date for Prom

FIRST PERIOD ON WEDNESDAY, Ms. Silverthorn asks me to stay after, promising to write me a pass. We started *Connecticut Yankee* today, and I may have over-talked, and I bet she's going to tell me to show off less and shut up more. My next period is chemistry, and I am happy to miss it, but she's giving off a not-excellent vibe, so I think I'm in trouble. I just don't know what kind.

She shuts the door after the last student. "How are you holding up?"

Somehow just the concern makes me a little teary, but I try to shrug it off. "I wrote my first dorm mail last night, so I'm already fitting in."

"Good, good," she murmurs, eyes dark.

"Did something happen?"

"No, no. Just . . ." I am not used to her being at a loss for words. It's very disconcerting.

"We need to focus on your situation. I have compared seventeen books about time travel, three of them nonfiction, to see what I would glean." She clocks the look on my face—seventeen books? Since she picked me up at the mall? "If I'm your English teacher, you can hardly be surprised that I read with alacrity!" A little frown, then she goes on.

"We have several things to consider. Some argue that Einstein's special and general relativity theories allow for moving along the space-time continuum, but no one has figured out how exactly."

"The Tesseract!"

"You mean like *A Wrinkle in Time*?" Apparently, the Marvel Cinematic Universe isn't a *thing* yet, or at least not the way it is in my day. It hardly seems worth explaining that there are these six stones that, when put together . . . Actually, now that I think of it, that part of the movies always confused me. (More Thor, please!) But I'm pretty sure the stones allow time travel.

She's still waiting.

"No. It's from these movies you'll tell me not to waste my time on someday."

"May I continue? Some argue you have to watch out for the grandfather paradox, that anything you do that hasn't been done before—"

"Will change the future. We call that the butterfly effect . . . in my time."

"It's a little late to un-room with Ernie, and there's no way around the fact that *I* am changed by your arrival, so I hope that this paradox is overstated, but try not to interfere with other people's choices, at least."

"What if you change a *bad* thing in the future into a *good* thing? That's a net win, right?"

"Unless that, in turn, changes a good thing into bad and so on, onward, endlessly." She trails fingers through the air as if showing ramifications rising like sparks from a fire. "One theory is the causal loop, that someone from the future changes something in the past, which of course then sets off the grandfather paradox by changing the future, which already exists, and round and round we go—hence, the loop, as no one can say where the actual origin lies." Now she's tracing a figure eight in the air.

"I like that one better. If you can't say where it started, then no one can blame me for what I screw up, at least not for sure."

"There's a third one that seems worth noting: The Fermi paradox explains why, if time travel exists—and it must, as here you are—we don't know other time travelers. The answer: they blend into the population for their own safety."

That makes sense. Some religious fanatic who finds out I'm from the 2020s might think I'm a witch or a devil and, I don't know, burn me at the stake. (Granted, I did go as a really *hot* demon for Halloween last year, though Mom drew the line at shirtless—I had red sequins on my nipples, so I was bummed—but agreed to a leather vest, which ended up looking super fetishy.) And I've seen enough movies to know that the government would weaponize me. *Would I get a name? I vote Glitter Bomb.* I'd probably just end up institutionalized, which would be like Oscar bait for some future actor playing me in the biopic, but really bad as a life experience.

I reassure her. "I'm a total chameleon. I'll just fade into the background."

Ms. Silverthorn tries to suppress a smile, one eyebrow arching in disbelief. "In that . . . ?"

Apparently, she doesn't love my new Chess King bomber, which I have paired with a cherry red popped-collar polo and jeans I added safety pins to. Or maybe the bandana I have tied around one ankle is too much? I think I look super cute!

"What? It's all from your time!"

She laughs. "One: Try not to say things like that too loudly. Two: Did you see *any*one dressed like Michael Jackson in English class?"

"It's too late. They've all seen it now." I know I'm pouting. "I'll make it my *brand*. I'll say it's a Connecticut thing."

For oh so many reasons, I don't mention my plan for Chaz. I really just want to find out if she's discovered her version of a DeLorean to zip me back to the 2020s.

"Did you figure out how to get me back? Like, a portal or a rift or some celestial whatever?"

She just looks at the clock and writes out my pass. "I'll keep you posted. But for now . . . chemistry."

Gordo isn't in class. Maybe he's sick. I would love that because I'm not digging running into him. Some kids who grow up missing a parent spend their lives wondering about them, trying to fill the gap. I just *don't*. My whole life, I've had Mom, and she's been enough, really and truly. It makes me *furious* when people diss single parents. I can recite a *roster* of messed-up kids with two parents. So maybe Gordo was my mother's grief, but he isn't mine. I can live without him in *any* time, but I'm glad I have her. (Not that she could tell when I was trash-talking her *to her face* on Monday.)

We're supposed to work on a lab in pairs today, and Ma Elena picks me. I'm so happy I could cry, but it's also so *weird*. She has on this perfume that smells like someone ran flowers through a car wash made of candy. And she's so energetic. She's chatting away about prom so excitedly and draws me a sketch of her dress. (No phone means no screenshot, so what else is she gonna do?) If she's an artist of any accuracy, it's got these Princess Diana sleeves and a strange buttoned bib and a huge belt. I don't tell her that she's too short for this look, which will box her in. I just ask the color and then wish I hadn't because her answer is burgundy. *Burgundy!* She'll just die if Becky Eberhardt wears the same dress, which happened their junior year, because they have the same style, and I agree, no one wants *that* horror on the big night. Meanwhile, I'm thinking: She always told me she didn't go to prom at all.

"What are you going to wear?" she asks as if I've been here long enough to have an outfit. She can't know that it burns me to think I'm going to have the very same prom experience here (by any other name) that I was trying to avoid by going to see (my) Ms. Silverthorn two days ago.

(Two days!)

I deflect. "I'm still deciding. What's Gordo wearing?"

Her eye roll is majestic. "His *band* suit." For a half-second, I picture marching band uniforms. *That* would be a sight. "Those suits are horrible—the polyester is so shiny. And he wears it to church all the time! This is supposed to be a special night."

I still don't understand what she's doing with him. "So . . . how'd you guys get together?" I try to sound neutral, but it's never made sense to me.

"When he got here, he had a huge chip on his shoulder, sure he wouldn't be welcome, so Frohmy and I made it our mission to change that. I introduced him to the kids from band, so he had friends right away. Frohmy gave him a shop job with Mr. A, who never loses his temper. He was so grateful to be included. By Halloween, when he told me he liked me, I thought, *You know what, I'm good for him.*"

"Okay. So that explains what he gets out of it . . . but, seriously, what do *you* get?"

She crinkles up her face like she smells something. "You're so intense all of the sudden! I mean, mostly if someone likes me, it's either 'I feel it, or I don't, and I decided I did.'" She sees that I still want more, and though it's not like I deserve some big answer, she comes up with one. "I guess what I like is that I finally have a boyfriend who's Cuban, which I've never had in *this* town, and it doesn't hurt that he's strong and handsome. And once he lets down his guard, he's really nice."

"Not if you're Chaz."

She sighs. "Poor Chaz." I wait for her to say more, but she goes back to prom drama, listing the on-campus girls currently not going with anyone. *Including Leeza*, she adds meaningfully.

"I'll just go stag," I say. "Too late to figure that stuff out now."

"You still have four days! And I bet you could borrow a suit."

"A band suit, maybe?"

She laughs, and it feels good. We used to watch *Parks and Rec* together, and it was the best, but she ended up on night shifts, and I ended up, well, too old to sit on a couch with my mother, so that trailed off. I forgot how much I loved seeing her green eyes flash with amusement, how it felt being a part of that.

"I like you," she says. "I'm glad you're here. I think you're going to make the whole month better."

Gordo enters, handing a late slip to the teacher, and is partnered with the odd kid out. Gordo's cheeks go into clench-overdrive when he realizes that I am paired with Ma Elena. I can feel his eyes on me for the entire rest of the class. Let's just say it is not a friendly look.

At lunch, Chaz is already sitting with Leeza and Tawny. I stand at the tray line, not hurrying over. What if he's still upset about yesterday? Or what if he got my note and it was a misfire? Vin Weasel leans over my shoulder and says, laughing, "Space cadet—you're holding up the line!"

By this time, Leeza has spotted me and waves me over, so I'm hoping that means Chaz is okay. I walk up, and he's telling a story. I slide into a seat next to Tawny. She whispers foot-notes while I just listen to him.

"And then our mother found the note! In his *laundry*!"

("Chaz's brother's English teacher had a crush on him!")

"The fool left it in his jeans like Eleanor would not be checking his pockets."

("He calls his mother 'Eleanor.' It's so formal!")

"And when he walks into the house for dinner, from, *hello*, a *one-person field trip* to the MOMA with The Flake . . ."

("That's the English teacher.")

"Eleanor is lying in wait. And do you know, she has taken the note, which was four pages long, and clothes-pinned every page to twine, then strung it like a garland over the dinner table."

"Tell me you're exaggerating!" Leeza's expression makes it clear she hopes he is not at all exaggerating.

"Lanford can do one of two things: He can take the 'How Dare You Invade my Privacy' approach, which will just about ensure a nuclear winter to follow, or he can fall on the mercy of Sister Eleanor Mudd Wilson, and claim The Flake has been

105

forcing unwelcome attention upon him, thus redirecting our mother's substantial arsenal on her."

We're all breathless.

"But my brother is a fool—he was born one and stayed one, and ever will be, and he says, 'What *is* that?' with a look of pure innocence as if he has never seen it. He has made the most wrong choice. Eleanor does not even give him time to claim he'd never read the note or that The Flake is delusional or any other ridiculous thing. She just scoops up the bread-basket and throws it at him, dinner rolls scattering like popping corn!

"The fool is so surprised she'd do such a thing, he just stands there, mouth open, until the basket hits him, and then he is running up to our room, Eleanor two steps behind yelling, 'I am not done with you!'"

"And then Trini—"

("That's the little sister!)

"—says, 'First rule of horror movies: Run out the door, not up the stairs!" Chaz pauses for the big finish. "'That fool is *dead*.'"

Chaz is a natural storyteller. He got the rhythms just right, and the punch line is both unexpected and perfect. If he could live past this place, there's so much he could do with this talent. How can I say that without, um, saying that? "That would make a good monologue for an audition!"

Leeza and Tawny both second that motion, but Chaz is cool. "Thanks," is all he offers, his eyes ever-so-briefly meeting mine. He's looking at Tawny, not me, when he adds, "That's not even my only story about a note." Wait, is he talking about mine?

Tawny blushes. "What I write to you in dorm mail is private!"

"I'm just playing," he assures her—or is he assuring me? I can't tell.

Leeza announces that I made her the cutest llama, and Tawny immediately wants me to show her how with a napkin, which I do, all the while dying to look at Chaz, which I don't. Somehow this situation is making me stupidly shy.

The bell rings, and we clear our trays, Chaz and Tawny heading off together. Leeza and I head to the shop building to work our campus jobs—my first day!—and she leads the way. She tugs at my sleeve as we walk. "Nice jacket." (So Ms. Silverthorn was right—the jacket draws attention. I hate it when other people are right.)

"Ms. Silverthorn thinks it's too much."

"You call her Ms. Silverthorn?"

Dammit, I keep forgetting she's my aunt. "Only on campus. She says it makes me like any other student."

"I don't think you're 'like any other' *here*."

"Um, thanks?"

"That's a compliment. I stick out too. Do you want to stick out together at prom?"

I hesitate a second, and she's on it. "Just a friend thing. *Trust* me. No need to freak out."

"No—that's—great. I'd love to." *Oh my god, it's so het.* "But I have to find a suit first."

107

"I expect something cool, you know! My dress is turquoise and sleeveless with an asymmetrical waistline that ends in a bow on my hip. Then there's like a black net under the skirt to make it fan out—street length cause I'm not some cutesy Little Bo Peep. So you can't be a sheep in a band suit. Do the blazer and skinny tie thing. Or go all *Miami Vice*." She knows I'm about to protest that I have neither. "Just ask Chaz. He has a closet full." Wait—is that code? Is she trying to tell me something? My heart pounds, but she doesn't linger on it. "He's way ahead of the rest of the school."

"I'll figure it out. Thanks for asking me." I smile, but we're at the shop building and have to part ways. She works in the broom factory, and I have to go to the cutlery room. She gives me a hug, and it feels so good to have someone here that I over-hug back, but she doesn't seem to notice.

The shop building is where concrete goes to die. I mean, *please*. Someone was paid to design this thing? Two floors of square cold rooms painted gray and off-gray, with these awful fluorescent lights the length of a surfboard. Upstairs are cutlery, direct mail, and buttons, while downstairs is entirely broom shop. The roof is flat, like dead flat, which is why it will collapse from the weight of snow and ice during an especially bad winter ten or fifteen years before I am born.

Ernie has explained that cutlery is the easier of the two shop jobs still available, even if it doesn't pay well as broom shop, the school's big moneymaker. I'll be making sets of knives, spoons, and forks, rolling them in paper, sliding them in plastic bags, and hot sealing the ends before the school sends them to the distributor. Boring but easy, and I can talk with the other kids on my shift. Sometimes, he says, you get to listen to the radio, a big deal because radios aren't allowed in the dorm. The best part is Mr. A, who he thinks is the coolest teacher, listens to music that some of the other teachers would call a sin. (God, they love that word.) He knows because he worked in the broom shop one semester. (I don't ask why they fired him: I'll just assume he broke something.)

Mindless as it sounds, I'm guessing cutlery will be a major upgrade from the noise and mess of the broom factory. I have my game face on until I open the door and see Gordo. I feel haunted. Everywhere I turn, there he is. I know he's not thrilled to see me either.

He surprises me by being professional when he tells me how the process works, making the rules clear, outlining the possible slipups and how to solve them. The Gordo running this shift for shop is not like any Gordo I've seen (or, for that matter, even heard about). He shows me the target board, with all the piece-per-hour goals and tells me he'll start me on a modest goal so that I can ease in.

As I roll little bundles of forks and spoons and knives (seriously, there is nothing this boring in *Back to the Future*), I see how he checks in with the other kids working cutlery. He scoops up stray utensils at the end of a table where a spacey-looking boy hasn't even noticed they've fallen. Gordo doesn't shame him, just reminds him to be careful, and when a girl has trouble with the plastic in a heat sealer, he steps in to solve things, joking about the equipment. He's so foreign to me:

Gordo the helpful, Gordo the diligent, Gordo the *nice*. I could see Mom dating *this* guy.

When he loops back around to my station, he nods approvingly. "You're doing great. We'll keep your target low anyway, so you don't have to stress."

"That's so sweet!" The words are out before I can recall them, and he freezes, then boils.

I just meant to thank him, but, unfortunately, I sounded exactly like myself when I did—and that was enough to flip the switch, igniting the Gordo I remember.

He stalks away from the table and then stalks back. "Wherever you're from? We're not like that here." I know what he means by "that," and I can't find a safe retort. "You can't handle that for an effing month, go home."

I wish I could. I really do.

When the Lights Go
Down in the City

MY DORM MAIL CONTAINS a surprise. Ernie is reading me his note from JJ (who I now know to be wallet-on-a-chain girl), a missive that is very funny in a deadpan way, mostly riffs on the school and classmates. I'm half-listening as I unfold the little paper sailboat Leeza made to keep up with my llama, but there's not much inside.

Meet me at the shop. 11 p.m. xo L

Um, *hello*. I would like nothing better than to hang out somewhere else instead of being trapped in the carpeted cinder block box, but there are RAs on duty, and one of them is my dad, who already hates me. (Okay, she doesn't have any way of knowing that, but *I* do.) And I can't afford to get kicked out for sneaking out because my "Connecticut" isn't real. Where would I go?

On the other hand, oh my god, I *love* being sneaky. Despite tripping over himself continually, Ernie is a nice guy, but I seriously cannot hear the mechanical sound of another inning of hand-held baseball or whatever. Without my white noise app, it's hard to fall asleep here, and I can't Houseparty my friends, who haven't been born, on a phone that hasn't been invented. I don't know how anyone else stands all the empty time, but this note feels like a lifeline.

Dorm mail only comes once a night, so I can't even reply. (God, the '80s are inefficient.) This means she'll be out at the shop building come 11 p.m. whether or not I am. Can't leave a sis hanging like that, right?

Good thing for me that Ernie sleeps like a log. When "lights out" comes at 10 p.m.—can you stand it?—and the RAs go room to room to enforce it, he climbs into bed, rolls toward the wall, and is *gone*. I don't know from this side of the door whether the RAs go to bed immediately after or whether they get some special late-night privileges. I have to trust that Leeza knows that they, too, will be in their rooms, and I have to hope the dorm doors aren't alarmed.

10:55. I slide out of bed with the grace and stealth of a panther. (Okay, sure, I have never seen a panther and can't really distinguish the big cats, but it's always a panther in a metaphor.) Ernie remains a fallen log as I crack the door open. The hall is empty. I can hear only the humming of window fans and an old-school wall clock ticking ridiculously loudly. *Or is that my heart?*

My options are complicated: the end of the hall farthest from my room has two doors leading outside, but is also directly opposite the dean's apartment. The end of the hall nearest me has only one, which leads to the basement and then out, but because the universe hates me, Gordo's room is closest to that exit. I think I *have* to choose that option and hope Gordo doesn't catch me, and if he does, I hope that having seen him at the mall is a teeny bit of leverage.

I'm barefoot and almost tiptoeing as I pass his room and find, to my relief, the stairwell door propped open. What was I worried about?

The basement stairs descend to a landing then reverse direction to lead to the exit. It's in my pivot that I see them: Vin Weasel and some redheaded giant blocking my escape. I could pee myself.

Nobody moves for a second. Surely as I'm sneaking out, they're sneaking back in, which means we are canceling out each other's rule-breaking. Vin's surprise gives way to amusement, and he advances, noiselessly clapping me on my back. "Just got here and already a player!"

Oh my god, really? I give them a thumbs up and scurry away, safe in the knowledge that they won't report me, and now sure there's no alarm. I slip outside in the cooling air, and the night is mine.

◎

I don't know where Leeza wants to meet. There's an on-all-night light by the main entrance that's currently a rave for frenzied moths. She can't possibly want to meet where we can be seen, so I try to stay in the shadows and head around back. It's so dark at first that I think she's not here until I see the tip of a cigarette glowing like the target of a laser. *Sis,* I want to say, *that stuff will kill you and ruin your teeth*, but then again, half my classmates are permanently scarring their lungs vaping, so public service announcements never work.

I can see her smile once I'm closer. Her greeting cracks me up. "You put your big girl panties on and came."

I love her sass. "I never take them off, sis." I wave away the cigarette when she offers it.

Above us, the sky is crazy beautiful. I mean, Antic Springs isn't a metropolis in my time, but it's a lot more developed then than it is here in 1985, where there aren't even streetlights. So I'm not used to seeing the stars I love quite this clearly. The contrast of brilliant white blinking against the deepest black makes the heavens feel more immediate. I'm half-convinced that if I reached out to touch the Big Dipper, I could.

"I saw Vin Weasel—"

"Who?"

"Vinnie. I saw Vinnie and some other kid sneaking back in. Does everybody do it?"

"No, most of these kids are too angelic or too scared of being caught. But, come on, we're at like the most hormonal age we'll ever be. They should be glad we let off steam before—"

"Before someone goes postal!" I complete her thought.

"What?" She laughs. Apparently, I am *not* completing her thought. "Is that a Connecticut thing?" (Honestly, I don't know. It's older than me for sure, and it's something you just say.)

Leeza takes a drag on her cigarette and it's long enough that I can so tell it's a segue to something. I was hoping the sneaking out was just to be cool and to bond with a new friend, but maybe there's an agenda.

"So you think Chaz is gay?" Her question is not casual.

That I wasn't expecting. I've heard about the '80s, how gay people were just starting to get a little freedom, then AIDS made everybody treat them like crap. (Later, being treated like crap won them sympathy, but that was in the '90s, which this is not.) I don't want to make his life harder—I just want him to be happy.

She lets me off the hook. "I mean, I wondered too." Another drag and then a long plume of smoke. "I'm not sure *he* knows, though."

"I'm pretty sure he knows," I say quietly. We all know. Our bodies tell us things, sometimes really nakedly—an erection watching the lacrosse team—sometimes more subtly. "But knowing may be its own problem. Maybe he works really hard to *not* know."

115

"Right? Like, what's Tawny about?"

I pause to think about that for a minute. Maybe I shouldn't be so knee-jerk. "He could be bi. Or pretty much gay, but really into Tawny specifically." Other options start floating to mind. "Maybe he's *ace*. Or we think he's gay because he's a little femme, but he's really just genderqueer, and we're boxing him with our cisnormative—"

"Stop!" She's choking with laughter and expelling smoke. "You're just teasing me now. Making up words." Shaking her curls, she looks me in the eye. "I've been to Connecticut. *Nobody* talks like that."

"Fine. You got me." Why not go for it? "I'm from the future."

"Totally," she says. "You totally are." The cigarette is down to a nub, still glowing, and she drops it to stamp it out.

I wonder why she wants to talk about Chaz. "Is Chaz upset about what I said that first day?"

"Not as much as Tawny." She pauses. "But he got your note."

Oh my god. It never occurred to me he would *tell* anyone.

"Oh . . . uh . . ." I am never speechless! "How did that go over?"

Leeza's laughs a smoker's laugh, throaty and warm. "Before or after he burned it?" My god. I'm an idiot.

"What did he say?"

"I'm not going there yet." She leans close. "You're actually gay, right, not just setting him up?" Everything about that—her tone, her concern for Chaz, her closeness—makes clear she wants the answer to be yes, that it's okay.

"OMG, sis. I'm so gay, I'm my own category, Ultra Gay, or GayPlus or—" It feels so good to say it out loud. I mean, my real coming out was so long ago (or, um, so far in the future), it's a hazy memory. And it wasn't like I needed to tell anyone, exactly. I'm not Danny Al-Hadid, who played lacrosse and lifted weights and went to NASCAR races and pretty much had to *beg* people to believe him when *he* came out. I am a natural Kinsey six and honestly would be an eleven if the spectrum went that high. It's only been a few days here, and the relief of not having to tamp it down is immense.

Leeza shushes me. "Okay, okay, I get it! But we snuck out, so shouting it is a wicked bad idea, and honestly, even saying that to anyone but me and maybe Laney is a really bad call, period."

What? "Why Mom?" I correct as quickly as I can, "*Laney*?"

She doesn't seem to notice the slip. "She's like me: the only person I know for sure who doesn't drink the Kool-Aid." *So that's a phrase I can safely use here.* "She gets that a lot of what the stuff the school teaches is just wrong. I don't have a kissing-up face at all, but she does, so the school thinks she's an angel, even though she's really got a mind of her own. And Frohmeyer adores her, so she's always getting kids out of trouble. Which is why all the kids love her."

Okay, wow. My mom, who stayed married to the crap husband all those years and who, if she's honest, doesn't *really* want me to be gay, was not always a doormat with a conservative streak? That she is Miss Independence (well, by First Secondary standards) is total news to me. And she never told me she was popular! Or did I never ask?

"Do you think she knows about me?"

Leeza shakes her head. "She was asking who we could set you up with for prom, so no. That's one reason *I* asked you—figured we'd both get to have a date without being saddled with someone we can't tolerate."

"Should I tell her?"

Leeza's jaw drops. "What? *No.* I know I said Laney's more likely to be understanding than most people, but the fewer kids who know, the better. And you don't want Gordo to hear, for sure. You've seen how he is with Chaz."

"What's that about? He can be all nice, I've seen it now, but then a whiff of gay and—"

"He's a beast. I know. But that's kind of every guy, every *straight* guy, right? It would be weirder if he was the opposite."

"Not where I'm from. Even the biggest bros are either cool with it or at least act like they are to fit in with everyone else."

"If they have to 'act like it,' is that really a big improvement?" Fair point. I don't concede; I change the subject.

"So . . . back to Chaz."

"He thinks you're setting him up. And he made a big speech about how even if he was gay, he's not stupid enough to risk graduation, this close to the end of school, for some kid who showed up out of nowhere with a bad haircut." She hears herself. "Sorry, his words. I think it's kind of cute."

I am not used to rejection. Confidence is my brand, and it is usually enough: if someone sees that you like yourself, it gives them permission to like you, too. Here I am coming all the way from the future to give this kid a gift of a better life—an actual gay one—and he's gonna do me like that?

Apparently, my face is all sorts of red, and Leeza does not get why. "Don't be embarrassed. Chaz *is* cute. I thought so too when we met."

When I can speak without shrieking, I push back. "You know what a gay guy wears in the closet?"

"What?"

"A T-shirt that reads 'Even if I *was* gay . . .'" She laughs, which lets me know I'm not going too far. "Nobody—*nobody*—starts a sentence, 'even if I was gay,' unless they're on the defensive."

"Can you blame him? What with his brother and all, and his family so strict, he can't be anything but what he is, and what he is is scared. *Tawny* is safe. *I'm* safe. You—you're a wild card."

This has a ring of the familiar to it. Cheng always says I push people too far. When I convinced the students to walk out of class for a climate change protest our freshman year (the cafeteria refused to switch to compostable materials), the admin team were already huffy about it. I guess the fact I made Kim Okemwa call her mom (who's a reporter for Channel 7) was a bit extra, even for me. In the end, the protest was on all the news channels, and the cafeteria switched to only recycled or biodegradable utensils, and I was very happy. But Kim got in trouble for inviting a camera crew without permission, and she never again listened to any of my ideas.

"So . . . leave him alone? That's what you mean."

She sighs. "That's what *he* means. He actually said, 'Tell him to stop sending me notes.'" She lights a new cigarette and takes a drag. "I don't know that *I'd* say that. It might be good for him to see the world has more than Gordo in it. Maybe he can become the person he's afraid to be."

"*Exactly.*" That's all I'm trying to do. I mean, it's almost charity.

"But I can't help you—he needs me to let him be who he is right this moment. You do what you think you should, but be careful, okay? Like, totally tiptoe around this. You don't want the other guys to get wind of it because they can be assholes. Not to mention he could get kicked out. And his parents—I can only imagine what they'd do."

Whoa. I hear her, but she's really taking the fun out of this for me.

"I didn't ask you to break curfew for nothing. Chaz is my closest friend, and I need him to be safe."

"How about you?"

"What do you mean?"

"Are *you* safe?" Befriending the school closet case, sneaking out after curfew, smoking (a prohibition meriting all capital letters in the student handbook)—I find myself wondering how Leeza herself has lasted this long.

She steps away, and even in the dark, I know she's looking at me. "Why wouldn't I be? Nobody cares what I do." Her voice sounds tighter as if she's speaking through clenched teeth.

"I just meant—you're not exactly a rule follower yourself."

She can't catch her breath. "What did you see?" Before I can figure that out, she speaks more softly. "Did someone say something?"

What? Now I'm curious. "About . . ."

She hesitates. Maybe because she sees me as an ally, or maybe because I'm out to her and straight people always use that as permission to discuss their sex lives, Leeza answers with a detail I *so* did not expect. "About Buckman."

"That old creeper?"

"He's twenty-six!"

"Right . . ." I realize too late I mixed up my timelines there for a minute, but that's hardly the big issue here. "But still, *ew.*"

In my day, Buckman is famous for his student conquests, a quasi-open secret that somehow goes unstopped. He chooses a girl on the fringe of the pack, someone unsupported at home or maybe prone to rebellion or a newcomer without a crowd of her own. From the outside, it looks like Buckman finds a girl who needs him in some way because she'd grieve the loss if they broke up, and she'd never trust her own status next to his position of power. No one ever seems to report him, or if they do, it's hard to tell because he's still there.

It's horrifying that Leeza's a Buckman girl. For all I know, she's the original.

"Seriously, did you hear something about us?"

How do I explain why I know what he's like? Once more with the truth. "I did say I was from the future. He's still chasing skirts in the twenty-first century."

"This isn't funny." She's shaking now. "Who told you?"

This might not be my best idea ever, but I'm going to lie. I need to concoct a story that will make her knock it off with Mr. Buckman. She deserves better.

"It was *Mrs.* Buckman." I spool out a story I hope is both plausible and that she can't verify. "The night I got here, she came by my aunt's, claiming she needed to borrow cookie sheets or something but really just gossiping for a hundred years. She didn't even know I was there, but I heard the whole thing. My aunt was trying to find a nice way to get her to move on, but then Mrs. Buckman started complaining about Mr. Buckman." Leeza is listening, so this detail is ringing true. "She . . . she said he was spending too much time with the girls on the campus."

This must also confirm something she already knows because she nods vigorously. "She says if she had her way, girls wouldn't even be allowed in shop."

"Sounds like her . . . but what did she say about *me*?"

"Uh . . . nothing specific. She just said she thought Mr. Buckman had a favorite, and she needed to do something about it." I'm hoping this will make her nervous, but it has the opposite effect. All Leeza hears is "favorite," and she nods, pleased. "And then I thought I saw him watching you when you left the shop today, so . . ."

"Hmmm . . ." She mulls this quietly. "He's gonna have to be more careful then, especially if she's telling people he's stepping out. We only have to sit on this till graduation, then

122

we're in the clear." The steely command is back in her voice. She's not even going to deny it.

My god. She thinks he's in love with her.

"What?" she barks. "Did I shock you?" I don't answer quickly enough. "You're gay! That's way more out there than me liking an older man."

"A *married* one, three times your age."

"Married to a frigid shrew, which is an unjust punishment of some kind. And come on: I'm eighteen, and he's only twenty-six! We could have almost gone to school together."

"When he graduated from high school, you were in, what, fourth grade?"

"I said *almost*." She looks away for a moment, shaking her head. "I thought you'd be cool." She turns her gaze to meet mine. "Why are you freaking out?"

"Because he's your teacher and a legit adult, and he has not only a wife but all the power here. He could ruin you."

"I don't think he's running to Frohmeyer to confess our relationship any time soon."

"I bet he's banking on you thinking that."

"Have you even met him? He's the nicest guy, the kindest." I shudder. If only she knew I really *can* picture him three times her age, still hooking up with seventeen-year-olds. "He's incredibly sweet—unlike you, 'cuz you're being a dick—and he gets me. We're going to get married as soon as I'm out of here."

"After the divorce . . ."

"Obviously."

"Which takes how long?"

"How would I know?"

"And is he moving to New York with you and Chaz? Are you going to be roomies?"

She is full-on mad. "You sound like Chaz. Are all gay guys so mean to their own friends?"

"Maybe we just watch out for people we care about. You said it yourself: you're my friend."

"Judging is not super friendly." She stares at the sky for a moment, and I do too. I don't want her to have anything to do with Buckman—I mean, nothing good can come from it—but I also hope I haven't blown it with her because my circle here is already small. Her voice is soft. "He loves me, you know."

What can I say? "Do you love him?"

More silence. More stars. "I think so. I mean, I'm pretty sure. He makes me feel things I've never felt before. And we've done stuff . . ." Her words are tinged with thrill, regret, aware-ness. There is so much color in her voice, which is lower than ever. "I already imagined our life together, so . . ."

I don't argue anymore. Instead, I slip my arm around her, and she rests her head on my shoulder. I make a promise I don't know how to keep. "You don't have to worry. My lips are sealed, and my ears are open."

She doesn't look at me. "Good." She relaxes. "Good."

Blinded by the Light

TODAY IS THURSDAY. SOMEHOW, I'm already on my fourth day in the old/new world, and I might feel worse about that if I wasn't so obsessed with what Leeza said about my mom before we got into the Buckman mess.

It's not like my mom has ever been capital *H* homophobic, and she has always been *majorly* loving, but her reservations come across loud and clear. The wince when she hears me "yassss"-ing my friends and the tightened lips when I say "sis." The refusal to let friends sleep over. Her insistence that I could go to Capitol Pride with the regional queer youth group only if there were adult chaperones—as if some crazy debauchery is ever gonna happen on the streets of Albany. (Does she know I've been to the real Pride in NYC *twice*, claiming I was with Cheng's family at their cabin? No, no she does not.) It's never directly about me *being* gay, only what the world is like for gays *like me*: those who don't play sports or dress like Sears models. Honestly, she could have handled being a mom to Cheng way better. It's a gentler, kinder way of disapproving, but if you have to deploy a "gentler, kinder" version of anything, the underlying sentiment is neither.

I want to witness this progressive version of her, the one before whatever happened to Chaz. So ignoring what Leeza told me to do, I'm lying in wait at the poster board near her locker when she enters the ad building. I pretend to be looking at the Last Call for Prom Council flyer, which turns out to be genius since she is the head of the team.

"Are you going to help out? I'm pumped! It takes forever to get all the streamers up, but if you don't do it, the cafeteria just looks like the cafeteria."

The cafeteria? Seriously? Instead of a hotel ballroom or a ship?

This place! I correct myself. This *time*.

"I'd love to!"

Lie. I hate crepe paper. So tacky.

"Do I need to sign up or—"

She trills a laugh. "Duh. I'm in charge, and you just told me! But walk with me . . ." She sets a pretty brisk pace with those short legs, and we're heading away from the classrooms toward what is the computer lab in my day but turns out to be a huge supply closet. The girl who didn't go to prom is actually the Shreya of the operation? She has some 'splaining to do when I get back to my time.

Along the storage room's back wall are two metal tables covered with bolts of shimmery blue-black fabric taller than I am and rows of glass vases shaped like stars. "Night Under the Stars?" I guess, a little bummed that Mom chose such a predictable theme.

" 'Over the Moon' actually," she replies. "But close. Our photos are going to be taken on a moon-shaped swing that Buckman and Mr. A have been working on, and there will be all these blacklights to make everything all glow." I like this a little better, but blacklight is a rookie mistake. I mean, the space will look amazing, but the prom pics are going to look like X-rays.

She hands me a bucket of "moon rocks," reflective white pebbles to fill the vases. "Fifteen in each vase exactly, or we'll run out."

I do as I'm told. "Aren't we going to be late for first period?"

"I'll get a note from Frohmy. Prom is the biggest event of the year next to graduation, so he only gives me so much grief about using class time." She holds up a vase critically. "Are you sure that's only fifteen?" I shake my head, and she counts them out—sixteen. Amazing eye. She's the one you want counting the milligrams of your meds, for sure.

Happily, she doesn't linger on my lazy handiwork. "So

127

you're going with Leez?" I nod. "And . . . are you just going as friends?"

Ha. "I mean, I've only been here four days!"

"Sometimes, a spark is instant!" She eyes my vases but doesn't count.

I can hear Leeza's voice telling me not to talk about this. But since when do I listen? "I don't think . . . uh, that's not what sparks me."

Ma Elena looks at me, eyes puzzled, and I hold the look, willing her to understand. For a moment, everything is weirdly intense. She's Mom *and* my classmate and it's the 1980s *and* the 2020s all at once—I see the unsettling electricity of the connection affect her too. And then it passes, and her eyes change. "Ohhhhh . . ." she whispers, even though there's no one to hear.

"Does that . . . uh . . . bother you?" I have to know.

Setting aside the vases, she looks me straight in the eye. "My whole life, I've been taught it's a sin. My dad says a *maricon* isn't a real man. And it's the punch line for all the jokes the boys tell. But I kind of know someone now and . . ." She doesn't want to say Chaz, but I'm sure that's what she means. Is she protecting him? And if she is, is the danger her boyfriend or me? She sighs. "I don't know. My friend . . . he's so sweet and so funny, and it seems wrong that God wouldn't love him as much as me. It made me think about all the divorced people in church and how nobody chases them away. I don't want to doubt God, *and* I don't want to hurt people, so . . ."

She trails off again, and I am not sure what to say. Probably not the time to mention that divorce isn't hardwired into your body the same way. I just wait it out until she comes up with something.

"I guess if you're like *he* is"—*my god, she's not any better at saying "gay" now than when I'm her son*—"it's just more reason for me to *want* it to be okay. And to stick to 'judge not, lest ye be judged.'"

There's something in her voice that I'm not used to hearing in my time: a yearning, a desire to make this all right, even a hopefulness. By the time she's my mom, Chaz's death will have sanded away the hope, replacing it with grim surety. It was easier for me to think of Chaz's fate as a relic from another time because I couldn't picture him, really—had never heard him tell a story over a meal. She could. From her senior year to mine, she carried this loss with her. Now, I get it. Even in her hesitation, I feel for her, and can't help myself: I throw my arms around her.

Just as Gordo opens the door.

Hey, universe: What did I do in a past life that earned me this douche as a father *and* forced me to go to high school with him?

"What the hell?" He sputters.

Ma Elena doesn't miss a beat. "Since my *actual* boyfriend didn't show up to help with decorations, I'm auditioning replacements."

Mom is sassy? This cannot be.

"I'm only ten minutes late! Cut me some slack!" Gordo's words are angry, but his eyes are something else: scared. He thinks she might really give up on him. It's so clear, so *painfully* clear that I'm *almost* sympathetic. (*Lots* of space between almost and am.)

"You!" he says, thrusting a thick finger at my face. "Get your own girlfriend!" (And that space just got a mile wide.)

"Who says he wants one?" Ma Elena lets her retort fly before she hears what she's said and then shoots me a panicked look. It's not even her words but the *look* that Gordo hops on.

"What'd you just say?"

She's fast. "I said he doesn't need to look for a girlfriend here because he has one in Connecticut." Gordo isn't entirely buying. His attention is squarely on me now.

"That so? You got a girl at home? You have her picture in your wallet? Is she pretty?"

"Well, she looks a lot like you, so *no*."

The buzzer for first period rings, and I totally feel the phrase "saved by the bell." Ma Elena throws open the door, exposing us to the rush of students, wisely assuming we're not going to break into a big fight with an audience. (Oh my god, it would be awful; I did jiujitsu for like two seconds in fifth grade, so I know Gordo would pulp me.)

Worse, Gordo and I have first period together, so we end up trudging the same way. I try not to look at him, but as we get to Ms. Silverthorn's room, I hazard a side glance. He's doing the same thing, and he looks away instantly as if burned by homo rays. Maybe he's one of the *deep* closet cases (the worst 'phobes always are), or maybe he's a classic bigot, just needing an Other to punch when he's mad. And maybe it doesn't matter: my attempts to play Dr. Phil won't keep me safe from either.

At lunch, Chaz, Leeza, and Tawny save me a seat, but Chaz seems strategically placed at the far corner, with Tawny at his side and the others opposite him, so that I cannot possibly sit across from or next to him. He manages to work the words "Tawny and I" into every possible subject: prom, drama, Pre-Cal, last Christmas, Darien Lake, even baby photos—theirs will be side by side in the yearbook.

Ma Elena comes by, sliding into the seat next to me. "Frohmeyer says we can start on the cafeteria Saturday night. They'll do bagels and sack-lunches in the dorm on Sunday, so we have the whole day plus."

"Hallelujah!" Chaz stretches a thin arm across the table to high five her. "It is not going to look right if we are throwing up streamers any old way in a panic on Sunday."

I chime in enthusiastically—and I'm not even faking. "Yay! It gives me something to do this weekend!"

Tawny turns my way. "Are you on the decorating committee?"

"As of this morning," Ma Elena answer for me. She looks pleased with herself, maybe too pleased, and I'm rethinking the wisdom of her being a confidante. I mean, how do I know she can keep a secret? "I think he's a *perfect* fit for this squad." Oh my god, she just went all gays-are-born-decorators on me—which is kind of homophobic even if, in this case, it's true—and I'm blushing. *Please, Ma Elena, stop.*

Leeza understands the implication and is shooting me a "what did I say" look, and Chaz does not seem thrilled. Tawny says she's glad she's on yearbook, not prom because she doesn't want to see any of it before the dance—it'll ruin the magic. Honestly, she wishes we'd stop talking about it in front of her because we're kind of killing the surprise.

Ma Elena's not done. "Note taken. We'll be totally silent." (Somehow, I doubt this is true.) "But for the rest of us, we don't have to wait to get to work. Weese helped with I *won't say what* this morning, but we still need to paint the I *won't say that either*, and Mr. A said we can get in the shop building tonight to do it." The smile she lobs at Chaz and me might as well have come from a matchmaking tía.

If she has at all noticed that neither of us smiles back, you'd never know.

Rec starts right after dinner at First Secondary. The boys play baseball on a real diamond next to a wan volleyball net just plugged into a flat-ish patch of grass for the girls. If this was not the dark ages, I'd start a campaign on Insta to shame the school. (Where's Megan Rapinoe when you need her?) Rec would not be my first choice for an evening, but on Thursdays, it's "sack supper," which means sandwiches, chips, and cookies in paper bags, and they're distributed here on the field. Even if it's cold cuts with (oh my god) globs of mayo on white, a sis has to eat. If there is any slim reward, it's that the ball field is the highest point on campus, the only place with a lake view.

Mrs. Buckman is here, pregnancy making her look fifty pounds heavier and yet not any less pickled than in my time, and she's strolling among the students who are camped out on the lawn. Every now and then she points at someone and makes a scissors with her fingers, but instead of making a snipping motion, the blades go up and down in an alternating pattern. *What the hell*? Vin Weasel is going by and even though it's him, I ask what that's about. He grins. "So they don't have the "One Up" rule in Connecticut, huh?" *Apparently*, Mrs. Buckman is the Social Monitor, whose sole job is to make sure there are no public displays of affection and that nobody cops a discreet feel. "One Up" really means "*At Least* One Up," meaning that if a boy and girl are on the ground next to each other, they can't both be lying down: at least one must sit up.

(Um, why? Because somehow they might have sex in front of everyone? Or does she think just being prone gets you pregnant?)

I start laughing and poke his arm. "Does the school not know how babies get made?"

He flinches at my mere touch, and his jaw tightens. We both pretend he didn't flinch, and I didn't notice. He works hard to seem cool. "I think there's a lot this school doesn't know." Gordo has told him what he thinks about me—it's clear as day. Why did I say anything to Ma Elena? He steps back—time to put me in my place.

His eyes glitter. "So Gordo says you've been holding out." I can hardly breathe. Is he going to— "You have a *girlfriend* you've been hiding." His smile returns, a Cheshire cat grin getting wider. He thinks he's caught me and is enjoying himself immensely.

"She's not hiding. She's back home. Where I wish I was." My throat catches on that.

Oh my god, I just went all girlfriend-in-Canada. How the hell am I, the queerest of my class, suddenly an effin' closet case? I came all this way to show Chaz how it's done, and now I'm Chazzing myself. I hate the '80s.

He's not done. "Does Connecticut Babe have a name?"

"Bianca? Yeah, obvi."

Not buying it. "Like Madonna? No last name?" He's so proud of himself.

"Bianca del Rio." I can't help it. I giggle, pretty sure he could never imagine *RuPaul's Drag Race*.

"Pretty name. Can I see her?"

"Yeah, move to New Haven." I've never pegged a specific place in Connecticut before, so this may be a bad call, especially since I've never been there. Here's hoping he hasn't either.

"A picture, doofus. Show me a picture." His needling has taken on more of an edge like he's tired of it taking so long for me to buckle.

I look down at my gym shorts. The shorts in the '80s are phenomenal: they go up over the waist and they are outlined in white piping, and stop way up the thigh, so they show off my legs *and* my butt. Mine are red with yellow trim, and I'm wearing them with a Devo tank in yellow with a red logo. I think I look really cute. What I do *not* look like is someone carrying a wallet. And I'm super annoyed that he thinks he can demand anything of me.

"Um, where exactly do you think I'm stashing it?" His eyes widen. I should *so not* follow my impulses here. I shouldn't, but I do. "Or are you offering to help me look?"

He shoves me, one hand right in the chest, and stalks off without a retort. The blow was surprisingly forceful, and my heart pounds.

What the hell?

That is more than enough rec for me, and I grab my bag. Decorating committee doesn't meet for another half hour or so, but I'm not staying for another inning.

Ernie is in our room, which I didn't expect. I mean, *everyone* is at rec. "Why aren't you up the hill?" I ask. And then I see it.

He's on the floor hunched over a big sheet of heavy paper covered with the most intricate pattern of fractal whirls I've ever seen. His canvas is probably three feet by four, and he has pushed our desk chairs up onto the beds to make room. The outlines of each curling swirl fill the sheet, inked in dramatic black, and more delicate lines within each reveals arcs, bubbles, and more swirls. About 90 percent of them have been filled in with color, each tiny part given depth from multiple hues. It's like the most intense paint by number I've ever seen.

"I'm trying to finish my art project for Monday." His eyes don't leave the canvas. "I spent too long on getting the outlines just right, but I don't want to hurry the light pockets." *Light pockets?* I love it. And it's not paint by number—he *made* this. I can't believe it came from Ernie. It makes me wonder why the hell he ends up a curator instead of an artist.

"This is too good for art class! This should be in an art show."

He looks up to see if I'm teasing, and it's clear I am not. His eyes brighten. "I win ribbons at the Syracuse State fair every year. Summer before senior year, I won the grand prize and got the Ontario County scholarship, which I can use for college at Cooper Union in New York this fall." (I'm awful. I don't even know where home is for him. Why don't I listen to people?)

"I had no idea." I kneel next to him to look more closely.

"Course not. Nobody really cares about that here. I'm just the 'Gale warning' guy." He doesn't sound sad or outraged as I would, just resigned. Which is worse. "I'm not actually that *clumsy*, just distracted. I'm in my head a lot."

"If that means you can do this—then distracted is a small price to pay."

"Tell it to the tractor I crashed." He chuckles, and I nudge him with my shoulder. Unlike Vin Weasel, he doesn't recoil. Either the rumor is still stuck among Gordo's friends, or Ernie just doesn't mind. He should've been born in my day.

"I'm your roommate—why haven't you shown me this?"

He shrugs and then is quiet, concentrating on filling in the tiniest bubble with three shades of blue. When it looks like it came from the depths of the sea, he replies. "I like having something no one else knows . . . for myself. When I knock over a bookshelf or trip up the stairs, that's the guy they expect. I like being more than that. They don't even know what they're missing."

"When you bring it to art class, they'll know then."

"Yeah." His grin is profound. "No one'll know what hit 'em. I've been getting *A*s all year for simple drawings of the admin building and a pinch pot that a baby could make. Even Miss Jarvis has no idea what I can do. I'm going to take this in the last day, and she's going to go nuts. They hang the three best projects up in the hall for graduation, and I'm not bragging, but there's no way this won't go up. My folks will see it and think I've been Ernie the Artist all along, the guy they know. They've never even heard about Gale warning." I hope that becomes true.

I glance up to the clock, and I'm ten minutes late. "I have to go decorate for prom." Which gives me an idea. He clearly has an amazing eye. "Come with!"

The look on his face borders on shock. "I'll probably knock something over."

"You're an artist! You *have* to help."

"I don't think anyone but you really wants me to . . ."

"Well, I'm the boss of me, and I'm asking."

He looks at the paper and mulls. When he starts gently

rolling his canvas, I know I've won. Finally, someone here is doing what I want! And hopefully, he won't break anything.

The lower floor of the shop building is all aglow. The broom-making equipment is quiet, and a sheen of straw dust coats everything, but the swing sits on a sea of drop cloths at one end. It's pretty clever, I have to say: a tricked-out love seat swing you'd see on a verandah, but fronted with a crescent moon, its lower sliver obscuring the bench, and its top sliver covering the bar the swing hangs from. Ma Elena sits in the swing, giving it a try, and it's kind of perfect, the way her legs dangle off the crescent. Chaz and Leeza stand to one side, disagreeing about something. They all look surprised to see Ernie with me, but Ma Elena seizes the moment.

"More recruits! Perfect!" She hops off the swing and strides over. "You can help us settle a debate. Leez thinks—"

"I can speak for myself! I think we should only paint the moon in white and leave the rest of it natural wood so the moon stands out. Otherwise, why—"

"And *I* say," Chaz cuts her off. "Natural wood is going to look ridiculous. The walls are going to be sparkling, twinkling lights outlining the room, the tables covered in satin with the moon rocks shining under glass, and after all that, we hang the moon on LL Bean furniture?"

"Oh my god, sis, you're so right." I did it again. I hurry on. "He's right. You can't have one element that doesn't fit and make *that* the star of the show, pardon my pun. Think about the photos."

He lets the "sis" slide because I've agreed with him, and he gives me a "thank you" look. "Okay, think about the photos," Leeza replies. "If the rest of the wood is also white, you'll barely register the moon." Or people's faces either, but I don't offer this thought because, well, they've already paid for it all.

Ernie has forgotten us for a moment and is wandering close to the moon. Chaz and Ma Elena see this and instinctively get between him and it, envisioning what he might do to their centerpiece. He backs up, looking at it from afar, then says, "Black."

Envisioning a black moon, Leeza looks like her head is ready to explode until he explains.

"Paint the entire frame flat black. Paint only the moon white. And then in the photos, the rest will disappear, so it really looks like you're swinging on a crescent moon."

I cannot believe I didn't think of it first, and they cannot believe that Ernie did. Chaz looks at Ernie like Iggy Stardust has descended from Mars. "That's genius! You totally win."

Ernie basks in the attention and keeps going. "Make sure you paint every bit of the frame—backsides, undersides, bolts—so there's no chance of any place not reading as black and pulling from the moon. Use flat black, not a gloss, so it catches no reflection. And have it on a black drop cloth, not the cafeteria floor, which is light gray and will act like a white."

Everyone is nodding approval.

Is this the first time in four years at First Secondary that Ernie has gotten credit for something good?

Speaking of which, Chaz is almost floating with excitement. "I'll run over to industrial arts and get black. You guys start on the white." I spot an opening and offer to go with. I'm happy to have a moment alone with Chaz and finally get my plan in motion.

As Chaz heads for the door, I take in the unexpected view of Ernie in the thick of things, and I start to wonder if maybe I'm here for a twofer: making life better for Ernie, too. But I'm already dropping the ball on my main plan—the clicking of a metal door tells me Chaz has left without me.

In the Closet

I KNOW CHAZ IS a little scared of me (I can be a lot, so I get it), which means I shouldn't dive in right away. Small talk is in order.

"What's IA?" I ask to fill the silence as we follow the lawn leading downhill from the shop building.

"Industrial arts." He doesn't sound too annoyed that I'm there. "That's where they hold what any other school would call shop classes, but since we already have shop, it's less confusing this way."

"Um, since the shop building is all the industries, wouldn't it make more sense to call *that* industrial arts and the other place shop?"

He laughs and shakes his head. "Tell me you think wrapping utensils is an art, and I'll tell you I have a girlfriend in Connecticut."

Whoa. He didn't. So much for my discretion.

"Has *everybody* heard?"

"No way. But Ma Elena told Leeza what she said to Gordo and—"

"Got it. Leeza's your bestie."

I'm suddenly grateful that cell phones don't exist because "Girlfriend in Connecticut" would be a meme by now, and everyone in school would already be doing parodies. It's a slim comfort that not everyone has to know all my business at once.

We are crossing the ball field, now empty of students, and shadowed in the gloaming. Chaz makes a surprising confession. "The IA building isn't this way."

"So . . . where *are* we going?"

My god, that came out flirty so fast, you'd think I'd met him on an app. But he misses the intonation. "The IA building . . ." he laughs. "We're just taking the scenic route. This is my favorite spot on campus."

"The *ball field?*" I didn't picture Chaz as Sporty Spice, if you know what I mean, and I don't bother hiding it.

"Hey now, I played Little League!" He's not really defensive, just teasing. "I mean, I was terrible at things like catching a ball or throwing it, but I was *fast*—if a pitcher ever walked me, I could run like a rabbit from base to base if my teammates got actual hits."

"Trust me. I'm not throwing stones . . . *or* balls. I mean, please." He just laughs as he climbs the bleachers, waves me up.

Far away, the lake is gleaming silver, just lighter than the dark fields around it. "That," he said, "is why I come this way. Most of the time, all you can see is the campus itself—it's everything, but up here, there's more. It's a reminder the world beyond this school is so much bigger and more beautiful than the world *inside* it. And in a month, that world is mine."

He sounds so hopeful, it hardly jibes with the suicide story. But what do I know? How can I tell what might change this in the next few days? And what to say?

"I'm glad you're in the world."

He doesn't say anything, but he smiles at that before leading me down the bleacher steps and onward to the industrial arts building, which, true to his word, is about as far from the ball field as you can get and still be on campus.

He stops in front of the main doorway into the building, which is completely dark. It takes a moment to find the nearest light, which illuminates only the worktable nearest the entry. Beyond us, a room full of welding equipment and band saws disappears into the shadows.

We can't find any more switches, so we're left in the semidarkness to try and find the supply closet. We're almost tiptoeing—we're not doing anything wrong, but there's something about the shadowiness surrounding us that makes us both nervous. I can't help it, and start giggling; so does he.

"We're the fog creeping in on little cat feet," he whispers. Apparently, Ms. Silverthorn has been teaching *that* poem forever.

We can't open the first door, but the second one seems to be unlocked. There's even less light once we're inside, and we have to feel the walls for a switch. I think, *now we're both in the closet*, which makes me giggle more, and soon we're both dying of laughter while still in the dark.

Maybe not being able to see me is what lets him speak directly. "You don't have a girlfriend, do you?"

"No." I stop trying to find a light. I hesitate. "But you do."

"Yeah . . ." He lets out a sigh so full I can picture it as plumes of smoke curling into the air. "I really like Tawny." I don't think he's trying to convince *me*.

"Cool."

"Yeah?" We've both stopped looking for a light. "So why'd you send that note?"

Wow. He's really going for it.

"Because it's true. Your eyes *are* flawless. And . . ." Where do I take this? "I'm far away from home, and I miss my boyfriend, and I was hoping I wasn't alone, and I guess I was wrong."

Good thing it's dark, or he'd see that my eyes are brimming. Cheng. Why did I have to think of him right now? His strong arms. His calm when I'm flying off over the latest thing. His kiss. The matter-of-factness of us. How long will it be before I know what it is to be me again? Oh my god, I'm halfway to a good cry.

Poor Chaz. He so wasn't expecting me to do an emotional dump. "It's okay, it's okay. You're not the only one who . . . who thought that about me. I guess people just see me that way . . ." There is a pause, a silence that sounds like a struggle. "Sometimes . . . I—"

He can't go on.

I want him to finish the thought. To say: sometimes he thinks so, too.

What does Ms. Silverthorn call it—a pregnant pause? When the air is full of words waiting to be said. We're in one of those. I know about romantic tension—about sexual tension. And this is something else entirely—coming-out tension. Not the moment before you tell your mom or best friend, but the moment you tell someone you hope is like you, someone you badly *want* to be like you, because maybe, *maybe* there's a chance with them.

He doesn't finish the thought.

When he finally speaks, his voice is insanely soft. "You have a boyfriend?"

"Cheng. Yeah. I mean, I did . . . but now I'm here and I don't know when I can go home." *And* I'm choking up again. Girl, I'm a mess.

"I'm glad you had someone." The envy in his voice! And the gentleness with which he wades through this minefield. "I'm sorry you feel alone." Now I'm not even sure who I'm crying for.

Chaz pulls me into a hug. He's comforting me, not being romantic, but we're alone in the dark, and he's handsome, and

145

I'm me, and I've so badly missed being held that my heart is racing. The sparks flying might as well be visible. I pull away just enough so that I can look at him.

And I see the tears streaming down his face now.

"Oh . . . god . . . Chaz . . ."

"It's okay," he says, leaving the hug. "Mama always said I'm too empathetic for my own good."

Nice try. I don't think those tears are for me.

He is wiping his eyes. "You should've seen me at the end of *Terms of Endearment*. Crying myself blind, I couldn't walk straight." (I can't tell. Is that a coded joke?)

He starts feeling the walls again. When he finds the switch, the light is harsh—we both blink and laugh. The moment is lost. Just steps away, I see an entire wall dedicated to paint cans, many drip-spattered and half-used. We grab more black than we need, then Chaz kills the light. I want to tell him to stay, but he is out the door. There's nothing for me to say or do but follow.

The Status Quo

EVERY TIME I'VE ENTERED a classroom today, I have been off my game. I just don't know what I'm walking into. The kids who were indifferent to me remain so (and really, indifference is not something I'm used to), though the friendly ones seem fine. Gordo and Vin Weasel glower at me every chance they get, and I have a strong hunch they've told more of the guys, including the acne-scarred giant I'll call Red, who seems to bristle when he passes me in the hall. Maybe I'm being paranoid? Or maybe I shouldn't have offered to let Vin Weasel look in my shorts. So much for the "girlfriend" ruse.

The biggest change is Ernie, who ends up padding around behind me to half of my classes as if I am his best friend.

I already have a bestie, and they bear no resemblance to my new roommate. Except, they both always carry a device: Nix an iPhone, Ernie that handheld game thingy. Granted, Nix is decades away, but with my status here still so uncertain, I'm not sure I'm ready to be paired with Ernie in everyone's minds.

I've been counting the minutes until lunch when he'll hang with JJ, the wallet girl, and I won't have to babysit. I know that makes me sound like a dick, but I'm tired. I couldn't sleep last night. There was so much to turn over: the sparks in the paint closet, Gordo and Vin Weasel treating me like the next Chaz as fodder for taunting, and all the what-ifs.

What if I'm here forever? Will I grow up alongside my mom? And then what? I'll never know Nix or Cheng or be *me*. Take my advice: don't time travel; it messes with your mind. A joke, obvi.

Time traveling, at least in my case, is like being gay—*so* not a choice. Today I can't be the-sun'll-come-out-tomorrow-Annie—I'm more Maleficent-at-a-baby-shower. Trust me, it's a whole mood.

Chaz and Leeza flag me from a different table than usual. It's the only round one in the cafeteria, and it's the opposite end of our usual seats. Worse, it's close to Mrs. Buckman, who is Lunch Monitor, too (yay for a skill set!), and I don't want her hearing anything too juicy. Why did they have to move? I know I've only been here five days, but I like a routine, especially one that cements my in-group status. A glance back at "our" table tells the whole story. Gordo, Vin Weasel, Red, and a few more of their buddies have taken it over. It's not accidental. As soon as I pass by with my tray, Vin Weasel loudly says to Gordo, "You're right, this new table is better. Guess it's ours now." I'm a few steps away by the time Gordo says something in Spanish, and I am *this close* to turning around and letting him wear my lunch, but I hear a splash and a ripple of laughter.

Of course, it's Ernie. He's trying to wipe up chocolate milk that is spreading right in the middle of the path and because he is flustered, he's decided to use his sweatshirt instead of running for a paper towel. Taking off his sweatshirt reveals that he is wearing the world's most beat-up T-shirt underneath, once probably forest green and now faded to bad AstroTurf. In my day, a hundred phones would surround him, snapping or streaming his embarrassment. For the second time, I'm glad it's the '80s.

It's Chaz and Leeza who get to him first, pressing their napkins into the brown slick, and then Ma Elena arrives with an entire roll of paper towels. I realize I am just standing there watching, not helping, so I drop my tray on the nearest table and join them, ineffectually patting at the spill with a lunch napkin. Leeza frowns at me, and I feel seen, not in a good way.

Why didn't I help sooner?

Leeza's frown tips over into a full-on scowl as Mrs. Buckman arrives on the scene with a mop and shushes us away. When the mess is cleaned up, I join my squad at the table, complimented by Ernie, who gushes about how nice it was to have

149

help. My day brightens a little when Chaz catches my eye and flickers the quickest wink. When Ma Elena slides in next to me, I feel even better: aside from Ms. Silverthorn, every person I like in this timeline is in one place. There's no excuse for me to be such a douche. Sunshine it is.

Almost immediately, permission is granted for my inner kraken to return: Gordo comes over.

Ignoring the rest of us, he leans over Ma Elena. "We saved you a seat."

"Did you? 'Cause it looks like a testosterone party."

"Ha ha. Come on."

"I'm good."

"Whatchu mean you're good? Unless you're dating one of these ladies, you can have a seat with your boyfriend."

"Or you can sit with your girlfriend. We can make room."

It's like we're watching beach volleyball, our eyes pinging from one side to the other.

"You think I won't?"

"Yeah. Kinda."

"You don't want me to."

"I do."

They have forgotten us entirely.

Now he's trapped. If the point was that they need to sit together, she's making it impossible. If he refuses, it shows the lie. But if he does eat here, his whole table-grabbing display was pointless.

As if tethered, Chaz and Leeza both stand up with their

trays. "Take all the room you need, Gordo." Tawny reluctantly joins them; no one is leaving her behind.

Now Gordo's thoroughly flummoxed, and Ma Elena is amused. She pats the seat next to her. "Sit, Gordito."

I get my tray, too (no chance I'm eating with Gordo), and nudge Ernie, who is eating so much, so fast, he hasn't really paid attention. But he gets up, too, happy to be included.

Gordo relents and sits, waving at his crew to come over. Vin Weasel looks a little put out, making the universal what-the-hell hand gesture, and Gordo mimes that he has claimed the table. Apparently, it looks like he has scared us off and *that* they like. As a unit, the boys cross the cafeteria and surround Ma Elena, who looks like the cat who swallowed the canary.

Gordo doesn't see that Leeza and Chaz have spotted that our vacated table is now empty. We swoop into our old places, with Ernie close behind. We are all laughing at how easily Gordo has been outmaneuvered, and this should feel like a big win, but Chaz isn't convinced we'll get to enjoy it. "Eat fast, kiddos," he says between bites of sandpaper-dry lasagna. "The cavemen will notice soon enough."

He's not wrong. Within minutes Gordo is at our table, fuming. "You think you're so funny."

Chaz plays innocent. "I think we gave you a whole table."

"I get what you did there."

"Do you?" Chaz asks. "Explain it. Use your words." Gordo's eyebrow twitches, and he can't think what to say, which makes Chaz even bolder. "No? I didn't think so." A lazy smile slides into place. "Funny that you'd rather be over here with us instead of with your girlfriend." I love it—it's like he's a dialed-back version of me.

No one trumps Gordo. He's almost spitting. "You little fag! There's no place for you here. I know what you're into, perv, and I can get you kicked out. And you'll be lucky if that's all I do."

Chaz's smile is gone. "Come on, Tawny," he says. "We don't need this."

"Yeah, Tawny, go with your 'boyfriend.' I bet he's a real good kisser." The whole room is watching now. And Gordo makes the most of his audience. "Ask your boyfriend why he's sneaking out at night with *his* boyfriend!" Chaz and Tawny stop in their tracks. Honestly, so do I, and I wasn't even standing.

CHAZ HAS A BOYFRIEND? How is that even—

Gordo is grabbing me by my polo before I get it: he means me. I can see Ma Elena trying to grab one of his arms while his goons crowd her away. My kraken awakes. I have like four shirts total, and he is not going to tear the buttons off this one, which is my favorite.

Nix and I signed up for a free women's self-defense class at the yoga studio in Auburn (they weren't like super happy to see either of us, but Nix is Nix, and I was in full face, and they had like two clients that day, so they let us stay). It's all sort of blurry, but I think for a front assault, I'm supposed to bring my hands up through the middle and pull back while dropping. Or maybe dropping and kicking? I try it all at once in a panic and

152

end up hitting my own chin with my hands, but a kick is a kick, and mine is square in his crotch.

Gordo goes down, howling, and his boys finally let Ma Elena through. But he only has eyes for me. "You kicked me in the balls, asshole! Who does that?" Like, what, I violated some bro code? He's actually crying.

"Then keep your paws to yourself." 2020s me has climbed over '80s me and is about to plant a pride flag right in his effin' forehead. "I know I'm hot stuff and that it's just about impossible to resist me, and *oh* I could give you the ride of your life, but if you touch me again, you'll be the one kicked out, and then what will you have left? Is there even time to find your fourth high school before graduation?"

Mrs. Buckman has finally made her way across the cafeteria to see what the fuss is, but she's missed the good part.

Gordo scrambles to stand, but Ma Elena is directly between us, hissing—not just at him, "Grow up! I don't have time for little boys!" She pulls him away, and he goes, but not without a red-eyed look back at me. It's the scariest thing I've ever seen. Kids are beginning to go back to their seats, leaving Mrs. Buckman (who hates to miss drama more than she hates anything else in the world) to canvas them, asking who did what to whom.

If I saw that speech in a movie, I'd be all finger snaps and "you go!" But I don't feel that way *at all*. "I could give you the ride of your life?" *Really*?

I may have just outed myself in the least welcoming time and space I can imagine without having been here long enough

153

to first gain general goodwill. If Frohmeyer hears the details, I'm out for sure. And for what? It's hardly a way to make Chaz feel *better* about being gay. If I'd just been smart enough to let Gordo knock me out, maybe I would have ended up back home.

Chaz is still standing there with Tawny. I'm expecting an angry face or a fearful one. But it's like he's seen fireworks for the first time: His face is lit with wonder. Tawny has to drag him away. As for me, I just flee.

I am in such a mood. I don't want to go back to my room and risk exposure to Ernie's newfound puppy-like enthusiasm. My cutlery job doesn't start for another half hour, but I head for the shop anyway. If nothing else, arriving early means I can score a table by the window; if I am meant to squander my youth in service of plasticware, I can have a better view. I suppose this will not increase my productivity, but there won't be any pleasing Gordo today, no matter what. Maybe we can just pretend not to see each other.

What I do see is Buckman walking Leeza into the lower level and looking both ways before ushering her into his office. The shades are already down in tryst-ready fashion.

I cannot possibly come up with a convincing excuse to go knock on that door, but I can't leave Leeza there. I don't know if I'm a white knight or an idiot as I approach the shop. I hesitate for a moment, hoping I'm not about to interrupt anything that will scar me forever. I know that Leeza may be furious with me, and I hate to risk that, but if #MeToo taught me anything, it's that friends don't let friends get played by lecherous older men. I can get one thing right today.

Taking a deep breath, I turn the knob.

Or I try. Buckman may be lecherous, but stupid he is not. The door is locked.

I have no choice but to leave or knock. I knock, making up a lie as I wait for them to open the door. I will tell him that Gordo and I had a fight, and maybe I shouldn't be on cutlery anymore. I know this means I will end up in the broom shop, which sounds even worse, but Leeza needs me—even if she doesn't know it.

Nothing.

I knock again.

Inside the office, I hear a phone ring and ring.

They've got to be freaked out—someone knocking, someone calling, as if the gods are conspiring to interrupt them.

The ringing stops.

And they don't answer the door.

If I hadn't seen them with my own eyes, I'd swear there was no one inside. Which is, of course, the whole point. Now I feel stranded and creepier by the second for lurking outside the door. Should I just bail? What did I think would happen?

Raucous voices float down the hill and, without turning, I know it's Gordo and Vin Weasel. I can't stand here any longer and risk drawing their attention to this door, which Leeza will have to walk through sometime. If I make her the object of their speculation—well, I can't imagine any good outcome.

I dart around the end of the building and trudge up the back stairs to the cutlery shop, defeated. Gordo is just as much my enemy as when the day started, and Leeza is still in Buckman's grasp.

Status quo for the win.

So Not a Fool

ONLY A RELIGIOUS SCHOOL would name all its teams The Flames. Tonight, most kids are in the gym for the game. I can only imagine what it's like for Gordo and the rest of the basketball players (the only team good enough to play other schools) to drive to, say, Oneonta and show up with tongues of Pentecost on their chests and the word Flames on their backs. I mean, seriously, even Frohmeyer can't be so innocent he doesn't know what the other schools must think. In a way, it's justice—it must make Gordo *insane*. I would kill to take over the cheer squad and help the team *really* earn its name.

While the other students are watching the game, the decorating committee is working on a new project. The swing looks ah-may-zing, so now we're onto the rest of the night sky. The shimmering fabric I saw the first day I helped Ma Elena is going to be the cosmos, and she's ordered hundreds of glow-in-the-dark stick-on stars. Leeza wanted to lay the bolts out on the floor for ease, but Chaz insisted that we hang them all around the room to see how the fabric moves. Ernie (who is now permanently part of the squad) suggests arranging the stars to replicate as many constellations as we can remember.

Leeza has brought her illegal boom box (we're not supposed to have them on campus) and a mixtape, so we have music. The whole time, Ma Elena's bopping about taking photos on this little Instamatic camera that is adorbs even if the flash is basically like something a second grader has on their starter phone. I'm doing everything I can to stay out of the photos because it's too trippy to think I might end up preserved for posterity in my own mom's photo albums before I am born. I dart out of the shot at the last second or pretend to sneeze into my hand or turn to look away so many times that she gets the message. "Are you running from the law or just weirdly self-conscious?!"

"I'm from the future, and if you take my picture, it'll mess with the space-time continuum!" Why not? They're not going to believe me.

Ernie hears this and vibrates with excitement. "Like *Back to the Future*!"

(Wait—is that out yet? God, I wish I could google it. Where is IMDB when you need it?)

But Chaz joins in. "My family thinks movies are sinful—"

"Your family thinks everything is sinful," jibes Leeza.

"I was *trying* to say I can't go to the movies without sneaking out, but I saw the preview for that, and it looks so good. I'll just have to find a way. That is if anyone will go with me . . ."

"I'm in!" Ernie is hopping up and down, and I feel a little bad for him. The invitation was meant for me, but Chaz can't say that, obviously.

I play it cool. "When does it come out?"

"July 3!" Chaz and Ernie answer at once. I had no idea it was such a big deal at the time.

"Bummer!" Leeza cuts in. "I'll still be working at Camp Cherokee, or I'd be there too. Where do you live, Ernie?"

"Canandaigua, but that's like an hour and change from Syracuse."

Ma Elena hates imprecision. "More like an hour and a half."

"Not if you drive eighty-eight miles per hour," I say in my best Doc Brown voice, and not only do they not react, Ernie thinks I mean it.

"The speeding ticket on that would be huge! My parents would kill me. But I can definitely come see it with you, Chaz. How about you, Maria Elena? Come with?"

"It's two hours to Syracuse!"

"Fine," says Chaz. "You'd just crowd my DeLorean anyway." She pings him with a star just as "Everybody Wants to Rule the World" comes on. Eighties music has never been my particular jam, but I love this song. I mean, the title says it all, right? And soon, we're all dancing around the vast room, the backbeat motivating us, the synth kicking as the chorus approaches. We're singing at the top of our lungs, Chaz crushing us all with his amazing pitch. Leeza is the only one who can keep up, and they do an air duet on the first chorus. Chaz steals a glance my way, and we both are smiling so hard, you'd have to be blind to miss it. I try to get Leeza's attention to see if she has noticed the obvious chemistry here, but I can't seem to catch her eye. It strikes me that she hasn't actually talked to me since we started, making me nervous. Does she regret talking to me about Chaz? Is she less cool than I thought?

The doubt flickers and then passes. How could it not with this music playing and everyone so high on it? Work on prom is forgotten. This is a dance party.

This tape is like thirty minutes on each side and has to be flipped to get the second half of the playlist, but I'm digging it. We all are. We do a "Don't Stop Believing" singalong straight (and I mean straight) out of a karaoke bar, and a dance-off to Amy Grant's "Wise Up." Ma Elena is looser than I've ever seen her, tossing her hair and dancing with her hands in the air. Leeza is all new-wavey, shoulders up, arms drawn in like a self-hug, eyes closed. Chaz—the way Chaz moves is magic. He's doing his own thing, every move as natural a link between limb and lyric as humanly possible. Seriously, I can't take my eyes off him.

And then there's Ernie. He's into it, in a spastic robot way. He dances with such abandon, I'm surprised he doesn't fall down, but not surprised that he does manage to trip Chaz *and* me. I'm glad he has friends, but a little personal space wouldn't hurt.

"If you do that at prom, you're going to bring down the house," I say, pleased with the double meaning. But this stops everyone, and they shoot each other looks that pretty much say, *You tell him.*

Ma Elena speaks for the group. "You know there's no dancing, right?"

"At *prom?*" What fresh hell is this?

"It's a religious school. Dancing's technically a 'sin.'"

"Oh my god, it's *Footloose.*"

Leeza shoots me a dark look. "Maybe read the handbook—it's just full of sins you can commit." Is it just me, or does her tone slide past cool snark into sharp dig?

"Prom comes from the word 'promenade,' which means walk." Ernie thinks he's helping. He is not.

"So we'll just walk all night? I mean, that's the dumbest thing I've ever heard."

Weirdly, Chaz defends it. "No! Some of the kids sing, and there's a movie—"

At prom?!

"And they cater instead of serving cafeteria food, which is worth it in its own right."

Ma Elena chimes in. "It's really just about getting dressed up and having a big night with your friends. Nothing wrong with that."

Chaz gently ribs me. "I bet you miss Connecticut now . . ."

161

I thought prom would suck if ASA wouldn't let me dance with Chaz. But First Secondary has gone and made it worse. Kudos to them for being so extra.

"It's going to be great, I promise." Ma Elena seems very invested in this, which is a little surprising since she will tell me for years that she *didn't* go. She bites her lip and then makes a decision. "I wasn't going to show you guys yet, but maybe this will help."

She tells Ernie to turn off the lights, and the room is a field of stars as if we're floating in the cosmos. That's not the surprise. She tells us just to be patient while we stand in this celestial night. We can hear her fiddling with equipment of some kind. She hits play on the boom box just as a faint hum of electricity kicks in.

All at once, "Drive" by the Cars fills the air with wistfulness, and a black light disco ball swirls a pattern of light through the space so that the glowing stars become twinkling ones. Oh my god. It's *amazing*.

We pretty much all gasp and then fall silent—the *yearning* in the song. I've never really heard the words before. The singer keeps asking someone—a girlfriend, maybe?—who's gonna watch out for her when things fall apart, but *apparently,* they're not together because he keeps asking who will drive her home that night. Maybe he's not even with her, just thinking about her and worrying. The lights flickering around us just ramp up the melancholy effect.

Leeza and Chaz have each other. Ma Elena has Gordo.

Who's going to be there for me when school ends? What if I've lost Cheng forever? What if I lose Nix too?

I had this really awful time in ninth grade. A boy I liked had talked me into texting him a picture of me in a Speedo. I mean, it's not like it was nude, okay? I'm not brainless, just occasionally impulsive. And he texted back the meanest things about how I looked. I mean, like, fired them off, rounds from an AR-15, so quickly it felt like he was loaded before I sent the pic. And then he blocked me entirely. I didn't want to go to school the next day, so Nix came over, missing two tests and a lab final, to sit in my room streaming *The Office* reruns, telling me that watching other people cringe would be just the right medicine. They were right, and now they're thirty-six years away.

I try to blink back tears and check to see if my friends are a mess too. Ma Elena and Leeza both are swaying softly, arms linked. But Chaz is transported. His eyes are closed, face upturned as if trying to catch the light of the moon, and he has his arms fanned out at his sides, palms open, as if he may lift off. Ernie and I both watch him, transfixed by this vision of Chaz as a mystic. What does Ernie see? Someone who moves through the world with a grace he does not have?

What do I see? I hate to admit it: I see boyfriend material. I know, I know I *have* a boyfriend, but Chaz is so beautiful right now I'd have to be a fool not to swoon a little if I'm going to be stuck here. And I'm so not a fool.

It strikes me that what's happening right now is different:

No one films our dancing. No one stops to check their DMs. We are present for it, *really* present, in the moment. Obviously, we *could* make this happen in my time, but we don't. Not ever.

When the song ends, no one moves. We let the spell linger. I know I will never forget this, not in any of my lives.

Not from Around Here

A RAPPING AT OUR door wakes me, but not Ernie—that boy is Sleeping Beauty, I swear. I stumble out of bed to answer, and I have an enormous woody, which is mortifying but totally fair. (It's not like I can masturbate with Ernie six feet away.) But who cares? Who do I have to impress?

To my surprise, it's the dean. He takes a full step back upon sight (seriously), but he's used to teenage boys by now. "*Some-one's* up." I want to die, which he clocks, and it amuses him. "Might want to cover that up before you see Silverthorn."

Huh? It's Saturday morning, and as far as I know, there are no special make-up classes for the kid who missed nine months of school.

He shrugs. "Don't ask me. She told me to get you." I thank him and close the door.

Maybe she's figured out how to get me home! I'm so eager that my fingers shake as I put on my tracksuit. Yes, I have a tracksuit. I bought it as my weekend look and, yes, it's women's, but it's all zippers, so who's to say? It's mostly black, which could make it unisex, but all the cutouts and bands slashing across the chest and one leg are in sherbet colors.

I don't worry about closing the door quietly—only hunger will wake Ernie—and I am down the hall in like three seconds.

Ms. Silverthorn is wearing a red buffalo plaid blouse, with linebacker-worthy shoulder pads underneath, and the effect of the enormous pattern and bulked-up silhouette kind of diminishes her head. I want to do an intervention, but she's not here for my opinion, and based on her face, I'd say she's feeling the same way about my look. "I'm taking you shopping for prom. I hear you have a date."

"Why would teachers know who's going with who?" It never occurred to me that they would care. They have lives, right?

"A good teacher has her ear to the ground. I listen. Kids have no idea what I know."

She's parked out front, and as we get into her car, I see Gordo in an upstairs window frowning. I smile my biggest smile at him, and he flips me off. Total lovefest.

☺

I'm dying over the name of the store she has brought me to, Rodolfo Men's Rentals. Yes, please, I'll take one boyfriend. Size? Mmm, let's say, large. Do you carry the Cheng?

I'm less amused inside. If Sears gave birth to a funeral parlor, it would be Rodolfo. The sales floor is somehow both too dimly lit and devoid of character all at once. But I can see that my choices are terrible: deadly dull, the stuff of a straight guy's prom fantasies. (Do straight guys fantasize about prom?)

The clothes are funereal too: rack after rack in black and gray. Either bright-colored tuxes are not yet a thing, or we're between fun-tux eras. There's no chance of me finding either look Leeza wants here.

I'm ready to give up when I see the sign on a small rack in the back corner. In signature swirling Rodolfo lettering, it says, "Vintage Selection." A similarly tasteful but much smaller sign, reads "Sale Items. Not For Rent. No Returns."

Seventies fashion isn't my thing—but the '60s hold some promise. There's a crushed velvet tux, but it's chocolate brown, and I cannot see myself wearing it. There's a Motown-feeling number that's cute but apparently was designed for an emaciated giant.

And then . . . Oh my god. *This*. It's a shawl-collar smoking jacket, black and teal brocade with black velvet trim. I know *exactly* what to do. Mom and I watched all those '80s movies with Molly Ringwald, and this is as close to a Duckie jacket as I've ever seen. (*Pretty in Pink* is so great and kinda messed up all at once, like we're supposed to root for Andie to fall in love with Duckie, the best friend, but he's a little obsessive and doesn't respect her agency so much. Even so, he's adorable, and his prom look is fierce. Everyone else shows up having shopped at somewhere like Rodolfo's, but he's in a smoking jacket, tux shirt, and bolo tie.) I can wear this jacket and be ahead of the curve but not crazily out of time *and* still match Leeza.

When I step outside the dressing room to show Ms. Silverthorn, her entire comment is, "I've seen stranger." We rent a tux shirt and pants, which I order in a size smaller than the tailor would like. He throws in a bowtie for free as a prom promotion, but there's no chance of it ever leaving its little plastic tomb.

I drag Ms. Silverthorn to Claire's and find the biggest, most '80s pin I can. A fake onyx orb surrounded by fake silver filigree fanning out in the four cardinal directions, like a really gay compass. It's more brooch than bolo, twin strands of silvery chain forming half-moons. (Sorry, Duckie.) Leeza will *die*.

We're back in the car before Ms. Silverthorn says anything. "Is that sort of outfit okay where you came from?"

"What?"

She is quiet, eyes on the road for a moment. "There are some questions I haven't asked, but I'm thinking maybe I should."

Got it. "You want to know if I'm gay? *One hundred percent.*"

She blinks. "The future must be different if you can just say that so easily."

I can't help but laugh. "Oh, you have no idea!"

She doesn't respond right away, and I'm dying to know

what's on her mind. It would be *very* sci-fi and paradoxy if it was me coming out in the 1980s that made her so open to kids like me in the 2010s. "So, I guess this is pretty new territory for you . . . ?"

She seems to be speaking to herself. "You're not the first student to tell me. Something about me being an English teacher must make it okay."

"Or something about you. You're the definition of welcoming."

She nods. "I try." A pause. "But it's not without effort."

It occurs to me: if this is her first year teaching, that means I probably know whoever came out to her. Was it Chaz?

She doesn't say any more, and I know I can't ask who it was, so we're both quiet. When we're nearly back to campus, she takes a left that leads us through cornfields and away from school.

She pulls into a gravel lot that has an even better view than the bleachers at school, taking in the whole campus, the fields in one direction, the thick woods in the other, and a full panorama of the shining lake beyond. "Antic Springs may be more, what's your word, *welcoming* in the future, but this is 1985. If a student's homosexuality were to be well known here and now, it'd only be a matter of time before he got beaten up by classmates—or Townies. And if he survived that, what would happen? The school would kick him out."

Oh my god. This is the same woman who will later let me write my junior research paper, *Art in the Aftermath of AIDS*, and give me an *A* for it. She really does sound like my

169

mom—which makes sense because my mom was her student when she was still this person.

"Did you not at all consider how you might look to the others if you wear a brooch to prom at First Secondary? Add that jacket, and you might as well be David Bowie."

"David Bowie is an icon. And he's bisexual, for the record."

"That does *not* help you. You're setting yourself up to be a target for Gordo and his crew."

Seriously, will there ever be a time when people aren't using queer people's safety as a reason to tell them to be less queer? How about telling everyone else to be less dangerous? "Um, maybe the problem is the *weapon*? No target ever shot itself."

She mulls this. She has always been good at hearing students out, even when we're melodramatic or reactionary. I don't think I'm being either here and by the look on her face, I see that she'd agree with me on this. But she also knows the world we're currently in better than I do. "It's unfair. I know that. You just want to be yourself. But I am telling you: pay attention to your context." She flutters her fingertips lightly on the steering wheel, a wave-like pattern from hand to hand as if rolling scales on the piano. "We need to get you back home."

She gets out of the car and walks to the edge of the hill, where an ancient-looking stone wall shores up the earth. Beyond it, the ground drops away dramatically. I join her and ask straight up: Has she made progress on finding me a way home?

She sighs. "It's all speculation. I want to have a concrete

170

answer, and I don't. I liked time travel better when it was something to dream about, not a problem to solve in real life. There's no single pattern—no one-size-fits-all explanation. The oldest stories—mostly time slips—are based on a rift somewhere in nature, and all the newest—the wormhole ones—are also about openings in space and time, portals and such. I don't think humans get to choose the space, only capitalize on it."

I'm way ahead of her. "So I need to go back the way I came. From the arts building."

"Where?"

I forgot it hasn't been built yet. "Oh! You get the academy to build a whole arts center for drama and music. It's your masterpiece, and they use it to death on social media—er, *videos*."

"*I* get them to do that?" Her face lights up. "I've spent most of this year expecting they'll find an excuse to fire me."

"Over *Godspell*?" Even *I* don't hate *Godspell* that much and trust me, I hate *Godspell*.

"I don't know about the twenty-first century, but being the only Black woman on staff right now isn't a cakewalk. Everything I do has to be twice as good for half the acclaim." I do not tell her that this hasn't changed so much. Her tone gets a little sharper. "I know about being a target."

God, I suck. "I'm sorry," I say. "I wasn't thinking."

"You're not the first." I'm guessing that's a massive understatement. "But let's focus on the problem at hand. If it *is* a portal, you can't travel back through a building that doesn't exist."

I'm not fazed. "The rift or portal or whatever didn't care. It

171

just dropped me in the field where the building will be in my time. So maybe I have to find that exact spot on the field again. Which shouldn't be that hard."

"I suppose. But the *place* is likely the easy part."

Ugh. She's right. "The time . . ."

"Some of the stories tag it to celestial events—an eclipse or a full moon. Most seem to use anniversary logic: the same day and time, but, say, a month later or six or a year." A year. My heart sinks. But she's not done. "And in some of them . . ." I don't want her to go on. "The people don't go back. They stay."

I mean, I know that. I've worried about this possibility. Not deeply, more like when you are sure you have a dreaded disease because your arm tingles or a freckle suddenly looks funny, then the tingling stops or the freckle is just a freckle, and you forget you were even worried. It's one thing to peek through the window at a horror and another to call it home. I *can't* stay here forever and never have my *real* life as a result. So I'm not gonna entertain the idea.

"Nope. Not me. We're going to have to figure the portal out. I'll start by standing in that field this next Monday at the time I arrived and then every Monday after school till I'm a scarecrow. I don't care. It's home or bust."

"That's the goal. You can even take me with you."

"No chance," I joke. "This school would never have two Black teachers at once, even if they *are* both you." The sentence is like a grenade, it's out so fast and lands so hard. Why would I say that???

172

The look she gives me is steeped in disappointment. "It never gets better?"

"Well . . ."

"I want to be surprised, but I'm not. I live in this country."

I need to throw her a bone. "We had a Black president!"

"*That* is news. Did they shoot him?" She waits, and I realize it's not a sarcastic joke. She means it. She assumes someone would.

"No! He was beloved. Well, at least on one side."

"The next guy was white, I'm guessing."

"Yeah." I don't say who—no need for her to live with *that* for thirty-six years.

"Figures. And what about you . . . gay people. Is that any better?"

"We can get married now. And be in the military. But . . ."

"People still hate you?"

"Yeah. Some do."

She says nothing, just absorbs it. "Sounds like you traveled the wrong way in time. Should've gone forward!"

"Preach!" The eyebrow raise she deploys in response suggests I should never say that again, or at least not in that voice. "Right. Maybe next trip."

She laughs. "Let's get you home from this one before you start packing your bags."

"If you do, I mean, if I find a portal or whatever, how will you explain?"

This, at least, is a question she has an answer to. "I'll say your mom got better, and you went home. Simple as that. No

173

one will think about it twice." But she pauses. "Except me, of course. 1985 won't be remotely the same after that."

◎

When I'm back on campus, I see Chaz coming out of my room. He's eager to see me. "There you are! Take a walk with me?"

It's a perfect May day. The sky is a vivid blue, the air dry, the lawn the color of green that tells you the heat of summer hasn't yet taken a toll. Our stroll can't take us anywhere all that amazing, considering we need to stay on campus, but just being here with a cute boy is exciting. I'm pretty sure this unexpected visit means he has started warming up to my presence, which makes me so happy, I find myself chatting nonstop until he asks a question.

"What did you do to piss off Leeza?"

Huh? I have no idea. I mean, she didn't love my opinion of Mr. Buckman, yet we've hung out together since, and she seemed like herself—

No, she didn't. She barely looked at me last night. But I was so caught up in the spell of the dancing that I just let it go. And I can't say any of this to Chaz, in case he doesn't know about the affair.

(Ew, I hate using that word for this.)

I shrug. "I don't really know." I look in his eyes. "What did she say?"

He rolls his eyes. "Something about you not being different than anyone else at this school no matter what you say." This

174

stings, and he can tell. He plays it off. "Sometimes, she can be a little dramatic. It'll blow over."

I'm quiet the rest of the way to the bleachers by the ball field. But Chaz is humming softly, and it makes me feel better. He's wearing a *The Wiz* tee that he has cropped by hand and blue jeans that cannot have been easy to squeeze into. The sun hitting his face makes his forehead, cheeks, and the bridge of his nose glow. I feel that current again. Maybe this is the moment he tells the truth. Maybe this conversation will change everything for him, and maybe that means no fall from the Ledges in his future.

"I broke up with Tawny."

Whoa. "How did she take it?"

"She said it was mean to do it before prom. I offered to still go with her but—"

"She has a shred of dignity and told you to step off?"

He grimaces. "Ouch."

"I am *not* judging you. If she's not the . . ." I stumble over the noun ". . . the *one* for you, she's not."

"You can say it, you know." His voice is just above a whisper, even though the field is empty.

I don't even pretend not to know what he means. "Okay . . . if she's not the *boy* for you."

Those violet eyes light up. "I can't believe we're sitting here having this talk. I've waited a long time . . ."

Looking at him now, I don't see how it is possible he'd hurt himself. I know that's not science, just a hunch. But I feel his love of life too clearly. Maybe the Townies rumor is right—maybe the choice was never his. I feel even more protective—I thought he needed me to help him come out, but now I wonder if what he really needs is someone to watch his back.

I want him to know that I do. "I'm glad you're having the talk with me."

"It helps that you're not from here. I'm not either, you know." He says this with such seriousness, it gives me pause.

Oh. My. God. He's a time traveler too.

"When are you from?" I can hardly breathe.

"When are *you* from?" He laughs.

"The 2020s!"

"What is that, like, the Jetsons?" He pushes me playfully. I don't know what Jetsons are, but I know that he thinks I'm kidding, which means he is not a time traveler.

I try to recover. "I just mean I'm ahead of my time!"

"*That* I buy."

"So where are you from, if not here?"

"We live in Syracuse now, but we moved from New York City. There were . . ." Again, his voice drops. ". . . these beautiful men there and they always seemed to travel in packs. I couldn't stop staring at them, and I was kind of afraid of them, too. My mother called them every name in the book—he-shes, halfsies, queers, sissies. You can*not* imagine the loathing in her voice. I decided at age eight that would never be who I was."

I feel for him. Even with Mom's limits, I never doubted who I was or whether she'd love me. Wanting to leap from the

Ledges makes more sense in this light. But I can't say anything like that. I just listen.

"We moved north to keep my brother and me out of a bad school, but Syracuse has its own problems. For years, Lanny has been nothing but worry for my folks, and I didn't want to add to that."

"So that explains the girlfriends."

"Plural? *Please.* Tawny's it." He sighs. "I really did like her. But I knew . . ."

I lean closer to let my shoulders touch his. "You did the right thing breaking up. If you know, you know, and it's better not to involve someone else."

He scans the horizon, maybe looking at the lake, maybe trying to think what to say next.

"I just keep thinking about when we were in the paint closet."

"Yeah, me too."

Here it comes. Here it comes. Here it comes.

"About your boyfriend."

Annnnd there it goes.

"I know you miss him, and you don't know when you'll see him, but he's a fact—a real thing. Not a girlfriend you talked yourself into because you were supposed to want one. A choice you made for yourself."

I can't tell where this is leading anymore, but the bleachers feel crowded now that Cheng shares them with us.

"I decided not to go to prom with a girl just because

177

I couldn't go with a boy. It wouldn't be honest. It wouldn't be fair."

"So ask a boy." I'm practically wearing a light up sign that says, "Pick Me!" even though that'll take some explaining to Leeza.

"Are you kidding? I plan to graduate and get myself back to a real city where I belong." He fixes a skeptical look on me. "Tell me boys go to prom together in Connecticut."

"They do!" I say. It stings because it's true and *still* doesn't apply to me. "All over the country even. There are Insta pages dedicated to prom photos of gay couples."

"What's Insta?"

"It's a 2020s thing."

"We're back on that?" He grins. "Hope I live that long." God, that line stings.

I like this conversation less by the second, but he sounds content. "And I hope I'll always know you."

This would be a perfect moment for a kiss. Which I shouldn't want. But I do. I'm torn between feeling guilty— *hello, I have a perfectly good boyfriend*—and feeling like a sixth-grader with his first real crush. I'm going to have to sort this out at some point, but all I want right this second is to enjoy the way he is looking at me.

"I found you!" It's Ma Elena, and she's waving a ring of keys. "I sweet-talked the deans into letting you come to the party supply store."

Chaz hops down. "What's our budget? Is it too late for a balloon arch?"

"Way too late!" she laughs. "You coming, Luis?"

I need a minute. "Um . . . I haven't even showered today . . . I'll head to the dorm." The kiss that didn't happen has left me feeling a little blue (and a lot conflicted). Chaz looks surprised at my answer, and so does Ma Elena, but they tell me they'll see me tonight and head off. I can hear Jefferson Starship on the radio as they drive away.

The Stars and the Cars

I'M SUPPOSED TO BE helping decorate, but my mind is on a new plan. I'm going to prompose to Chaz. I mean, obviously, it can't be public, but still.

Cheng promposed to me in, like, the best way. I had gone home to the apartment after lunch, and when I returned, we were supposed to meet at the arts building. He had claimed his team needed props for a fundraising calendar they were doing: "Legs of Lacrosse." (Those boys never lacked confidence in their looks, a kind of self-esteem premised heavily on ASA being too small for any serious competition.)

He wasn't in the lobby, so I headed into the auditorium.

There must have been fifty students in the front rows, and for a dizzying moment, I thought I had missed something on the social calendar. (Like I ever would.) Before I could process that the crowd was entirely a mix of kids from drama and lacrosse and our English class, I felt arms on either side of me: Taji and Cree, the modern dance squad co-captains, were gliding me down the center aisle to the stage.

Someone cued up "Bloom" by Troye Sivan, and the rest of the troupe materialized around me as a flash mob. They were all doing this sexy flower thing, and I was dying because I suddenly understood what was happening. As the song reached its chorus, Cheng appeared from the wings, holding a sign with the lyrics changed to, "I PROM JUST FOR YOU."

He verbed prom—can you stand it? And seriously, the whole school started using it to describe their dream dates. "I prom for Katrina . . . I prom for Vikram . . ."

I know what you're thinking: I'm lucky enough to have a boyfriend who started an entire prom meme, and yet here I am whipping up a promposal for someone else. If I ever get to tell him this story, I hope I have not discovered the end of Cheng's chill. I'll just say the truth: I'm doing this for Chaz, not me. Cheng and I have had so many good times—our Darien Lakes trips alone are right out of a rom-com montage, and Gay Pride was Insta gold—and he's not even my first boyfriend. But what has Chaz had? A girlfriend with a terrible name and no love life. I can give him one special night, a night where he's closer to his true self than ever before. One that absolutely won't end in tragedy. It's practically public service, and if Cheng minds—well, I'll cross that bridge when I time travel to it.

There are limits to what I can come up with here on a few hours' notice and no access to amazing props. And first I have to talk to Leeza. I'm not asking to ditch her—it wouldn't be safe for me and Chaz to be *out* out at prom (ugh, *now* who sounds like Mom?). If we all go together, it provides cover. Plus, she's bound to have good ideas.

I'm the first one at the cafeteria, which is a huge surprise because Ma Elena is usually way ahead of us. There's not much to do but wait because the supplies aren't even here, so I busy myself thinking up a plan. I'm not going to be the idiot who writes "Prom" on the inside of a pizza box and calls it good. Obviously, a flash mob is out, and I doubt a drama department which has only done *Godspell* is where I want to look for costumes. I could slip a note inside one of the balloons (do we have balloons?), fill it with confetti (if there's confetti), and hand him a pin. I could do the boom box thing from that old movie—*Say Something*, maybe?—but that only works if the movie is already out, and I can't remember if it is.

Leeza enters with a huge box of star vases in her arms. When she sees me, there is a moment where she clearly considers heading back out the way she came. Instead, she slams the box down on the table, and starts unpacking it icily.

Whatever it is hasn't yet blown over. "Did I do something?"

The way she looks at me makes it clear that not knowing my crime is a crime unto itself. "Are you serious, Weese? We could *see* you lurking outside the shop the other night. And then you had to knock too? Andrew is pissed at me now like it's my fault!" It takes me a second to get that Andrew is Mr. Buckman. "Are you trying to get him to break up with me?"

"He can't break up with anyone but Mrs. Buckman . . ."

"Which he will! Unless you ruin everything!"

"I'm trying to protect you!"

"What the hell? I don't need protection from Andrew. What I need is protection from backstabbers like you."

I reach for her arm. I need to make contact. She needs to know I'm serious. "Look at me. You're my best friend here. I wouldn't do anything to hurt you."

"Too late." She is trying to read my eyes, figure me out. "I don't get you, Weese. I don't."

"I'm sorry."

"Don't stalk us again. Just leave Andrew and me alone, and I'll believe you mean it." The way she keeps using his first name, the ownership in her voice, the trust—ugh. I don't know what to say, but she fills the space. "And forget prom. If we go together, he'll be furious."

"Are you serious?" It's one thing for me to propose a third wheel and another to be dumped instead.

"Tawny's pretty sad about Chaz, anyway, so I told her we'd get a group of girls together in solidarity. I'm asking Ma Elena too—she's pretty annoyed with Gordo these days. It'll be girls' night, and we'll all be better off."

I must look shocked or bummed or something because she

softens just the tiniest bit. "Make your own stag party with Chaz or whoever." This sounds half like an olive branch and half like a dig: *You know my secret, I know yours.* It's not entirely a friendly suggestion.

Without cover at prom, Chaz and I will be a lot more exposed. Who exactly can I fill a squad with? *Ernie?* He'll break someone's leg. I'm not asking Vin Weasel for sure. I'm roiling as I follow her outside, where the crew is unloading boxes and bags of supplies.

Ernie just about decapitates me with six-foot-long bolts of starry night fabric, and I have to literally dive out of the way onto the grass. "Sorry!" he shouts, but as he turns to look at me, he swings the bolt wildly and wipes out Chaz, who ends up on the lawn a few feet away from where I've landed.

"Funny meeting you here!" he says. It would be a *perfect* meet-cute in a movie.

Doing my best ingenue, I croon. "Do you come here often?"

He just rolls his eyes and leaps up, offering me a hand. He's got a strong grip for someone so lithe. Who knew?

Ma Elena hands me two boxes full of streamers. (Have I mentioned I hate streamers? Crepe paper is a nightmare to work with and screams '50s sock hop to boot.) I see a tractor pulling a flat trailer approaching, bearing the swing, which looks amazing. Mr. A climbs up to steady it, but Mr. Buckman is driving, so I take my cue to flee inside. I stay in the bathroom, admiring the only-at-a-church-school graffiti. Someone has taken time to scratch a trio of crosses—a full Golgotha tableau—onto the stall wall, and another person has written in pen: "You're never standing taller than when you're on your knees," and I cannot tell if this serious or satirical. I mean, the *setting*.

When I emerge, the swing is in place at the opposite end of the room from a little stage someone has set up with wooden pallets. Chaz is trying it out, his legs a little too long for dangling, Ernie trying to push the swing even so. Leeza busts out a whole new mixtape, which she has titled "Deco-Raver." However mad at me she may be, she seems like herself.

Ma Elena grabs my arm. "Hey, Weese, we're still short on a few things. Wanna make a run to the party store with me before it closes?"

My real answer is no: I want to be here with Chaz, who I need to prompose to. But I can't exactly say that. And maybe a party store will inspire me.

Leaving also lets me do a sorry-dash, which is what Nix calls my bad habit of delivering an apology and then fleeing. I'm sure therapy could explain why I can't just sit with it when I admit I'm wrong, but my method does at least get the apology out, so it's not all bad, and the next time I see whoever it is, we're good, right?

I squeeze Leeza's arm on the way out the door and whisper, "Sorry I suck" as she raises one eyebrow.

"Mm-hmm." It's a noncommittal response, but the eye roll is actually kind of sweet. I hope it means she's already moving on.

Before we hop in Ma Elena's car, a lemon-yellow Ford Escort that was never a sweet ride in any decade, Frohmeyer appears.

"Silverthorn!" he barks, and I'm nervous. What did I do? "What's this I hear about you sneaking around at night? That true?"

Did someone see Leeza and me at the shop? Vin Weasel couldn't expose me without exposing his own curfew-breaking excursion. My heart is pounding, but I feign puzzlement. "Huh?"

"Mr. Buckman says you were out past curfew last night."

Whoa. Buckman's good. He's already ahead of me, seeding the notion that I'm trouble so that anything I say about him and Leeza will be taken with a grain of salt. "But I wasn't!"

"Where were you?"

"Shop and then my room."

Ma Elena is frowning. This debate is not helping her schedule. She turns to Frohmeyer. "*You* gave us permission to decorate starting last night, and we did. He left when we all left, which was right at curfew, so maybe Mr. Buckman got confused. I made sure every single one of my crew went to their dorms on time."

Frohmeyer focuses only on me. "That's not what Buckman said."

"What?" Now, I wonder whether Leeza has told "Andrew" about our meeting. Whatever. I'm just going to lie because anyone who could fight me on it has a secret I could spill. "That's just not true." And now I will deploy the skills which got me Best Actor superlative in last year's *Intrepid*. "With everything I've been through this year . . ." I tear up, which I can do on cue; it's a real gift. "I'd never do anything to lose what I have. I'm glad to be here, and I want to stay."

He looks like he isn't entirely buying what I'm selling. "Good to hear it. Prove Buckman wrong then, and keep your nose clean. And get me those transcripts, or you'll be watching your friends march across the stage while you sit on the floor with the audience."

Once he's gone, Ma Elena slaps my arm. "Don't get yourself kicked out, mister. If you're breaking curfew, you're toast. He has no problem kicking people out before graduation. Last year, three seniors went to an off-campus party where there was drinking, and they weren't just expelled but banned from campus. And you know what Frohmy did at graduation? He put three empty chairs onstage to make a point. Do you want to be an empty chair?"

What I *want* is to not still be here then. But I can't say that. "No. Trust me. That's not on my agenda."

Time to change the subject. "So how did Gordo ask you to prom?"

"What do you mean?"

"Did he surprise you or do something extravagant?"

She looks at me like I'm an idiot. *"Gordo?"* Her laugh has a little edge to it. "He never really asked. He's my boyfriend, so it's implied." But then she thinks about it. "I heard through the grapevine—perks of working in the office—that he put in an order for the nicest corsage the florist carries. He's more a shower than a talker."

"I guess." I'm not a huge fan of giving my dad credit for things. "Okay, so, what's the coolest promposal you saw?"

Her blank face confirms that promposals are a new thing. At First Secondary, you just use your words and ask, or if you're shy, you ask by dorm mail. When I explain how we do it in my imaginary Connecticut, Ma Elena is deeply jealous. I tell her about the kid who hid themself in the salad bar and popped out (breadcrumbs and kale flying everywhere) to surprise their vegetarian boyfriend. Then there was the guy who hired mariachis to serenade his Mexican girlfriend in the middle of lunch and practiced his Spanish long enough that he didn't just sound like a white politician trying to be cool. I even tell her about Cheng's promposal, but I don't say it was to me. (Really, do normal rules even apply if I'm time traveling? I think not.)

"Did you do something like that for Leeza?"

"Oh, uh, no, she asked me. Just as friends, obviously. And now we're not going together anyway. Chaz and Tawny broke up, so Leeza is going with her for solidarity." I skip the part about how Leeza's also pissed because I spooked her married teacher-boyfriend.

"I heard, actually. She keeps hinting that I should go with them."

"Hinting?" Leeza isn't really the subtle type.

"Okay, big hints. Like 'why be stuck with Gordo and Vinnie

all night when you could be with us?' That sort of thing. Part of me wants to say yes to the idea, corsage or not. I don't like how he's been acting lately." That makes two of us. Ma Elena slaps the steering wheel. "Maybe I will."

"What'll Gordo say?"

She glances my way quickly and then looks away. "Honestly? Since you got here, and he's had *two* people to pick on, it's harder for me to keep saying he's really nice inside, you know?"

"Wait—" I'm confused. "I thought he was kind of a jerk to everyone—not just Chaz."

"If he was, do you think I'd date him? Like, seriously?"

"Well, I haven't seen much of the other side."

"He's cocky, but in a way that just says he's a scared kid inside—in Mrs. Ham's psych class, she calls it overcompensating. You have no idea the things he went through as a kid. The stories I've heard about his dad and the way he treated the family. It roughened Gordo up. He fights against it most of the time." I fail at not rolling my eyes. "Yes, he can be mean, but not always. He was meanest to poor Chaz."

"And that was okay with you?"

"No!" She falls silent. After a beat, she sighs. "Why am I dating someone I have to apologize for?"

We're driving down a street which in my time, has two coffee shops, a yoga place, three ATMs, a pet store, and competing cell phone providers. Currently, it's mostly empty, except for a dollar store, a lunch place with floral curtains, a Sears "catalog store" (whatever that is), and a family dentist. The dentist closed when I was little, and Mom used to say my cavities (okay, I had a few) were his last.

Finally, Ma Elena goes on. "I figured I balanced things out by being nice to Chaz, and always giving Gordo a hard time about how he acted. But you're here, and he's worked up about you too."

As nice as Mr. I Got the Good Corsage might be, it sounds like he officially was (or still is—who knows?) a homophobe, not an all-purpose jerk. Still an asshole, different brand. "I guess he doesn't like gay people very much."

"He's been raised not to. I mean, we all are, right? Some of us just get over it."

We turn into the parking lot of Confetti Fun City, which is kind of a fantastic name. I'm torn between the sting of my mom saying she was ever like my dad on this and knowing I need to validate that she has changed or, at least, is trying to. "I'm glad you did. The more that hets change—"

"Hets?"

"Um, straight people. Nothing will change until straight people do."

She nods at this but turns the subject back to prom. "Maybe what I need to change first is my boyfriend." She doesn't laugh when she says it, turning the car off and stepping out.

It's a good thing she can't see my face because I am having a bite-size panic attack right now as I realize what I have done. I have planted the seed in her mind that her boyfriend is crappy, which he is, but if she follows through, and he doesn't stay her boyfriend now, maybe he won't someday be her husband, and if he's not her husband . . .

Holy Marty McFly. I've Back-to-the-Futured myself.

You tell me: if you knew your dad was a self-absorbed, immature baby who would eventually leave your mom, wouldn't you want to spare her? I mean, it's hard to root for that couple, right? But I like existing. That's hardly a surprise when your life is as good as mine. I mean, maybe if I was miserable, I'd be more open to a venue change to the afterlife. But if you don't have a life to start with, there's no afterlife. There's a void. There's nothing. The thought of just blinking out of existence makes me gasp. Loudly.

Ma Elena turns around. "Are you hyperventilating?"

Girl, yes. I'm doing what Nix calls "clutching my pearls," which is funny because no one under a hundred even wears pearls anymore, but if I did have a string, that's what I'd be doing. I have one hand on my breastbone like I'm trying to still my heart.

I try to pull it together. I need to change the subject.

"I want to ask Chaz to prom."

Her eyes get huge. "Oh. Wow. No . . ."

"I mean it. And I want to find a cute way to do it." My heart rate returns to normal. Having a task is *so* my thing—it feels good.

"He'll say no, you know."

"Why?" Seriously, who else is going to ask, right?

"I keep telling you: He's First Church. He can't say yes even if he is, for sure, like you."

"Trust me, he is. But knowing that he could turn me down doesn't make me want to ask him any less. It'll make him feel good just that I did. You know?"

"Maybe." She doesn't say more as we get to the celestial aisle of Confetti Fun City. We are surrounded by suns, moons, paper planet series, rocket ships, and aliens. Ma Elena rifles through racks of plastic stars to find the right shape, netting a handful the size of dessert plates. I'm sure there's a "but" coming, and I wait.

"There are a million good reasons you shouldn't do it, but big ones both begin with G: One is graduation, and the other is Gordo. If the school knew, you'd both be toast."

"But they couldn't know for sure."

She considers that. "Maybe faculty couldn't tell, but you know Gordo's obsessed with you. He's already going to be watching you like a hawk—if he thinks even for a second that you guys are there together, it'll be awful. The scene he'll make . . ." She shakes her head. "'Together' . . . I mean, I can't believe I'm even saying that."

I guess I need to write off getting her help. But then she surprises me with a thoughtful look. "I mean, it might be the sweetest thing he's ever experienced. You *know* it's never happened before." A light glows in her eyes. "I love Chaz. I want him to know that feeling. If you're right about him, I mean. But you can't make a big deal of it. No one can know, or they'll kick you both out, no question. Can you 'prompose' where no one can see you?"

"I can do *anything*."

Six days ago, I was shaming Mrs. Somboon-Fox for having me pretend that my prom date was not my prom date, and now I'm all giddy to deliver a stealth promposal. Does this make me a hypocrite or adaptable? The '80s are messing with me.

While we wait in line at the register, I ask her what Chaz likes—what he's into. Drama, which I knew, so maybe a line from *Romeo and Juliet*? She says he digs art, which I didn't know, but maybe Ernie could help with, except Ernie doesn't know he has a gay roommate, and I'm not about to tell him.

"He likes to dance, too"—(I knew it)—"but not here, cause it's a sin."

"How is he getting his family behind dance school in New York?"

"They think he's going to major in business."

"Isn't lying a sin too?"

She crinkles up her face. "He says it's a kind of sin that they're so controlling." And then she trills a laugh. "Maybe it's just easy to sin."

We turn down another theme aisle full of inflatable keyboards and guitars. She lights up. "Oh—that's it—music. He loves all the new-wavey stuff. Like bands with a lot of synthesizers."

Thank god she didn't say like heavy metal (not that I could picture that) or *rock* because I could not play along. Let's be honest, most of what I know of '80s music is from TV commercials or oldies stations, but there's a "Sweet Dreams (Are Made of This)" remix I like on TikTok, and "Tainted Love" has been in a zillion movies.

All at once it comes to me; I know what I have to do.

"When we get back to campus, can I borrow your car?"

I know she's considering whether maybe she's going to add to Chaz's sins, but to my relief, she says yes. She is doing what she does best: taking care of me, taking care of Chaz, trying to do the right thing as much as she can. Tonight, I see it so clearly, even though I'm pretty used to taking it for granted at home. Someday, I'll thank her for all of it.

I am sitting in Ma Elena's parked car, engine off, on the lawn where recreation is held. The baseball diamond lights aren't on, so the field is just a dark expanse stretching all the way to where the school's property ends. The field is far enough from the dorms and other buildings that they cast no light my way. If you were to walk up this hill now, as Chaz is about to do, you might not even notice the car. I have borrowed Leeza's mixtape, without telling her why. I changed into my best outfit (thanks Chess King!), and now I am waiting for his appearance.

Ma Elena has cooked up a little lie: she told Chaz to go to the field because she saw me on the bleachers, and I looked upset. She said he's such a total Care Bear, he'd never question why she was asking *him* to go instead of just checking on me herself. I hope she's right because it occurs to me now that if Buckman or Frohmeyer show up, my cover story is weak. I had

194

planned to say that Ma Elena needed something from her car but, duh, she has already taken all the decorations we bought inside.

Listening to a symphony of crickets, I seek out my constellations in the velvet sky. I look to the Big Dipper, its stars twinkling. The stars all look especially brilliant, and I swear there are more of them than ever. If you flung diamonds into the air and they never came down, it would look like this. If I were home, I'd text Nix a photo, and they'd get it immediately.

Finally, Chaz appears over the hill. He is heading for the bleachers, puzzled at my absence, and I let him get to the bottom step, where he stops, completely baffled before I turn on the headlights—two beams of white sluice across the grass, ribbons of illumination on the shadowed field. He faces the light but hesitates. "Weese?"

Tentatively, he takes a step toward the car, and I turn on the song "Drive."

The question of who is going to drive him home tonight floats on the air, closing the distance between us.

A puzzled smile becomes a deep one as he walks toward the car, and he's shaking his head. He knows it's me now. And then he's singing! Okay, that's stealing my thunder a little, but let's go with it.

I step out of the car and walk toward him, both of us singing now. Instinctively, we keep our voices soft, so they don't float down the hill to campus, but we sound beautiful together. And then Chaz starts spinning, arms out, during the synthesizer bridge, and I do, too. We are laughing and singing, and the stars are shining, and it's one of the most romantic moments of my entire existence and now is the time.

The music is fading, the last synth riff fading to a single note on the guitar. I take his hand. He looks so surprised (the benefit of never having heard of promposals).

"You light me up, Chaz. Will you go to prom with me?"

Crickets.

Literal crickets. Noisy, insistent, ignorant crickets heckling me as the silence stretches between us.

"Oh, I already said I was gonna go stag with Ernie."

Leeza's stupid plan has spread like wildfire before me. Does no one care about romance at all? What is wrong with everyone?

"Oh . . . okay . . ." I can feel my cheeks burning. Why can't Chaz take advantage of the opportunity right in front of him?

He sees my face and does, swear to god, a pearl clutch. "No, Weese, don't look that way. I . . . no one, *no boy*, has ever asked me before. I didn't think anyone would dare." His violet eyes are so tender. He reaches for my face, both soft hands cupping it. "You are so sweet."

I'm so confused. Are we about to kiss? Or is he letting me down easy? (And if I've been doing this all for him, why are *my* feelings hurt?)

He drops the hands. "We can all just go together, and I'll still know you asked. Is that okay? Or . . ."

I'm going to try and take comfort that he's not rejecting me so much as honoring his word to Ernie, who has gone from

Gale warning to Spoiler in less than a week, but this is so not how I expected things to go.

"Sure." Do I sound convincingly chill? I can't tell. "It'll be fun." *Apparently*, I am not selling this because he's wearing a full *"I'm sorry"* face. I do a little spin. "But my look is going to crush both of yours." He laughs, and I take my cue to turn off the car lights.

Of course, Buckman appears and ruins what's left of the vibe. "What are you doing up here?"

Dammit, now I have to produce invisible decorations.

Chaz doesn't even blink. "Laney left her keys in the car." God, he's fast, and his story is better than mine. I hold them up as proof as he continues. "She sent us to get them." He doesn't even let Buckman respond. "Have you been to the cafeteria? We're almost done, and it's amazing. Best prom ever."

Chaz chatters so constantly, striding on long legs back down the hill, that Buckman has no choice to follow us partway. "You guys don't have a free pass to just roam the campus. Stay where you're supposed to be."

I try on my best sycophant voice. "Thanks, Mr. Buckman. We will."

He sees right through my faux sincerity and curls his lip, ready to snarl something, but Chaz starts praising the star swing he made and talks so much that Buckman raises his hands to stop him before retreating back the way he came. I'm so impressed with Chaz's diversion skills. I could kiss him. I really could. Why does he make it so hard?

I see Chaz with new appreciation. "You shut *him* down!"

"I wasn't about to let him ruin things." He tenders a sly smile. "I've never been asked out before. I want to remember tonight just this way—the stars, the Cars, and you." And then he's through the cafeteria door, leaving me beneath the night sky, totally confused.

This boy. *This boy.*

Second Best

A BAGEL BAR IS set up in the dorm lobby, and there's a lot of grumbling about a cold breakfast. Chaz is nowhere in sight, and Ernie is, per usual, a log fallen in a forest where it made no sound. My choices are a cinnamon crunch bagel the size of a hub cap, strawberries, which look a little too pale for consumption, and melon that I swear is perspiring. Honestly, is poor quality fruit even *healthy*? I take the bagel.

My internal debate over food has me so preoccupied, I don't even see Vin Weasel behind me in line until I turn and crush my cinnamon crunch bagel into his Styx T-shirt. (I can still eat it because it didn't touch the floor!) I apologize, but the bagel isn't his focus. "You like making trouble, dontcha?"

This is how I learn that Ma Elena has broken up with Gordo. "And he knows you put her up to it."

"I did no such thing!'

"Sure, you didn't."

"What is your problem? Why are you guys so obsessed with me?"

His face is red. "Gordo knew there was something up with you from the moment you arrived."

"I was barely on campus before he was threatening bodily harm!"

"Coulda been worse. Still could be."

"Is that supposed to scare me?" If so, it's working.

"You think you just can show up and ruin people's senior year—"

"I have that power?"

"—and it won't come back to bite you?" He pretty much sneers in my face. "Dream on, asshole."

He stalks away, and I'm trembling. I've been teased before but, seriously, no one has *threatened* me. And so openly, with other guys milling about, bagels in hand. It's like he isn't even worried that he'll get in trouble. Maybe he wouldn't?

But that's only half of it. If Ma Elena and Gordo break up early, have I doomed myself by changing the timeline too much? I want to call Ms. Silverthorn and find out what precedents there are for a time slipper who prevented his own birth. I mean, I'm here—I can feel me. If they don't have me in the future, do I disappear here too? Or do I just stay here, *Connecticut Yankee* style, continuing to age even though I haven't been born?

I need to sit down.

I can't even go back to my room because Vin Weasel and Red are teasing a freshman in front of the entrance to my hall. I can practically hear my bones cracking. Bagel in hand, but with no will to eat it, I stand there making small-talk with some boy in my English class who asks questions about Connecticut, my old school, and eventually about my girlfriend, whose existence he doesn't doubt at all. I play along as he talks about girls and murmurs things that sound like agreement, even as I steep in my own shame: this is what it means to pull the closet door shut on yourself. As soon as Vin Weasel and Red are gone, I bolt.

Too restless to hang with Ernie for long, I head out across campus. I've heard a florist is setting up shop in the cafeteria, and though I didn't get to 1985 in time to place an order, I'm hoping maybe they have some spare boutonnieres lying around.

I find an Asian family in the kitchen, loading corsages and boutonnieres into one of the walk-in refrigerators to distribute to the dorms later. If they have enough extra, I could get flowers for Leeza and Ma Elena just to be sweet, and maybe even some for Tawny. (Would she know that hers are compensation for guilt?) What I actually want to do, of course, is buy flowers for Chaz. I mean, I know it would have to be discreet, nothing more than a boutonniere. But, wow, I really want to.

An older woman is busy sorting plastic-wrapped packets and paying no attention to me, but when her helper turns

201

around, it's Malee Somboon-Fox, or just Somboon at this point, I guess. She's so crazily young and pretty, it's hard to reconcile her with the principal she will become.

"Hey," she says. "I remember *YOU*! You bought the jacket."

"What are you doing here?" I sputter. "You don't go to First Secondary!"

"Jeez, way to make a girl feel welcome."

"Sorry, I—"

"Lighten up! My parents have a chain of florists, and I help out on weekends."

"Malee!" Her mom looks me up and down and then nods at a pile of bouquets. "Enough with the boys!"

Her dad catches my eye. "She can find a boy anywhere!"

I've *never* seen Malee look so mad. "*STOP!* You guys are the worst." She rolls her eyes. "Be glad you go to an academy . . . *AWAY* from your parents."

I'm about to repeat the sad story of my dying mother and then remember it's false and that Malee will grow up to be Mrs. Somboon-Fox, who knows my living mother, and my brain melts. Instead, I say, "Has your school had prom yet?"

Both of her parents shoot her looks that Medusa would endorse.

"Not my thing!" She leans across the table, dramatically lowering her voice. "I was going with Dane, who's Black, and my parents said no. They said I could go with an Asian boy, like our town is so full of them, or just with my girlfriends, but I was *NOT* going to roll over. So I skipped prom and met up with him anyway to make a point."

202

My head may collapse into itself. The ruiner of my prom was a prom rebel herself?

Her mom hates not knowing what we're talking about. "Malee! Work."

I help. "Um. Do you have any extras?" God, what a dumb question. I don't even say extra *what*.

Malee's face lights up, happy that her parents haven't scared me away.

"I can probably work something out for the right boy . . ."

Her mom swoops in. "Orders only. Nothing more. If you tell her your order number, she can put extra baby's breath in it. I'm sure *your girlfriend* will love it."

Malee's dad is visibly amused at his wife's move. I tell them I'm all set, and Malee mouths *"SORRY"* as I back out of the kitchen.

I encounter Chaz and Ernie, who looks like he was roused from slumber too soon, in the dining room, where they are putting finishing touches on the photo booth. Leeza and Ma Elena are nowhere in sight, but Chaz says that Leeza is probably already starting her hair and makeup. When I joke that I should be doing the same thing, Chaz laughs and Ernie, naturally, takes it seriously: "You wear makeup?" He looks scandalized.

The three of us head back to the dorm together. Ernie is talking about a new cartridge for his video game thing, but I'm half-listening. I'm focused on how perfect a day it is. It's sunny, and the sky is an open, clear blue. The air is dry and cool. It would be perfect for an outdoor wedding or a romantic drive along the lake. I want to hold Chaz's hand and stroll across the green like a couple in a movie, but I think Ernie would have a stroke.

Plus, Gordo is barreling our way. Or, I guess, my way. "You're dead!" He pushes me in the chest hard. "You told Ma Elena she could do better than me?" Sweat gleams through his fade. "She was fine before you got here, you little fag!"

The word hits the air like a bomb. Chaz goes perfectly still, like, literally stops moving. Ernie starts to sputter about bullying, but Gordo turns on him. "I'm not surprised that these two," he says, nodding toward Chaz and me, "are fruiting around together, but I thought you were smarter than that, Gale."

"I'd rather hang with them than . . . than . . . a moron."

Okay, so Ernie isn't the best at comebacks, but it gets under Gordo's skin.

"My GPA is as high as yours, you little freak, and *I'm* not a walking car wreck!"

Chaz finds his voice. "Ignore him, Ern. He's just jealous because you have two dates for prom, and he has none."

This sets Gordo off. "That's it!" He readies a punch, but the dean has been watching the scene and barks orders for us to cool it. There's no way to tell what he has or hasn't heard, but we take the opportunity to race for our rooms. I think I hear more shouting from Gordo, but I don't look back.

I'm dazzled by Chaz's quick retort, too, but Ernie looks like he might pass out. He's a terrible color, the shade that makes people say "green at the gills" about a white person on a sailboat.

Chaz is trying to be soothing. "He doesn't mean it, Ern. There's no chance Gordo really thinks that of you. He just lets his mouth run." I get it, trying to placate the freaked-out straight boy, but it still irks me a little. *Gordo's* more comfortable saying gay than Chaz.

But it works. Ernie shrugs and starts talking about an idea he has for graduation decorations, moving on to the next big thing even before this one is over.

When Ernie sees my prom outfit—smoking jacket, tux pants, oversized pin—he is pretty overtly torn between straight-up disapproval and wanting to be a good roommate. "Guess I'm not moving to Connecticut," he tries to joke, but it comes out a little strangled. I think I look really cute, like if I saw this thumbnail on iTunes, I'd buy the single.

Meanwhile, Ernie wears a three-piece suit I would never have guessed was in his closet. It's navy pinstripes, and it makes him look kind of Wall Streety, which weirdly works on him. The art, the suit—this kid is way more complicated than I thought when I moved in. He's the reason why you're never supposed to judge a book by its cover.

Now, we're just waiting for Chaz, and I don't know what to expect. If anyone is going to rock the *Miami Vice* thing, it's him. But I wouldn't put tails and a top hat past him either.

When he opens the door, I am speechless.

He can't be. He is. He *can't be*.

He *is* . . . dressed like Prince.

A shiny deep purple jacket with wide shoulders cinched at his waist, full-on British Lord ruffles spilling from neck to navel like a waterfall. Lace cuffs pour from the sleeves like waves. Sleek black pants end in black Capezios. Just like that, I'm second-best-dressed.

Ernie looks apoplectic. "Will they—will they even *let* you wear that?"

"Can they stop him?" I ask. It's a real question.

Trying to backpedal a little, Ernie stretches for a compliment. "I mean, that might be cool for MTV . . ." He can't sustain it. "Frohmeyer's gonna freak out."

Chaz looks serene. "My collar is buttoned. I'm not in jeans. It's half the outfit I wear to church every week. It's all dress code—what can they say?"

Ernie isn't sold. "I don't want to make a scene. I *always* make a scene. This was the first time ever I wasn't worried about it."

Chaz furrows his brow. "I didn't think you'd mind so much. You always seem . . . cool with me." He looks wounded.

I think back to when Ernie and I first talked about Chaz. The cream puff line. The implication that "acting gay" is a bigger problem than bullying. Instead of green, his face is red now. I see him working through his feelings. He'd gone through most of high school with only JJ, the wallet girl, as a buddy, and he finally finds a crowd—even has friends to go to prom with. But this, *this* is too much. His defense is weak. "If . . . if there was no Gordo . . . it wouldn't matter."

Chaz is heating up. "I'm done letting that fool define my

senior year. We don't all have to go together anyway. It's not like it's a *date*." He underscores the word with a sharpness that can't be missed. "This stag party thing was all Leeza's idea, and it seemed harmless enough. But if I'm too *gay* for you, I'm sure there's room at Gordo's table."

"You're not listening to me!" Ernie's head is nearly plum. Is this what an aneurysm looks like? Oh my god. I don't even know CPR. "You're not *safe* like that!"

"What's he going to do—attack me in the middle of prom? Get himself kicked out with less than a month of school left? Color me wrong for thinking I'd have my friends to keep me safe."

"You still have me." I squeeze his arm, but his blazing eyes are on Ernie.

Ernie sits on his bed, looking defeated. "I want to go with you. I just . . . this was supposed to be my night, too. Being on Prom Council made me feel—more part of things, ya know? And I thought we were going to have fun." He's wiping his eyes, head in hand.

Chaz opens the door to leave. "Do what you need. I'm going to prom."

I feel bad leaving Ernie there, but Chaz is striding away on fleet feet, and I've come all the way to the '80s to see him through this night. I have to follow, right?

And as we step onto the lawn, the sun leaning late in the sky, two gay boys in fabulous attire, it hits me: we're alone. I've gotten my date after all.

Glowing

A WHITE VAN, EMBLAZONED with the words "Land of Smiles Flowers," is pulling out of the dorm parking lot as we head for the cafeteria, and the side door opens. Malee is in on the passenger side and, when she sees me, she makes her dad stop. She pops out and slides open the side door, where her mom glares at me from the dark. A quiet debate ensues, which Malee wins, and she produces a clear plastic box with a corsage and a boutonniere.

"We did have extras!"

She's so proud of herself that I feel bad, especially when Chaz, also thinking it's for him, demurs. "I don't think that's going to work with these cuffs."

She is looking at the scene before her, Prince, and a fashion revolution. Her eyes flick from me to him and him to me and *ohhh*. But as soon as the light is on, she extinguishes it with a kind of denial that requires a lot of self-talk.

"*RIGHT.* You didn't say corsage . . . you meant boutonnieres . . . because you're both going *SOLO* and why be left out of the fun? Right. Good point! Why shouldn't singles get the whole package? It's *UNFAIR* that only the couples get flowers! We should have made flowers for everyone! Just a sec!"

Chaz's eyes are bright with amusement, and he cocks an eyebrow at me, curious as to how I know this tempest. She's back before I can explain, matching boutonnieres in hand.

"That's better! Boutonnieres for all!"

We thank her, Chaz copiously praising how nice his is (though, honestly, how interesting can it be: a white rose, green tape, and a hatpin). I impulsively hug Malee, and she holds it longer than I do, generating a shout from the van. "See you at the mall!" she says and gets in.

Even with the van door closed, I can hear an argument ensuing. I grab Chaz's hand and pull him away, but not toward the cafeteria.

"Where are we going?" He looks genuinely surprised.

"In Connecticut," I tease, "it is considered *so* basic to arrive right on time. Let's give it a minute."

"Okay . . ."

"Let's go to our field," I say that like it's an established thing. He doesn't argue, but he also doesn't let me hold his hand.

209

The rec field is, predictably, empty. I climb the bleachers to the very top for the lake view. This is my favorite time of day. The sun leans so heavily toward earth that all the light is slant, casting elongated shadows that stretch and stretch and soon will steal away. Everything the light touches is rose gold, a beauty I know to be fleeting. Once the sun is down, darkness will mute everything. For now, the world shines.

"May I?" I ask, pulling the pin from the boutonniere I'm carrying and hold it up to his chest.

That smile! It's a light of its own. "You may."

Trying to pin it on without stabbing myself requires a little concentration, but I manage and then step back, waiting for him to do the same.

"May I?"

"You may." My heart is beating faster as he fixes the rose to my lapel with the grace of an expert.

If I am going to kiss him, it has to be now. We have lighting worthy of Instagram. We're not so late that anyone is going to miss us yet. And there isn't a squad around to make it impossible.

And yet.

I suddenly am thinking about Cheng. Cheng, who hikes and plays lacrosse and dresses basic and is nothing like me. Cheng, who most likely will not be my forever guy (I mean, we're in high school) but is my guy.

Cheng, who holds me so tight, like I am a treasure never to be lost.

Cheng, who kisses me deeply. Cheng, who supports my

campaigns for every damn thing because he says the world needs more people like me. Cheng, who calls me on my bull without anger. Cheng, who deserves to be appreciated. Who smells good and makes the best waffles and whose arm draped around my shoulder is just about my favorite thing.

Can you cheat on someone thirty-six years away? This is a terrible moment to be so homesick, to miss what I had. But god, it's flooding me all at once. What about Cheng?

Oh my god, I'm crying. Chaz is open-mouthed.

"What . . . what is happening?"

I have to focus. This can't be about me. This is the night in one timeline that Chaz dies at the Ledges. I can make sure he never goes to the quarry at all by making sure he has a memorable night right here, complete with the kiss he deserves. (And I'm sure as hell not letting him out of my sight where the Townies can find him.) For once, I can forget what I want.

"I was just thinking how far away from home I am . . ." I wipe my eyes and smile the biggest smile, focusing on the great guy in front of me. Maybe one heart can race for two. "And how lucky I am that you're here."

"Aww . . ." Chaz crosses his hands on his chest. "Weese."

Based on old movies, I'm not sure consent is a big '80s thing, but I'm still twenty-first-century me, so I don't spring a sudden move. I fold my hands over his. "Can I kiss you?"

His lips part, in surprise maybe, or maybe because he was going to say no, but then he leans toward me.

The closeness is thrilling. His forehead almost touching mine. I can smell the soap he showers with and the pomade in his hair. Our lips meet, then our tongues. We pull away, just a little, and then kiss again.

It's fine.

Which means it isn't.

The chemistry I have with Cheng—it's not there. My giddiness leading up to the moment has been replaced by calm awareness that, in the end, I may have done what I set out to do, but there were no fireworks. Not for me at least. I hope to god that he can't tell. And since it's his first kiss with a guy, I think I'm safe.

He steps back. "*Huh*."

I step back. "Huh?"

"Nothing. I mean . . . thank you." This comes out so half-hearted. I know the jig is up.

"'Thank you'? That's a weird thing to say."

"I . . ." He looks away for a moment. He's deciding how honest to be. Apparently, *very* honest. "You weren't very into it."

"What? I . . . no! I—" Who renders me speechless? No one. No one! And here I am.

"I mean, it's been clear, kinda for days, that you wanted to, but then . . . that didn't feel like a real kiss."

Is he insulting my technique? "How would you know?"

"What does *that* mean?"

"Be honest: that was your first kiss!"

"You don't know what I do or don't do." Chaz looks about a half-second away from stabbing me with his boutonniere pin.

"You were playing straight till, what, yesterday? You might not like my style, but how much do you have to compare it to?"

He shakes his head as if he can't believe what he's hearing. "I wasn't criticizing your *technique* . . . I was just surprised that you weren't into it." He sees I'm about to interrupt. "And I could tell because I wasn't either."

His voice leaves no room for doubt.

"You weren't?"

"Okay, I admit it. I haven't kissed a boy before. And I *was* hoping to have my first kiss—a real kiss, thank you—tonight. Just not with you. That's why I broke up with Tawny!"

A change comes over him, a shy pride. His eyes take on something new—not a twinkle, but a gleam.

Knock me over with a feather. Who, what, where—I haven't a clue.

"I've been spending a lot of time with him," he says as if I should know who he means. "And he told me he's like you and me." He whispers though we're all alone.

"He *who*?"

And then. Oh my god. No. Does he mean . . .

"Ernie." He says Ernie's name how I say Cheng's, that note of belonging, that delight in someone being yours.

It's absurd and amazing and hilarious and wonderful and perfect. I've always said there's no accounting for chemistry; you just *know*. I have my Cheng. Chaz has his Ernie.

I start laughing. It's not at all a mean laugh; there's so much relief and honest joy in it that Chaz joins in. That's what I get

213

for assuming. "I'm happy for you. I really, really am. I thought you were alone . . ."

"I kinda was before you came. But you told me about your life, and I thought I want a life, too. And this week showed me an Ernie I never knew, so . . ."

My being here really is a twofer: Chaz lives, and Ernie will be happier than ever (well, after I send Chaz back to the dorm to get him). Mission accomplished.

Who knows where that leaves me? Right now, all I know is that I feel pretty good.

The sun is nearly down, yet we're still both glowing.

Over the Edge

THE FIRST ROCK HITS me square in the side of my smiling face, and I'm so shocked, I don't even process that I'm falling down the bleachers.

Chaz barely manages to cry out, "Weese," before he takes the second, in the gut, and goes into crouch mode, scuttling down the riser to me.

It's Gordo. And he's not alone.

Vin Weasel and Red are with him, along with a guy with a dark buzz cut. We're outnumbered two to one. They're all in their prom attire, minus the bowties as if they'd just stopped by for a quick gay-bashing on the way. There are no more rocks in their hands, but their eyes promise awful things to come.

"Hey, you little faggots!" Gordo spits the word out and chases it with one just for me, *"Maricones!"* He and his crew form a phalanx, a wall between the school and us. "You think you could do that here, and nobody would notice? Nobody would care?"

"We're not doing anything," I say, as lame an answer as possible.

Vin Weasel's smirk is terrible. "Um, just seconds ago, you were sucking face on top of the effin bleachers."

Chaz is too quick. "So you came to take your turn?"

Gordo crosses the empty space between us and lifts Chaz to full height by the collar of his shirt. "Say that again, fag."

I'm on my feet, trying to pry my future father's hands off Chaz's neck, then Red and Buzz Cut are on me, pulling me away and tossing me to the grass. Apparently, I'm less of a concern than Chaz because Gordo has him in a headlock, and Vin has his arms pulled back to keep him from wriggling away.

"You've been flaunting your fairy ass at this school, and all the girls treat you like you're special when we know you're just a dirty homo." Chaz doesn't struggle, doesn't speak. He looks only at me.

I try to stand up but Red immediately shoves me back into sitting position to witness the scene.

Gordo's face is close to Chaz's, forcing Chaz to look him in the eye, their noses as close as if they are seconds away from their own kiss. "You disgust me." He turns to me. "Like one fairy wasn't enough, you turn up, ruin things between me and my girl, and now you want to prance around holding hands.

216

Not gonna happen." Buzz Cut grabs my collar to make sure I understand I'm not going anywhere.

Chaz remains absolutely still, but his eyes are telling me: *run, get someone, help.*

I always hated old books and movies with gay people in them because something terrible always happens: the characters die or get beaten up or get AIDS. I was always like, that's so *tired.* Why always tell the bad stuff when there's so much more? I only wanted the happy stories, stories about the Chengs and Nixes of the world. We deserve it, right? I mean, I knew that stuff like that was still happening, and not just in like Chechnya or Zimbabwe. But I figured if we could focus on the better stuff, people would think that's how it should be, and they'd become better too, and that'd be progress.

Now, I have blood dripping from my face onto my fancy jacket, and the guy I just kissed is about to take a beating, and I am helpless to stop it.

"God wiped out a whole town to get rid of people like you, you know. So he won't mind if we teach you a little lesson."

"Both of you!" Vin Weasel laughs to make sure I don't think I'm safe.

Red and Buzz Cut lift me up and strong-arm me away from the bleachers. Gordo and Vin do the same to Chaz, and we're soon being forced across the road and into the field. In my time, the woods are only a half-mile deep before a housing development starts. But in this time, the trees stretch uninterrupted all the way to . . .

Oh my god. The Ledges.

I don't know if that thought has occurred to Chaz yet, but I can barely breathe. I'm lightheaded, picturing the eighty-foot drop to the jagged limestone floor of the quarry. I was never one of those daredevil kids who played there, especially after the summer I was twelve, when a pair of teens fell off while making out, one dying on impact and the other ending up a paraplegic. I can still see the newspaper photo of her being airlifted on a stretcher, black and blue face peering from between pads and wraps meant to stabilize her neck.

"Are you insane? You won't just get kicked out! You'll be arrested!"

Buzz Cut smacks the back of my head, and I stumble, sagging to one knee, before he rights me, and we keep going into the woods.

Vin Weasel looks like a kid in a candy shop. "Arrested? For what?"

"Assault . . . kidnapping . . ." I don't want to say "murder" out loud.

They all laugh at this idea. "How could we do anything like that? We're all at prom. We took pictures and everything."

Chaz mutters, "Someone's going to notice, morons."

Gordo shoves him hard. "It's not my fault you dickwads planned a black-light party. Can't see anything in there but stars, actually, so thanks for that."

"Yeah, it's heavenly," sneers Vin Weasel. And they all laugh again.

They fall silent. Night has come, and the woods are dark enough that I'd be scared even without all this. Our footsteps crack fallen branches as we go, each snap going off like gunfire.

I wish I could see Chaz's face. I wish I could hold his hand. I wish I could apologize.

The walk seems forever and apparently not just to me. "We should leave 'em out here," grumbles Buzz Cut, and Red agrees.

"Don't be pussies. We're almost there." Gordo doesn't hesitate for even a moment.

"There" is an opening in the woods, where trees give way to rocky earth that stretches forward less than five feet. The edge of the cliff is uneven in both directions, remnants of a long-abandoned quarry. The cliff face is far from smooth— small outcroppings here and there form shelves that give the Ledges its name. Fall from the top, and your pain choices are plentiful: smash into a ledge on the way down or plummet straight to your death.

I'm crying. I can't help it. I think I hear Chaz say, "Weese," but I can't be sure, and Red and Buzz Cut jerk me to a stop.

It's so dark here, even with stars in the sky, that I can't see their faces clearly. However, Gordo's voice is distinct: the righteousness of someone who has gotten to act on the worst of his prejudices. "You ever been out here, Chaz, or are you too big a pansy to know about this place?"

"I know where we are." His words come out heavy.

"Then you know what would happen if we threw you off the edge right now."

No one says anything. There is no sound from the woods behind us. There is no wind.

Gordo almost purrs. "And culo, I *want* to. But I'm a Christian, and so I'm gonna offer you a little grace here . . ."

My head is pounding. Does he mean that? I can feel Red's grip on one arm so tight it's digging into my skin, and I think he's wondering, too.

Gordo is pulling Chaz to the edge, and Red drags me forward too, and my heart is beating so hard it hurts. What are they going to do?

There is a little outcropping about five feet down from the lip just below us, maybe six or seven feet wide by three feet deep. "You're going to have a romantic night on your own private ledge."

"And we'll even help you get down there cause we're that nice." Vin Weasel is loving this. "If you want to climb back up, that's on you. I wouldn't recommend it—one false move and . . ." He trails off, laughing.

They can't be serious. If they leave us on the ledge, who will find us? Even if neither of us overshoots and falls on the way down, it's almost worse to be stuck out there. We can yell for help all we want, but it could be days before anyone comes.

All at once, Buzz Cut and Red have me going over the side. Oh my god! Oh my god! I'm holding onto their forearms for all I'm worth. I don't want to die. I'm trying to keep my body close to the rock wall as long as I can, and when my toes find the ledge, I start crying again. I kneel on the narrow outcropping, and my wail echoes off the stone walls.

I don't think they expected that, or maybe no one likes to

hear the terror of a victim because Gordo is telling me, over and over, to shut up. All four of them are looking down at me, Chaz momentarily forgotten.

The veins in Gordo's neck look like they may burst. "Jeezus, cabron! Stop acting like you're gonna die!"

"I'm . . . I'm not?"

"Like I'd really kill you?" He shakes his head, notes of pride coloring his explanation of his plan. "I just want you out of here. When you miss curfew, we'll tell the dean we saw you guys sneak off campus. No matter what you say happened, no one is going to believe you. *We* can prove we were on campus, while you will have to explain why you two were off in the woods alone. Frohmeyer's no fool. You'll be gone, and we'll get our school back."

The plan is half terrible and half smart and 100 percent dangerous. But I want him to keep talking, and I want all eyes focused on me. Maybe for the first time ever, I want the spotlight for the noblest reason.

"If I jump, what happens to your plan, then?"

Gordo's face twists, and he leans toward me. "You wouldn't."

I nod emphatically. "The police will start looking for me after all, and I bet they're harder to fool than the dean."

They're all leaning toward me now. I have their full attention, as I hoped.

Vin Weasel's voice is higher. "You'll die, moron."

"I'm a filthy, dirty homo—right?"

"We're just trying to teach you a lesson!" Red finds his voice, and it's panicky.

And Chaz? He says nothing at all.

Because Chaz isn't there.

Alone

CHAZ IS RUNNING THROUGH the woods right now, running on those long, thin legs, and I'm banking on him being nimbler than our attackers. He only has a few seconds' head start, but a few seconds might as well be a year for a whippet being chased by bulldogs.

When I was on the ledge, I noticed how Gordo and Vin relaxed their grip on Chaz once I had their attention. Gordo would never have admitted it, but I could also see fear creeping into his triumph—he didn't actually want me to fall. He wanted—who knows what? Vindication? Relief? An outlet? Whatever it was, Chaz faded from view for a minute, and where Gordo's attention went, so did his buddies'.

Chaz had locked his eyes on mine, and I'd tried for all I was worth to send him the bravest message of my life: *Run*. He'd gotten it, and when I'd nodded, it wasn't for Gordo, but for him. While they were shouting at me, he stealthily drew away and disappeared into the woods.

By the time they clued in, it was only a dark forest behind them.

They realize this now and bolt into the woods, swearing.

And . . . I'm left out here alone.

My eyes are closed, and they're going to stay that way. I don't look over the edge of the outcropping because I don't dare. I sit with my back against the cliff, my legs—one knee gashed from slamming against rock on the way over—folded yogi style. My face throbs from the thrown rock that now seems a million years ago. I sob into my hands and taste iron. How can it be that I started the week in glitter and ended in blood?

I'm so tired. Worst-night-of-my-life tired. I almost sink into the rock. I could sleep for a million years. I just want to lie down. Down . . .

I jolt upright. I can't fall asleep here. I have to stay awake until Chaz sends help.

With the goons gone, it should be quiet, but it's not at all. The quarry holds the sounds of nightlife like a bowl. An owl lets its call fly: *hoo-hoo-HOO*. Some bird I can't guess keeps chirping *Beet.* (Hard pause.) *Beet.* (Hard pause.) *Beet.* A bell-like song chimes above a bass line of grumbling, and I think both are frogs, but maybe they're insects, and now I wish I had paid better attention in sophomore biology. I practice imitating the sounds, though the *hoo-hoo-HOO* gets more insistent when I do, which unnerves me a little.

I have a lot of time to think.

All this time, I thought there were only two options about what happened to Chaz in the original timeline: he jumped, or some Townies threw him. Now I wonder if there were Townies at all or if it was always Gordo and his crew.

I think about all the work Ma Elena put into decorating the cafeteria and how the night is probably ruined, and then about how she will someday grow up to be a nurse who people think is amazing, but who I often treat like she's nowhere near my level.

I think about Cheng enduring all my whims and how mad I got because he didn't just indulge me one time. I'd blamed him for being a bad boyfriend when I was the one acting like a brat. I think about his arms and how safe it would feel to be in them.

I think about Nix listening to me talk about how I rule the school, and how I must have sounded, making prom all about me. Nix was right, of course, about all of it, and if I ever find a way back home, I'm going to tell them that I finally appreciate this.

But I do not, not for two seconds, think about jumping. I want to live, to make guys who think they can treat people this way *pay for it*. I want my living to cost them.

I've had the chance to know what it's like to really be me, to feel loved for who I am, to walk through the world believing there is not just one place for me, but many places. Yet I realize now that I didn't understand what it was like to constantly look over your shoulder, fear what your gayness means all the time, and walk down the halls of your school thinking that it could be years before you get to be who you want. How could I be so stupid to think confidence was all it took to make a person safe?

As I look down into the dark, I think about how this night played out for Mom in the life where I never time traveled. How she has lived with the idea of beautiful, funny, talented Chaz crumpled in the bottom of this quarry. No wonder she could never truly shake it off. I wish I'd tried a little harder to see her fear as love.

But now I'm alone, and it feels like it's been hours. What happens if the guys catch up to Chaz? Or if I fall asleep despite my best efforts and tumble into the dark? What if the fate I've spared Chaz ends up my own?

Hate Did That for Itself

FLICKERS OF LIGHT SWEEP across the trees on the opposite wall of the quarry. It takes me a second to realize they must be coming from the forest above me. I don't care who it is.

"Help! Help me!"

"Luis?"

It's Mom. I can't see her; I hear only the voice that sang me to sleep, the one that nags me to empty the dishwasher, the one who told me I could live without a prom.

"I'm down here!"

When two flashlights shine down at me, I can't see who else is there, but it doesn't matter: I know they're here to save me.

At least until I hear Ernie's voice. *Oh my god*. Why would you bring the clumsiest person on earth to rescue someone from a cliff?

Well, you bring him because it turns out that he is a Cheng: which is to say, he hikes, and he has these ropes and spikes and little metal cinchy bits I have never before appreciated. Ernie disappears from view long enough to attach the rope to a tree away from the lip of the cliff and then dangle it over, telling me to clip the lead to my belt and, um, maybe wrap it around my torso, too. He and Ma Elena start reeling the rope in with an arm-over-arm sailor move. (Now that I can see those spray bangs, bigger than ever, she's back to not being Mom.) Ernie commands me to grab onto every cranny I can find in the rock wall with my hands and my toes for balance.

There's an awful moment when my feet have left the ledge and fingers have just found the top of the cliff where it's clear to me that it's all or nothing now: if my belt breaks or the rope comes loose, I will fall backward and into the deep. I'm shaking so hard my teeth are knocking.

But then I am over, heaving on the ground, tears streaming down my face, and weirdly giddy. I laugh, a truly insane laugh that echoes through the trees, a song the owl and the frogs have never heard. Ma Elena rubs my back, telling me it's okay. After Chaz reached Ernie and Ernie found her, she sent Chaz to Ms. Silverthorn, who was now calling the police.

My first thought is *sweet*, and my second thought is *crap*. Yes, people who commit a hate crime (does such a thing exist yet?) deserve to face the police, but if my dad goes to jail,

228

I really have done it: I've pretty much ended any chance of my own future life. I try to focus on the incontrovertible fact that I do exist, right here, right now. (Can I just say how much I'd like a day to not worry about my existence?)

When we emerge from the woods, a lone cruiser is just pulling up. Two officers, one who looks as if puberty has just begun, step out and greet us. "Are you all right, kid?" the older one says, and I start laughing again.

"Define all right, sis." The shocked look on everyone's faces! But for a moment, I feel like myself.

We are at Ms. Silverthorn's, drinking hot chocolate. Chaz sits on one side of me, Ma Elena on the other, and Ernie sits on an ottoman, his foot bouncing madly. He was pacing for a while, but then he knocked over an end table and then, trying to recover from that, backed into the wall and wiped out James Baldwin. (That explains the new frame!) Ms. Silverthorn told him to *sit down*, and he did, but he's fretting.

Ernie has now said, "If I had come with you . . ." so many times that it's useless to rebut. He doesn't know about the kiss yet. In his mind, since we were only alone together because he was afraid to be seen with such flamboyant creatures, it's his fault. In a way, he's not wrong. Gordo and the goons might have been less likely to take on three of us. But I get it. Ernie didn't know he was trading his safety for ours. His fear didn't throw rocks or lower me over the edge of a cliff—their hate did that for itself.

Chaz has been nearly wordless since I got here. He gave me a brief, tired hug, but he has been mostly withdrawn. I think about the stories I heard that he killed himself after being tormented, and I wonder if I have saved him or only moved the deadline. I squeeze his hand. "I'm glad you got away."

He looks at me searchingly, violet irises dark. "Did I, though?" I don't know what to say. "When my folks hear about this, it's all over. Forget New York."

Ms. Silverthorn is firm. "You will go to New York, Charles Lawson Wilson, and I will make sure of it." *His name is Charles!?*

A rap at the door makes us freeze. When Ms. Silverthorn answers, it is the older officer again, but this time with Frohmeyer at his side. The officer asks to see Chaz and me. "We've taken the other boys down to the station for more questioning." He pauses, a little uncomfortable. "You should know that they deny it all."

"How can you believe them? Why would I do that to myself?"

"Hold your horses, Silverthorn," Frohmeyer interjects. "Danny here's just telling you what they said." Clearly, the officer and the principal have known each other for a long time, and just as clearly, "Danny" doesn't like Frohmeyer using his first name in official business. "You think we're so old we can't tell when a kid's lying?"

"Oh, I, uh—"

"Clowns didn't even change, so now they're sitting downtown in stocking feet with their muddy dress shoes in an evidence room."

230

"What your principal *means* to say is that we have them detained, but we're going to need you to come down for official statements yourselves."

Frohmeyer tells Ernie and Ma Elena to go back to their dorms but beckons me to follow him. I'm confused. "What about Chaz?"

The officer shakes his head. "He's with me. I shouldn't have left you two alone to begin with. I need your statements separate, no comparing notes. You can see each other later."

Ms. Silverthorn gives me the tightest, deepest hug. She whispers in my ear. "I'll be here when you're done."

During the interview, two things become obvious: Officer Danny absolutely believes what I am telling him, and Officer Danny also thinks it's just a very bad case of "boys will be boys." He keeps asking if I believed Gordo meant to kill us. There is no complex answer he likes: When I say, "Maybe not, but he could have easily," that's not good enough. Pointing out that any part of it (a rock in my face, a wrong move on the ledge) could have killed me is also not what he's looking for. I'm so frustrated, I could cry, and Officer Danny doesn't seem any happier about it. "Listen to me," he says, "I am asking a direct question that has legal ramifications. Do. You. Think. He. Wanted. To. *Kill*. You."

No. No, I don't. Hurt me? Yes. Make me go away? Yes. Calm some fire in him that I never started? Absolutely. But kill me?

"No."

"Okay. Okay." He sits back. "What happened to you was *not* nothing. But the law has very different categories for things, and you don't accuse someone of attempted murder if all they did was assault."

If "all they did" was stone you and drop you over a ledge . . .

Officer Danny sees the mix of anguish and judgment on my face. "They're in trouble. Don't you worry. We just don't want to ruin a whole life over dumb behavior."

Dumb behavior. They could've *ended* a life, and the best he can muster is "dumb"? The word is so puny next to what we've been through. It defangs the hatred, sprinkles sugar on the pleasure they took in our fear and pain. It's so gross, I could vomit.

And then I do. All over Officer Danny. I guess I'm not "all right."

Blue Monday

WHEN I WAKE UP, everything hurts. I don't have to look at my cheek to know that it will be a canvas of bruises. Ms. Silverthorn put some horrible goo on it last night, promising it would keep the cut from becoming infected, but gash-eraser doesn't exist, so I'm going to be monstrous. My knee looks like someone used a cheese grater on it, which is expected, but I didn't expect the tenderness around my chest from the climbing rope or the aching shoulders from trying to pull myself up over the ledge.

I don't get out of bed right away. I am in Ms. Silverthorn's guest room, a snug nest of jewel-toned fabric. She has drawn the blackout blinds so I could rest, and only a sliver of light sneaks in. I could stay here forever, and maybe I will—after what happened, who knows what the rules will be?

Last night changed what I think happened to Chaz in the other timeline, the one in which I never landed here. I traveled across time to save him from loneliness, only to find that hate always finds a way. In the end, I just shared the blow.

But he's alive. That's not a small difference. So sharing the blow was everything.

He wasn't alone because he had me; I wasn't alone because he went to get Ernie and Ma Elena. We're not alone now because Ms. Silverthorn said there was no chance we were going back to the dorm until we knew what happened to Gordo. Having a crew who knows you as you are and still stands by you—oh my god. I took it for granted, but I never will again.

Tap tap tap.

"Hold on a sec. Getting dressed." I look at the wreckage of my prom outfit—no chance of me ever touching any of it again. Next to it, a pile of clothes has appeared.

I start laughing when I approach it. They're Ernie's. The sweet fool has brought me clean clothes to wear, but not my own. I am grateful no one from my time will see me wearing a T-shirt emblazoned with a Tetris screen and tan corduroy pants. (Or smell me, in my secondhand Brut.)

When I open the door, I'm surprised to see not Ms. Silverthorn but Chaz. And he has suffered the same fashion fate as me, which is even funnier because he has a good three inches on Ernie. His Ms. Pac Man shirt is actually cute, partly because it barely reaches his waist, so it almost counts as a crop top.

There's no ignoring the ugliness of the pale Wrangler jeans, loose at the waist and high-water length, which he has tried to fold to pretend they are pegged and ended up creating the capris of your nightmares.

"*Some* things belong in a closet," I joke, and discover it hurts to speak. My jaw is so stiff and tight; I think I may have been gritting my teeth all night.

Chaz hugs me, and it's not romantic—it's a hug only your closest friends can deliver. We stand in the hallway a long time, just like that, and instead of missing my future world, I am grateful for the embrace I am in right now.

"Boys?" Ms. Silverthorn calls up the stairs, maybe worried that she has left two of her gay students alone and out of sight too long. She might be liberal, but there are limits.

We head down, and she tries not to laugh at our outfits. "I would have made Ernie go back and get you your own clothes, but he was already such an emotional mess by that point. I figured I'd drive you over after everyone has left for class and let you change yourselves."

"Don't you have to teach?" I ask.

"I got a substitute after I agreed to be your advocate."

"Advocate?"

Chaz seems to know what this means, but I don't. He looks grim. "That's what they offer students in big trouble." He sinks onto her sofa.

"Elder Frohmeyer wants you in his office at ten to discuss what happens next. It's not entirely up to him, but he is the one who makes the recommendation."

"*We* didn't do anything." I'm so mad, I could Gale warning the room myself.

She hesitates before replying. "In a school like this, sometimes just being the wrong person is as bad as doing the wrong thing."

Chaz leans forward. "What can you do . . . as advocate?"

"I already talked Elder Frohmeyer out of calling your family last night, Chaz. I convinced him that since you were physically fine, there was no urgency. And since we were still sorting out what happened, that it would be better to wait. I also reminded him that your family . . . they're going to have some strong feelings about . . . the accusations made."

"That I'm gay. Just say it."

"That you're gay. And that you were kissing a classmate on campus." She chooses her words carefully. "I understand why you wanted to. A lot of people kissed their dates last night. But I'm not the principal."

He sags again. His eyes close. "Thanks for trying . . ." he murmurs.

My turn. "So what else does an advocate do?" If buying us a single night is as good as it gets, well, that ain't much.

"He may recommend expulsion, but I will have a chance to plead your case. Then it goes to the Student Life Committee, which makes it official. But I can also make a pitch to them."

"Does that usually work?"

"It's my first year, and no one has tested this yet since I arrived. But in theory, it can, or why else make it a rule?"

Chaz sits up. "It never matters. When Frohmeyer makes up his mind . . ."

"Well, Elder Frohmeyer never had Anisha Silverthorn to contend with." Still, doubt reads large in her eyes. She glances at the clock on the wall. "School has started, so let's go get you changed. We don't want to be late for this."

Frohmeyer keeps us waiting till almost eleven, which is torture. When he opens the door to his office, we look as wholesome as possible. We both wear clothes that fit, and we have intuitively chosen our most conservative outfits: Chaz a light blue polo and khakis (he owns khakis?), and me a ring tee and jeans. Frohmeyer wears a suit—he always wears a suit, but today it looks especially funereal. His expression matches. "Anisha," he barks, "don't go far," before ushering us in.

We sit across the desk from him, letting him settle into a huge rolling office chair. I've never looked at his desk before, and I pore over its contents trying to decode signs of hope or warning: a small American flag, a silly plaster figurine of a golfer swinging his club into his own head, a photo of his wife from thirty or forty years ago, a bonsai plant that is either fake or reveals him to be a master of the art, and a glass bowl of wrapped candies, labeled with a *Take One* sign. Nothing useful is revealed.

"I know you two had a rough night, and I want you to know that you are safe. The boys are already home. Once other students confirmed their absence from prom, they admitted their part. I called their parents myself. No one does that sort of thing at First Secondary and gets away with it."

I feel like some knotted cord in my chest is unraveling. "Oh, thank god."

Chaz sounds less relieved. "You expelled them?"

"No . . ." A frown. "They were suspended. For the month. They'll finish up at home."

"So they're just going to come back and walk with us?"

"You know me better than that. They will not be on that stage. But this close to graduation, it doesn't make sense for them to lose credit for the year."

Right. Why slow up their promising futures just because they tortured a classmate?

Chaz says nothing else. I want to but can't either. We simply don't dare push back. The room is dead silent, but we don't want to ask what happens next for us.

Frohmeyer's eyes drift to the office window. The first gym class of the day, the juniors are jogging past, the sporty ones in the lead, followed by a few try-hards and then an ever-slower stream of kids just counting out the minutes to the next class. We all watch them.

He clears his throat. His eyes stay on the windows. "The boys said you were engaged in homosexual relations on school grounds."

Chaz is indignant. "I have not had sexual relations with anyone ever. I would swear that on a Bible."

Um, personally, I better keep mum on that score, but

Frohmeyer isn't waiting to hear from me anyway. "Wilson, I think you know better than that. You know what flies at First Secondary, and I'm not asking about sex."

Chaz shrugs as if he has no more to add. Frohmeyer eyes me. "You may be new, Silverthorn, but I'm guessing you know boys don't go around kissing other boys here."

I find my voice. "I know *I* don't." I don't "go around" kissing *multiple* people anywhere.

He lays both hands flat on his desk and raises his shoulders, then takes a breath and blows it out.

"You're saying you weren't making out on the bleachers."

I'm not leaving this to Chaz. "Seriously? Of course not." Honestly, you cannot call *one* kiss—with no magic—"making out."

"Why would they say you did?"

"They've been picking on Chaz since I got here. Ask them why!"

"I did. And they said it's because he—both of you—are gay. They admitted to chasing you through the woods—"

"Uh, the woods didn't throw rocks at us." I touch my face to make the point, and the wound throbs.

"I told you they admitted to it. I'm not splitting hairs. They went home, and that's that. But they owned up to what they did. That's why they get to graduate. Now I'm asking you to own up to what you did."

Because an attack and a kiss are equal crimes.

Chaz's eyes are narrow, trained on Frohmeyer. "If we say we're gay, we'll be suspended too, won't we?"

239

"Suspension is the least of your problems, Wilson. You have a family and God to deal with."

I cut in. "What if we don't say *anything*?"

"You clowns really think four boys gave up the rest of their school year by telling the truth, and I'm going to let you pretend they did what they did for no reason?"

"I'm not making assumptions about anything"—I have the good sense here not to call him sis—"I'm asking a concrete question."

His face is turning red. "Then it's four on two, four witnesses with nothing left to hide, saying you did, and two of you saying nothing at all? Letting them take the fall, a big one when you had a chance to tell the truth. You do the math. No way I'm letting two kids fool around on a Christian campus while I just look the other way."

"So, to be clear: we say yes, and you suspend us?"

"Count yourselves lucky."

"We say nothing and you expel us."

"That's correct."

I am a half-second away from telling Frohmeyer what he can do with his patriarchal, homophobic, blame-the-victim bull, when Chaz speaks.

"There's one thing you haven't told us."

Frohmeyer is surprised. "Yeah? What's that?"

"How do we stay? What would *that* take?"

I know the answer before Frohmeyer says it. "Tell me it's not true. Look me in the eye, both of you, and tell me you are good Christian boys who have not once looked at another boy here and who I can safely, before God and your folks and the Student Life Committee, proclaim innocent."

"And then we stay?"

"If I believe you."

He sits back, arms folded across his chest, waiting for us to sell him on a notion he clearly doesn't want to buy.

I look at Chaz. Beautiful Chaz, those eyes troubled, and think about what it would mean for him to go home now. Will his parents take away college? What happens to his dreams? Chaz needs to do whatever it takes to be safe. I will respect whatever he says; he has walked a different path toward this moment than I have, and it's okay. He can disavow it and feign shock when I don't. He's alive, and I want him to have everything he deserves.

But there is no way I'm going to say I'm not who I am. I'm not going to lie about my true heart to keep the peace with people who despise it. If I agree, I might as well throw rocks at myself.

I sit back. I don't say a word.

Chaz does the unthinkable. He reaches over and takes my hand. And holds it. Together we are a gay wall, and we've left the principal no opening. Whatever blow comes, we're sharing it.

Frohmeyer's lips part, then close, settling into a line of disgust. He doesn't even speak to us before going to his door and waving us out. When Ms. Silverthorn sees our faces and his, she knows the story.

We can't meet in her classroom, where a substitute teacher is offering the quiz on *Connecticut Yankee*, so we end up in a study nook of the library. There are the jankiest looking computers sitting where the Macs are in my time.

Ms. Silverthorn tells us we're not actually expelled until Student Life agrees in a meeting she imagines will happen right after lunch. The vote has to be unanimous, not just Frohmeyer but all four members. The bad news is that Mr. Buckman is one of the four. When Chaz says Mr. A and Mr. Blue round out the team, I feel like I'm in a Margaret Atwood novel. "They're all men? How is that allowed?"

"*Allowed?* It's the norm."

"What if a girl's in trouble?"

"Worse for her. No one said it's a fair system, just *the* system." She holds up four fingers. "You know there's two against you: Elder Frohmeyer and Mr. Buckman for sure. Mr. Ableman is close with Mr. Buckman, but he's also young and a little bit of a hippie, if that guitar means anything. I still think he's more a third vote on their side than a first on ours. Your best bet is Mr. Blue. He's been the senior class sponsor forever, and a lot of the kids love him because he takes the job seriously."

I don't tell her that I overheard him describe one of his students as "pure garbage" my first day when I got lost on the way to my third period. Or that Leeza says he snapped that her makeup made her look like "a Jezebel," which was an insult before it was a fun website. Somehow, I doubt that I'd ever become one of the kids who "love him," but maybe Silverthorn is right about him being a defender of his seniors.

Chaz asks, "What're you going to say? What's your defense?"

"I don't think trying to *defend* you against something you wouldn't say is going to get me much mileage, so I'm going for heartstrings. They all know you and like you, Chaz. You're part of us. When I remind them that expelling you on the brink of graduation could cost you your shot at college and send you back to a home where your family is already dealing with your brother's penchant for ill-considered choices, I'll help them see that it's not the Christian thing to do."

"Will it be enough?" He sounds doubtful.

"And what about me?" I mean, in case I'm stuck in this time forever, I should probably have a diploma.

"You? Well . . ." She bites her lip. "Here's the thing. I don't lie. Ever. It's one reason I'm not going in there arguing that you aren't gay. You may not have noticed, but when I took you into Elder Frohmeyer's office that first day, I just raised my sister's name and sounded all sad and looked at you and let him fill in the blanks. I never said I was your aunt or that you were her son or that she was sick . . . I prayed that would work, and it did. Everything else everyone knows, all the details came from you."

She's right; I *hadn't* noticed. That was some flawless sin-of-omission work. Chaz is looking back and forth like we have just pulled off a magic trick. He *so* has questions.

The bell rings. She rises, and we follow her into the hall.

"You two go to lunch. See your friends, and say goodbye, just in case."

Here Is Where I Am

WE FIND LEEZA SITTING with Ernie, Ma Elena, and Tawny, who unexpectedly leaps up to hug Chaz when she sees us. Girl is forgiving!

Chaz looks so relieved, it's almost funny. "You're not pissed at me?"

"If you're," she lowers her voice to a whisper, "*that way* . . . then I don't have to wonder why we broke up." He hugs her back fiercely, then she pulls away. "I deserve a real man!"

"Okay, sis, those are fighting words!" I say and am about to explain the inherent homophobia in this, but she just laughs at me calling her sis.

"You're so funny, Weese!"

Chaz shakes his head as if to say, "Let her be." He's more concerned about the other tables, where a hundred eyes keep looking at us and then sliding away. "So, everyone knows?"

Ernie answers. "No. It's like a major mystery. Gordo, Vinnie, Tad, and Arvis are gone, but no one knows why." (I cannot be at all surprised that Red and Buzz Cut have such terrible real names.) "Then you and Weese skipped morning classes, and people thought *you* were gone too until someone saw you waiting outside Frohmeyer's office."

Tawny nods. "In History, Missy said it was a drinking party in the woods, and the cops came." Oh my god—*that* is an image: me and Gordo clinking beers by a fire.

Leeza slaps Chaz on the arm. "We only know because Laney and Ernie filled us in on it. Why am I hearing what happened from Gale warning?"

"Hey!" Ernie's face floods with color.

"I'm sorry! I'm *sorry!* A week ago, I barely knew you beyond diving out of your way, and now *you* got to rescue *my* best friend." Her voice trembles a little. She turns to Chaz. "When you missed prom, both of you, I was so worried. I just knew you were in trouble, but I didn't know how or what. I had to wait to find out, and it was torture."

I try to lighten the mood. "Cell service at the Ledges is the worst." Of course, that brings four blank faces, duh, so I adjust. "We didn't have time to write dorm mail while they were chasing us."

My quip has the opposite effect intended since it reminds

us all what really happened. Chaz is grim. "I've never been so scared in my life. I prayed all the way back to campus."

Tawny frowns. "I can't believe they did that to you. And for what?"

"Right?" I say. "I mean, one little kiss, and they were out for blood!"

Chaz looks at me, mouth open. In fact, they're all in various versions of slack-jawed surprise. Ernie's face, barely returned to white from the moment before, starts to darken. Here I go.

"Chaz wouldn't have told you, to spare my feelings, but I kissed him. Blame the excitement of prom night—and seeing him in that suit—" I'm really selling it now. "Poor guy had no idea it was coming! It was, like, three seconds long, and it was terrible."

Tawny gives me a look that says she knows how I feel. Ernie relaxes so visibly that I wonder how I didn't notice anything between them before.

But Ma Elena purses her lips. "That was an incredibly stupid thing to do here!" (Now *that* sounds more like her.)

"Well, sis, *here* is where I am!"

"Not for long." Chaz decides we need to tell them what happened in Frohmeyer's office. When they hear that we are likely to be expelled, little explosions detonate around the table. Tawny starts to cry, and Ernie looks like he might faint.

Leeza sits erect, padded shoulders wide, eyes blazing. "No. Way." A look comes over her that can only be described as possessed. "I'm not letting that happen."

Tawny tilts her head. "What can you do about it? You're not exactly Frohmeyer's favorite."

Leeza can't argue. Spend four years being an outsider, and you have no favors to call in. "I am so done with this school." Leaving her tray behind, she storms away, well aware that some of the other kids are watching. She flips off the last table before she's out the door.

Ma Elena takes my hand. "Where will you go?"

What else can I say? "Back to the future, I hope."

Student Life Committee looks exactly like a witch tribunal, minus the pilgrim hats and, I don't know, straw. Ensconced in wooden chairs with the school logo, the four men line a table facing us, Frohmeyer and Blue in dark suits and Mr. A and Buckman in their button-downs but with fat blue ties. Ms. Silverthorn, like Chaz and me, sits in a folding chair, her status made clear by which side of the table she's on.

While we were with our friends, she was pleading our cases. Whatever she said to them, the grim set of her face has told us it was not well received. The men seem to consciously avoid letting their eyes land on her now. Buckman looks not just smug but hungry to deliver the final blow. Ableman—Mr. A—looks wistful, probably for his youth, remembering a time when he wasn't responsible for kicking kids out of school. Blue does not look beloved of seniors at this time; he can hardly untwist his face, so disgusted is he by the accusations leveled.

Frohmeyer settles heavily into his chair. "We're in agreement. What happened to you boys was terrible, but you did bring it on yourself. Your refusal to take real ownership of what happened, even after the other fellas did their part, is not acceptable. You're both expelled."

Chaz's eyes are brimming, but he fights not to let the tears overflow. I am so mad, I could leap across the table at these buffoons.

Ms. Silverthorn is steaming. "I am ashamed to call you colleagues today. And Christian? I don't think so."

"You watch your mouth!" Mr. Blue's face screws up into even more unpleasant form. "Students aren't the only ones who have rules!"

The door flies open, and everyone jumps. It's Leeza. And oh my god, she's gone full Pat Benatar: her hair is teased wildly, her lips deep red, her eyeshadow an extreme blue even by her standards. She wears a purple zebra-stripe bodysuit with a wide red leather belt and towering red pumps. She looks fierce. Like Wonder-Woman-taking-on-Nazis fierce.

"You can't be in here," Frohmeyer barks, and only I notice how frozen Buckman is right now.

"What are you going to do? Expel me?"

Ms. Silverthorn reaches for her. "Leeza, what are you doing?"

"Just making clear they have no power over me. Fun fact: one of the perks of being an A student with a love of extra credit is that I already have enough points to pass all my classes. If I don't do another thing, they'll still have to give me a diploma."

Ableman looks at Blue, who shrugs. She's right.

Frohmeyer rolls his eyes. "You want to skip class and lose out on being valedictorian, be my guest." (She's valedictorian? She never let on!) But we're in a meeting, and you're going to be in trouble if you don't walk out that door."

"The trouble's *inside* the room—this stupid school with its sexist rules and constant judging, and now this. You're going to kick out two guys who got attacked, and you're going to do it simply because they exist. Real nice. Real 'love thy neighbor' of you."

"We don't make the rules, Leeza," Ableman finally speaks, and he sounds pitiful. He doesn't like this, but he knows how things work. "We can't let them stay here."

"Really? If you're going to kick them out for one kiss—" Dammit. I probably should have warned her that we never admitted anything to Frohmeyer. "Then what are you going to do about Andrew? Because, let me tell you, we've had a lot more than one kiss."

Frohmeyer is on his feet. "What?" He turns to Buckman immediately. "What is she saying, Andrew?"

I see the way Leeza looks at Buckman: defiance mingles there with doubt. In her heart, she must know that he will fail her in this moment even as she hopes maybe he won't, that maybe they can Bonnie-and-Clyde this meeting together.

That isn't what happens. Buckman rises, face contorted in denials. "I have no idea what she's talking about." He makes his voice as commanding as he can muster, turning to Leeza. "If you think you can make up some wild story just to distract us from your *sick* friends—"

Her eyes blaze. She doesn't let him finish. "What was it you said to me last night at prom? *'I'm glad it's so dark; no one will see how I look at you.'* Yeah, especially not Helen."

"You shut your mouth!"

He reaches out—to grab her? to hit her?—but Frohmeyer gets between them. "Start talking, Andrew."

Chaz gets my eye and makes a "What the Hell is Happening" face.

"There's nothing to say!" Buckman spits out the words, eyes panicked. "And that's not why we're here . . ."

Leeza reaches into the bust of her catsuit and produces a black-and-white photo strip. Even from here, I can see the Darien Lakes logo in the corner. Buckman lunges for the strip, but Frohmeyer snatches it. You'd have to be an idiot (which I'm not) to doubt that it's Leeza and Buckman in the cozy confines of a photo booth. Blue and Ableman crowd around to see, while Buckman starts protesting that she dragged him in there and he thought it was all innocent.

Frohmeyer commands Chaz and me to leave. But Leeza isn't done. "Nope, boys, I want you to stay for this." She faces Frohmeyer head-on. "You need me. If you expel my friends, I will mail photocopies of these photos to every board member of the school and every pastor whose church sends kids here. *Maybe* I'll send some of the notes, too. Andrew is *quite* a writer."

250

Buckman opens his mouth, but Frohmeyer glares at him so hard, he shuts it. "What game do you think you're playing? If what you're saying is true, you'll be expelled too."

"I beat you to it. My folks are on the way. I have a whole life ahead of me that will obliterate my time here if I'm lucky." She is on fire. Like Katniss-rides-a-chariot fire. "Are you getting it yet? I. DON'T. NEED. YOU. *You* need me. If I go down shouting, you'll have to fire Andrew and then what happens to that grandbaby of yours?"

My head is going to lift clear off my shoulders in surprise. How did I not know that Helen was a Frohmeyer before she was a Buckman?

"You leave my daughter out of this."

"That's what he did whenever we were alone."

"I'm serious."

"So am I. You promise not to expel the boys, and this will stay our little secret. You can buy time for the happy couple to see their pastor or whatever, and no one has to know what goes on between students and teachers here. I think it's a fair deal."

Chaz goes to her. "You don't need to do this."

"Need to? *Want* to. I'm loving it if you haven't noticed. And it's done."

Ableman is just about moaning. "This has all gotten out of hand. I think we need to pray together."

Frohmeyer looks about six seconds away from a coronary, but Chaz decides if Leeza is stepping up, he should be, too. "Are you a man of your word?"

Warily, the principal nods. "Yes. And?"

"Then suspend me: I'm gay." He is glowing as he says it. The release of coming out and the pleasure of how transgressive it is to do it here and now! "I should have said that the first time you asked." I know he's pining for Ernie, but I could kiss him.

Chaz turns to Leeza. "Truth at a price is *still* the truth."

Leeza beams at him. Ms. Silverthorn looks like she has seen it all now, Blue is trying to give birth through the veins in his forehead, and Mr. A—wait. My god, is he jealous?

Frohmeyer has had it. "Fine. You're all suspended. Blue, go call his folks." Mr. Blue springs away from the table and darts out of the room like a prisoner freed. There is no tenderness left—the principal eagle-eyes Chaz. "Off the campus today and don't come for graduation. We'll mail you your diploma. Ableman, walk him to the dorm. He's not going back into class." Is it just me or does Mr. A look too pleased at the prospect?

He turns to me. "You have anything to add?"

"I'm so gay, I almost boomerang back to straight. I did not run around kissing boys all over your lovely, progressive campus, but you should probably suspend me now, before I start. Some of them are cute, sis."

That is Frohmeyer's last straw. "Anisha, get them out of here!"

Out of the board room. Out of the hallway. Out of the school.

Dropped out. Kicked out.

Out, out.

Perfect Plan

IT DIDN'T TAKE LEEZA more than an hour or two to pack, so her folks will be here any time. Chaz was slower, more meticulous, but his parents can't leave until his dad finishes his shift at work, so it'll be dark before they arrive. And me? Depending on how you look at it, my parents are either decades away or here in 1985 but useless: one suspended, the other in class.

I try not to focus on what happens next for me. There are no transcripts for Ms. Silverthorn to produce, and there never were, so I guess not much has changed, but the illusion of normalcy—going to class, hanging with friends—is gone because I can't go to class, and two of my four friends are suspended.

I have no idea how long Ms. Silverthorn can let me stay with her, and what other choice do I have?

We're all in her living room, but she's not here, having returned to campus to meet with Frohmeyer. Leeza is giving Chaz a pep talk about his parents. The reality has sunk in as he thinks about what life will be like in the months between now and the start of college—if they don't try to stop him from going, that is. Leeza points out that he turns eighteen in a few weeks, so really, they can't prevent him from attending a school he's been accepted to. He just has to find a way to pay for the parts his scholarship doesn't cover. " 'Just,' " he murmurs.

Ma Elena arrives with trays of Wendy's: four Frosties and four large fries. I know before she says it that she's going to call this "The Cure" because she has been calling it that my whole life. You eat your French fries one by one, dipping each in the Frosty as you go. Because I've been doing this since before elementary school, it seems perfectly natural, but Chaz and Leeza react like it's gross and horrifying. All it takes is one sweet and salty bite to convert nonbelievers. I mean, *please*, chocolatey and fried all at once? It's a pleasure delivery system. Mom always deploys it when she's blue or I've had a bad day at school. I may even have broken up with a boy or two just to deserve "The Cure."

Dunking a slender fry into her cup, Leeza asks where we think we'll be in ten years. Ma Elena is crystal clear: By then, she will be done with nursing school and working. She'll be married, but she won't have kids right away, because she wants to travel. (Mom? Travel?) Obviously, she can't go to Cuba, so maybe Puerto Rico first and then Spain. Chaz says he's going to be in the Alvin Ailey Dance Company or doing whatever leads up to that. He says he knows he'll have to work other jobs on the way, so he wants to get a teaching certificate and become a drama coach.

Leeza says she's going to be a singer. "New wave, cool stuff, none of that rock crap. My parents don't think it's realistic and I'm like: *Watch me.* I'm only going to college to appease them, but if I get my break before I'm done . . ." She shrugs. "When have I ever conformed to expectations?"

Chaz ribs her. "You're just going to drop out of every school you can."

"And probably date all the wrong men, too." She doesn't look upset at this prospect. She turns to me. "When you tried to tell me to stay away from Andrew, I was working hard to really believe in him, but, you know, I think I just wanted to have an excuse to keep fooling around. Sue me; I liked it."

Chaz and I both go "Ewwww" at the same time, and she fires back. "Not everyone is a bad kisser, boys!" (I so need to make sure I get her contact info before she leaves because there is no way I'm letting her live the rest of her life thinking the only problem with their affair was him not standing up for her.)

Ma Elena has reached her threshold. "Please, don't say more!" Trying to get that image of her head, she points out that I never answered her question about the future.

Ten years from *now* or from my time? 1995 or 2030? I can't say "I hope to exist" (though I do), and the careers that interest me (high end: Netflix series showrunner; low end: YouTube influencer) haven't been invented. "Um. I guess . . . I hope you'll remember me."

"That's not a career!" Mom will say that *exact* thing to me when I tell her I want to be an influencer in the future. "It's sweet of you to say, but you must have plans."

Who knows why I decide to just tell the truth . . . again. "Um. Here's the thing. I keep trying to tell you all . . . I'm not Ms. Silverthorn's nephew. I'm her student, in another time. I really did come here by accident from the future."

Chaz has heard this before. "Yeah, yeah. We know."

"I don't know how to get back, but we're hoping there's like a time slip or something . . ." It occurs to me that today is Monday, and if the slip occurs at the same moment it did last week, I should really be out on the field and not here, and that maybe I've already missed my window.

"Like *Connecticut Yankee*?" Ma Elena gasps. "Is *that* why we're reading it?" (Hmmm. Is it? Is this a causal loop thing?)

Chaz laughs. "Yes, Ms. Silverthorn has us reading it because it's *all* true, and she wants the new time traveler in class to feel *welcome*."

Leeza has one eyebrow raised, but her words are firm. "I think he means it." She leans toward me. "That's why half of what you say doesn't make sense."

"Finally!"

"You can't believe it—not really . . ." Chaz is incredulous.

I can see that Ma Elena and Leeza are both near trembling with excitement, wanting it to be true. We're in this together.

Leeza is excited. "It's fantastic, right? So, Weese, tell us about the future."

What to say? I start with Ma Elena. "You're a nurse and a mom, just as you said." I don't mention that her recent ex-boyfriend is her husband or that I'm her son. Instead, I look at Leeza. I make up a best-case scenario. "You're a pop singer, more Madonna-like than Duran Duran." I don't have an answer for Chaz, so I refocus their attention. "But I'm only seventeen then. So . . . we're not friends like we are now."

"Then I have *no* interest in the future," Leeza teases.

Chaz thinks we're all insane. "Are you guys really considering this?"

She laughs it off. "I don't know. It's fun. And what does it matter?"

"I half think it's possible and half don't," says Ma Elena. "I mean, it's not in the Bible."

Just as quickly as it seemed they believed me, the spell is fading. By tomorrow it will be a silly thing, a little joke between friends who won't even be together to share it.

A car horn plays "The Yellow Rose of Texas," and Leeza says it's her family. Who has musical car horns? And why that song? The fact that they are honking means her dad is royally pissed and her mom is afraid to argue with him. We team up to carry her things to a Lincoln Cadillac as long as a tugboat, helping her red-faced, wordless mother pack up. Her dad never leaves his seat, and every time she passes by in that catsuit, I swear he ages a little more.

Leeza tells us all she's going to call us and that she means it, keeping her hugs brief but fierce. "See you in New York," she says to Chaz. "And no more secrets." When she's in the back seat, she rolls down the window. "Trust me, Weese, in ten years, I'll remember you." She blows us a big kiss and then her dad pulls the Cadillac away, driving her off into the rest of her life.

Ma Elena shifts her weight from foot to foot. She doesn't want to leave if it means not seeing Chaz off, but her shift at the nursing home is about to start. Chaz teases her that the patients can live without *People* magazine and Doublemint for an hour, but when he sees she is tormented by the mere thought, he gives her a big squeeze and tells her to go. "Don't be a stranger," she says.

Before she heads off, she says, "You'll still be here, right? At least for now?"

"Unless I travel back to my time without warning."

"Ha ha! Not funny."

"Wait," I say. "I never asked—how was prom? You worked so hard on it!"

"Honestly? I don't know. I missed most of it because of what happened. And the photo booth photos are terrible: the moon is glowing, but you can't see anyone's faces!"

I resist the urge to say *duh* and just hug her tightly. And she, too, drives away.

As soon as we are alone, Chaz asks for my help. He wants to have his first *real* kiss—*apparently,* I don't count (tbh, that's fair)—which will also be Ernie's first kiss period (as far as Chaz knows), but it has to happen now before his parents arrive. He's going to ask Ernie out and, okay, it'll be a little long-distance for a while, but why not? No one has to know.

Ernie should be in cutlery shop by now, so all we have to do is sneak into my old room and get his fractal painting, which Chaz wants to mount inside a frame he has already snuck out of the art department. Then we're going to sneak it into the empty house on Faculty Row and hang it over the fireplace. I'm supposed to bring Ernie to where Chaz will be waiting. Oh my god, he's planned this like a promposal! I mean, it's no "I PROM JUST FOR YOU," but I'm still a little jealous.

"What do you think?" he says, dying for me to validate the most adorable plan ever.

This is what I think: it has now been exactly a week—maybe the most memorable week of my life—since I landed here, and the place I need to be is on the field. If the portal (if that's what it is) works, I'll be listening to the marching band, hoping they disappear from view, then waking up in the arts building with my life back. If there's even the smallest chance that we were right about the time slip, of course, I want to try.

Chaz is still waiting, eyes expectant but showing the first signs of worry that his plan may not be a good idea. I think of Ernie, who went from "Gale warning" to Prom Council to a guy who bailed on his friends to a guy who saved the day in the end. I consider how Ernie had once made peace with being on the fringe of school life and how it would now feel to be at the center of Chaz's. Even as much as I miss Cheng and Nix and (real) Mom and my own life, I know my answer.

"It's perfect. I'll do it."

Take on Me

THIS WEEK IS GOING to leave me with a permanent fear of heights. The second most scared I have ever been is right now, trying to pull myself up into the window of the room I shared with Ernie. I couldn't just walk into the building like a normal human being because today, of all days, Buckman is helping the dean replace the carpet in the lobby. Ernie's room is on the first floor, actually making it the second story from ground level because it's on the side away from the hill. I tried going through the basement door at the other end, but it was locked from the outside. (Seriously? Why now?) Climbing was my only choice.

I started on Chaz's shoulders, trying not to fall, him lifting my feet by the soles to get me high enough to push up the lower windowpane. Like Cirque du Soleil for profusely sweating gay boys of color. But now, to pull myself in means leaving the safety of Chaz's hands and, for the second time in twenty-four hours, I imagine falling.

I practically hurl myself through the window in fear, executing a tuck and roll that Simone Biles would be proud of. (Okay, she'd be more like *girl, please,* but, seriously, I took expressive movement for gym, so go me.)

For a moment, I'm a little nostalgic. I mean, the posters are still crazy, and there's a towel on the floor, but it's a space I shared with Ernie, who saved my life, during a week that has changed me forever. But there's no time to linger; carefully, *very carefully*, I grab the rolled-up fractal print and turn back to the window. Except Chaz is gone.

It's basement or bust, so I do my best gazelle impression and leap down the hallway and into the stairwell, grateful everyone else is in class—no sign of Buckman or the dean as I speed across the basement and out the door. I'm giggling maniacally now as I run to where I see Chaz hiding behind a tree. He apologizes for bailing—he saw the dean and panicked—as I hand off the artwork, but my work is not done.

I have to brave the campus a little longer. It's my job to lie in wait—literally in the shrubs—for Ernie to leave the shop building after his shift in half an hour. I hope it's long enough for Chaz to prepare his surprise, but not so long I get caught.

For the first time all week, things go effortlessly, though Ernie kind of whinnied when I leaped out of the bushes at him. Now we're trying to creep up Faculty Row as stealthily as possible. Which is to say, not stealthily. There are no trees, and the most coverage would be a wagon-wheel planter with some really mangy geraniums. As we pass the Buckmans', we see Helen furiously throwing luggage into a minivan.

Ernie's lugging his baseball game. Was he worried he would be bored on the way back to the dorm? I suppose it would seem more ridiculous if my cell hadn't been conjoined to my hand since eighth grade.

Ernie is gloomy. "I'm not supposed to be off campus! I didn't sign out!" I remind him that the school has probably used up its suspend-the-student-body quota for the year and that this may be his one chance to say goodbye to Chaz.

He thinks we're going to Silverthorn's, so when I steer him toward the empty house, he's confused. "Huh?"

This is my cue to bow out. "It's a surprise. Go with it."

Before he opens the door, I pry the video game out of his hand, which only makes him more nervous, but I figure Chaz deserves his full attention.

I swore to Chaz that I would send Ernie in alone, but there is *no* chance of me missing out on this. I mean, *please*. I know these faculty houses plenty well, and I dart around to the back door and slip inside, as little-cat-feety as I can. There's a hall from the kitchen to the living room that I sneak down, hoping they won't notice.

In the living room, Ernie's face is alight with the discovery of his framed painting over the fireplace. Chaz is nowhere in sight. Then I hear a click (a real drawback to the romance of a boom box), and music starts. It's "Take on Me" by A-Ha, and Ernie goes red, blushing with delight or embarrassment or both.

Chaz waits till the chorus to make his entrance, slowly walking down the stairs in a blazer and skinny tie, holding a parchment roll in one hand. He's singing along. When he gets to the part about being gone in a day or two, Ernie starts to cry.

Suddenly, they are kissing—not just a first kiss, but a dozen. If it was night, you'd see the fireworks painting the room, and even in the sunlight, I swear I can see the colors. They're holding each other so tightly. It's everything a first kiss should be. I feel bad for spying and yet so happy like I'm the mother of the bride or something.

They keep the embrace until the song ends, and Chaz unrolls the parchment, facing Ernie. It reads:

You're a work of art, Ernie. BE MINE?

"Your what, work of art?" Oh, Ernie. Gale warnings apply to sentiment too.

Chaz's laugh booms across the empty surfaces. "MY BOYFRIEND!"

And then, they're kissing again. *Really* kissing. Like, I bet he's glad his hands are free now. It's getting a little, um, grindy, and I feel bad for spying.

I should go. It's not my story. It's theirs.

Get Used to It

I HEAD TO MS. Silverthorn's house because there's no point in going to the field; the time of day I first arrived is well past, so it's too late to recreate the exact conditions that brought me here. I'll try again next week or hope we discover the time slip is imprecise, and any day will do.

I speed past Mrs. Buckman's minivan, now so thoroughly loaded, it'll be impossible for her to see out the windows if she actually tries to drive away. She's not in sight, and I count my blessings.

Ms. Silverthorn is sitting in her mother's rocking chair when I open the door. The lights are off, and the house feels gloomy.

"What . . . what are you doing?"

"Just sitting. Gathering strength."

"For what?" I already know the answer.

"Elder Frohmeyer pretty much said he thinks I knew about you boys and that I sanctioned it because of my 'liberal tendencies.'" She lets out a soft laugh. "He all but fired me. He suggested I might want to find a school 'where anything goes' if I don't want to honor this one's values."

"What are you going to do?"

"Do? Cross my fingers. And hope to outlast him. That man was a baby in the Great Depression. He may not like what I believe, but the world is not his for much longer. Today, I'm sitting with my feelings about his world and gathering the strength for mine."

"You do, you know . . . outlast him. By decades! In my day, you *define* the school."

"And you're welcome there, yes?"

I want to say yes. But I think about how my week started. "Um, like eighty percent? It's still working out a few things . . ."

With a sigh, she rises and goes to the window. I feel like I'm supposed to follow, so I do.

The view is of the fields across the school, leading to the woods and the quarry. I shudder at the vision, and she senses this. "You okay?"

"I don't know." A few minutes ago I was focused on Chaz and Ernie, and it was like nothing terrible had ever happened. Now I'm shaking a little. "I know it's only been a day, and yet . . . I don't think it'll ever go away—that feeling."

"No, probably not. But it won't be the same. It'll become a wound you're used to carrying."

She says this knowingly. I have to admit because she's my teacher and everyone loves her, I've never stopped for even two seconds to think about what she might carry. What it is like to move through the world—in any year—as the woman she is, knowing the dangers that she may face. Her dangers are greater than mine, I know, and more constant, but we share the walk.

"I think . . ." she begins, clears her throat, and starts again. "I think you may have to get used to being here. I don't know how to get you home."

I'm crying because I know she's right. I was focused on my '80s school life all week—watching out for Chaz and Leeza—but now both things have taken care of themselves, and I don't even have that. Unless I dedicate my life to figuring out how time slips work or invent a time machine (which so isn't happening because, sis, I am not fix-y), my own life, my real life, is lost to me.

"What am I going to do?" I know I sound pitiful. Why not? I *feel* pitiful.

She turns to me, dark eyes serious. "Light the way for others. Be your true self—that's what will make the future possible for kids like you. You've already changed things for Chaz and Ernie. Imagine how much more you can do."

Okay, but what about me? How do I make peace with a world that seems less than the one I gave up? What about my future? Like, literally, what do I do tomorrow? How do I graduate from high school? How will I go to college?

But I don't say any of that. I hear what she's trying to tell me. The big picture is that, whatever else I do, I need to make the road more walkable for everyone. I need to make it safer for kids like me by being me, right here and right now.

A doorbell chimes. I laugh at the look on her face because I remember how much she hated that bell. (Oof. I'm already thinking of my future in the past tense!)

It's Ernie, looking sweaty and keyed up. "What are you doing? You're going to miss him!" Without explaining—I assume Chaz's folks are here—he darts off. Ms. Silverthorn nods for me to follow, but I really want to hug her. So I do.

She extricates herself from my grasp. "I'm your teacher, not your aunt, and you will mind some boundaries." I'm pretty sure she sounds as amused as she is annoyed, but I toss off a quick apology before I race toward the dorm.

Chaz stops Ernie and me about twenty feet away from his family's Suburban. "Don't go any closer unless you want the demons cast out of you!" He's making a joke, but he looks weary.

"Is it awful already?" I can't help but feel this is my fault. Maybe because it is.

He shrugs. "I can endure *anything* for two months. Just watch the night sky on my birthday, and you will see me blasting out of there!" His mom's voice floats our way, reminding Chaz that they have a long drive. ("Get away from the homosexual deviants" is like a silent e: you can't hear it, but it's there.)

Chaz pulls me into a tight hug, and we both say "Ow!" at the same time. When he releases me, he says something I never

267

expected. "I am happier right this minute, even suspended, as myself, than I ever was when everything was 'fine' but I was hiding. Thank you for *seeing* me. And . . . thank you for Ernie." He takes Ernie's hand in his own.

Ernie looks like he might combust. "Um. I still go to this school, so . . ."

Chaz frees his hand. "All right, my sweet closet case, but in New York, we're going to play by my rules."

"We're in New York now . . ." Ernie says, helpless to avoid a technicality. Chaz gives me a "see what I'm getting myself into?" look and, would you believe, blows Ernie a kiss.

I want to stop time, to linger in a moment when I still have them. But we have established that time is not mine to steer.

"CHARLES!" His dad is now bellowing from the front seat, and with a playful pirouette, Chaz leaves us.

Who do I have now?

Ms. Silverthorn, if they don't kick her off Faculty Row, and Ma Elena, as long as Abuelo keeps the farm. And Ernie, after school, for a few more weeks before he's gone. I'm feeling nostalgic for my weird roommate already, even though he's right in front of me. He, of course, is thinking of more pressing matters. "Do you have my game?"

I don't, actually. The last place I remember seeing it was at Ms. Silverthorn's, which I guess I may have to start thinking of as home if the school even allows it. We head back to Faculty Row, but Ernie begs off. He can't risk yet another unsanctioned off-campus excursion. I tell him to wait at the edge of school grounds while I retrieve it, and he does, looking a little lost. What will school feel like with Chaz suddenly gone?

Trudging up Faculty Row, I picture ASA in my wake. Assuming I disappeared there the moment I arrived here, what did they think happened? And what will they do next? Will they hold the drama club banquet without me? And what about prom and graduation? Did I improve life for Chaz and Ernie but ruin senior year for my friends?

I'm way down this rabbit hole when I hear Ernie's voice in the distance. I turn to look back just as I process what he's shouting.

"VAN!"

I see Buckman's van too late, and somehow, the seconds are not mere seconds but a gooey morass of time in which my mind races, but my body does not. I understand that she will hit me, that it is going to hurt, that I can't stop it, and, oh my god, I really am going to die before I was ever born.

There's no stopping it. The blow is so hard, so complete, I don't even see stars.

Even the Space-Time Continuum

MS. SILVERTHORN IS LOOKING down at me with real concern. "I called EMS. You wouldn't wake up!"

Her hair is sleek, a perfect weave, and her eyes are rimmed in familiar crinkles. My head hurts, but my knees do not, and I get it instantly: it's the 2020s, for the second time in my life.

I'm just going to sit here and howl for a few minutes. Everyone looks so freaked out, but there's no chance of me explaining yet. They keep asking what hurts and if I know where I am, which makes me laugh and cry, and seriously I am a mess. The crowd parts to let Cheng in. It is so nice to be held that I can almost forget that my head feels like a hovel after a wrecking ball.

Cheng walks me to the nurse's office, with one arm around me and the other keeping me steady. It's sweet and totally overkill. "I'm fine. I am!"

But he doesn't loosen his grip. (And, really, I don't want him to.) "Yeah? Let's ask the nurse. I'm not letting go till then." The mixture of worry and protectiveness in his voice *slays* me.

The nurse checks out my pupils and then my limbs and seems convinced I am in no danger beyond bruising and a few days of headaches. As soon as she steps out of the room to get an ice pack, I kiss Cheng for all I'm worth. I don't care where or when I am: I've earned it.

When the nurse returns, Ms. Silverthorn is with her, eager to see how I'm faring. Nearly as much as I needed to kiss my boyfriend, I now need to talk to her, so I ask Cheng and the nurse if they can leave us alone. The nurse seems a little surprised but agrees, and Cheng, the living embodiment of roll-with-it, just gives me a quick hug and is out the door, no questions asked.

Ms. Silverthorn looks worried, and I can see she's wondering if there's more to the story of how I got injured. It's almost funny, because she has no idea. So I tell her.

"It happened *today*."

No reaction.

"*Connecticut Yankee* happened." I see a flicker of something in her eyes. "To *me*."

There we go! A quick succession of emotions—*No! Yes! Finally!*—fill the canvas of her face like Bob Ross brushstrokes making happy little trees.

"Well, it certainly took you long enough!" And she laughs a laugh I've never quite heard from her before, an intimate one that says we share a secret.

She doesn't want to have this discussion in the nurse's office, so we head back to her classroom, which emptied out a few hours ago. She sits at her desk and leans back, savoring the chance to talk about a secret she's carried twice as long as I've been alive. (That's a trippy notion, let me tell you.)

"When you showed up your freshman year, I had a flash that you looked like my Luis. But it was confusing because you came to orientation with Laney. You never told me, back in the day, that she was your mother."

"I know . . . it seemed like an impossibility on top of an impossibility. I thought maybe one thing at a time would be enough."

"I have lived decades making peace with that craziness." She looks out the window, and I'm guessing she sees that last day. "You can imagine my heart rate when Helen stopped the car and you were gone. I told her you ran off, and she was so upset about everything she actually went with it. But Ernie saw it . . . that poor boy! Picture me trying to explain to a church school student that you were a time traveler. If he hadn't seen your disappearing act himself, he'd never have been able to digest such a thing. I convinced him that we needed to keep this to ourselves. Though, *of course*, he told Chaz."

"So Chaz lived?"

"What do you mean? He didn't just live—he took off. He was a principal with Alvin Ailey for, I don't know, a decade, and is one of the most sought-after choreographers in the country."

My eyes fill with tears. Oh my god, he *did* it.

"Chaz and Ernie are ASA's biggest donors."

She says their names the way one says, say, Barack-and-Michelle, and I gasp. "They're still together?"

"Despite me telling them, separately of course, that no one should marry their high school sweetheart. They have defied the odds and I couldn't be happier to be wrong.

"Frankly, that whole experience you all went through . . . it made me rethink what's possible. You were only the second student who had ever come out to me and it was so soon after Ernie, I didn't know what to make of it." (*Ernie* was the first?) "That week changed me permanently. I unlearned some old notions and educated myself about what you boys were going through. From then on, I worked on every faculty member who would listen—a number that didn't rise all that quickly, at least in those first years. When people started using the term 'ally,' I thought, 'That's just what Luis said I was.' It's been a little mission, really.

"We were the first school in the county with a GSA and the first to have gay couples at prom. And all because of you."

I almost fall off my chair. "But—I mean—in *my* time—"

"Your time?" She looks amused.

Oh god, this is as tricky as figuring out past versus present. "In the *old* version of *this* time, same-sex dates were banned. That's what I was coming to see you about when the beam wiped me out."

She shakes her head. "I can't even imagine. Inclusion is literally on the school letterhead."

"They said it wasn't safe . . . because of what happened to Chaz." This earns a blank look, and I explain what was *supposed* to have happened and would have if I hadn't shown up. "After the tragedy, everyone acted like they had to protect us from it for the rest of all time. I mean, seriously, Mom never let it go."

"Really? That's not like her at all. We host the GSA pizza party at your house every year."

"We?" This is too much. "You hang out with Mom?"

"*Of course*, we hang out. She's one of the only people on earth who knows what happened."

Now I'm dizzy again. "How does Mom know?"

"She was so upset by your sudden disappearance. Ernie broke down and told her."

"And she believed it?"

"After I confirmed it, of course. It was fascinating to see her adjust on the spot. She said she'd wanted to believe it when you tried to tell them. That time travel was like you being gay—not something she could accept until she had a face to put on it. Once she decided to go with it, she was all in." (Wait—did I inherit this trait from Mom?) "But really, Luis . . . she should be telling you all this, not me."

As usual, Ms. Silverthorn is right. I do want to hear it from Mom. But that doesn't mean I'm done with questions. "Mr. Gale is married to Chaz, and my mom believes in time travel . . . so the butterfly effect is real. Everything is different."

"Everything? From what you've told me, that doesn't seem true."

She's right. The school is here, and Cheng is here, and I recognize my classmates. "I don't get it."

"I only know the current timeline, so I can't compare in any depth, but you're still my student, and the school is still here. However, I do have a thought." From her desk drawer, she produces a stack of books on time travel. From mid-pile, she retrieves a slim volume titled *Limited Ripple Theory*. "I try to keep up with all the latest, but perhaps I can stop now— you've proved one theory true." Silverthorn taps the author photo, a black-and-white shot of a commanding-looking Indian woman. "She's an astrophysicist who argued that time travelers only influence the trajectories of individuals upon whom they have made enough impact. And of course, the lives they change make their own impacts, and so forth. But they won't change everything—no more than a freak storm in Antic Springs can affect all eight billion people on earth. Ripples are real, yes, but they eventually smooth out."

"And everybody in this version of our time knows about this?"

She chuckles. "No, not at all. People think this woman has gone off the deep end. As they will also think of you if you run around telling your story. Your mom and I have been waiting for this moment so we could both warn you off. You can be out about anything you like except this."

I don't care what others do or don't believe anymore. "Sis," I say, "you know me. I am never shutting up again!"

Nix drives me home. All the way, I keep staring at them to make sure they're the same. Despite my boast to Ms. Silverthorn, I'm suddenly nervous about spilling the beans. I'm also wondering how much of my high school experience did or didn't happen. Oh my god, will I have new memories in this timeline and lose the old or keep both sets, and how will I tell the difference?

To say that Nix is not used to me being quiet is an understatement. They park next to the Wormwood Apartments sign—apparently, my ripples never reached the building's crappy name—and then fix me a serious look. "Are you okay or not?"

So I unload it all. I sound manic, but I can't stop. And Nix doesn't ask me to, never says "slow down, tiger," or tells me I need help. Nix just lets me go on and on and on. Until, finally, they say I should go in and see Mom.

"Is that all you're going to say?"

Nix considers the right response, settles on a friendly dig. "It's a whole new level. You've somehow even made the space-time continuum about you."

They laugh as if hoping that's enough. Nope.

"But do you *believe* me?"

Nix cocks an eyebrow. "Um, the details *are* killer . . . so . . . can I leave it at 'I'm open to it' for now?"

" 'I'm open to it' will be on your tombstone."

"What tombstone? If you can time travel, I'm going to be immortal."

I'm a little sad. I'd like everyone to react like Ms. Silverthorn, but I guess the world hasn't changed enough that time travel is the sort of thing you drop on a friend in the middle of the afternoon. Nix drives away, and I head inside for an audience I'm pretty sure will be an easier sell.

Mom is waiting at the door, clearly tipped off by Ms. Silverthorn. She's a sopping wet tear-delivery system, but I let her squeeze me. "It's really you," she says, again and again. "It always was."

It's All Ours

THE DOORBELL RINGS, AND I think it's Nix, but it's one of those food courier guys, carrying a Frosty for each of us and a big bag of French fries. "The Cure!"

Mom doesn't so much eat her food as play with the fries while she talks. "Your time at First Secondary was huge in my life, especially once I understood it. When I got pregnant, I insisted we name you Luis, ironically enough, after yourself—though of course, I didn't know yet that you were you . . ." She starts to laugh. "There is no way to talk about it that doesn't sound absurd!"

"How did you get Gordo to agree to the name? He hated me in 1985!"

A sigh escapes. "He would do anything for me in those days. He was so happy when we got back together after all those years and when he had a chance to have a family. I could have asked him to name you Frosty, and he'd have said yes."

"That doesn't sound like him."

"Some people . . ." She pauses, trying to put it into words. "Can't sustain joy. Some people are so primed to be unhappy, they have to make it true. I tried, for a long time, not to see it. He tried too."

"Did he know?"

"About the time travel? Ha! He wasn't quite as open to things as I am . . ."

"When did you know I was Weese?"

"You were five or six when I began to see 'him' in you. Your dad didn't notice anything unusual, but his eyes were on other things. By the time you were twelve or thirteen, I knew it wasn't just a resemblance. It was unsettling, and I couldn't deny it. Every time I looked in your eyes, I thought about Weese's face as we lifted him—you—up over the edge of the cliff."

Ah. "That's why you're so—" I stop.

"So what?"

"That's why you don't love me being this *out*. It's why you don't want me to go to prom with Cheng."

"Who else would you go with?" Her voice is thick with surprise.

"You really don't remember saying it wouldn't be safe?"

"I worked extra double shifts to rent you a limo. You *better* go with Cheng!"

This is a Mom I never knew. Not the one so scarred by the past that she made it her job to tamp down my present. This Mom sees me as I am, and sees only the possibilities of a teen in his golden hour. In her new eyes, mine is a life to lift up, not rein in. I'm crying now, and she really doesn't get why. How could she?

All my memories of her doubts and fears have been translated into only that: *my* memories. And I guess it makes sense—in this timeline, she only knows the life she has lived since I went back to the past when she was seventeen, and made her this person.

It's a hard concept to swallow: No one but me knows both lives.

A new thought. If she's like the "New & Improved!" model of herself, maybe Gordo is, too?

"Is Gordo cool with all this?"

Her grimace tells me I was aiming too high. "When I hear from Gordo, it's just to complain that child support is expensive."

"So, in *this* timeline . . . he still left us?" She nods. But a terrible new question arises. "How did you even end up together after he was kicked out—after what he *did*?"

She starts clearing away the fries and shakes, mostly to avoid looking at me. "He was so *sad* after he was suspended. He called me all the time. At first, I held out—how could I answer him? But when I was in nursing school, he wrote me all these letters. He begged me to forgive him, said God was making him a better person. The Bible says we *have* to forgive, and I was trying to live my faith. I prayed about it a lot. In the end, I told him I believed him but that I had moved on past high school, and I thought he should do the same.

"I didn't see him again until he came to an alumni reunion seventeen or eighteen years in, and, you know, he seemed to be all the things I liked best with none of the anger. I thought about how I changed, and decided to give him a chance, too. For a while, I thought he had." Her voice gets soft. "But some people never become the best version of themselves."

I go to Mom and draw her close. "He never deserved you, in any timeline." I say what I now know to be true, "I'm glad to be yours, even so."

Cheng comes over, and we sit on the flat rooftop of my apartment complex. We're not supposed to be up here, and it's probably dangerous, with all the hot air vents and a generator and, you know, a forty-foot drop to the lawn. But it's not the Ledges and, this week, I've broken more than a few rules—mostly involving quantum physics.

Imagine telling your boyfriend—hours after he has taken you to the school nurse with a head injury—about your time-traveling adventure. I mean, it's a hard sell. Chill as ever, he just nods a lot, quietly stroking my back. Even when I talk about kissing Chaz, which I downplay *hard*, he just listens without comment. When I am all done, he offers up only one conspicuously noncommittal response: "Okay."

" 'Okay, I believe you' or 'Okay, drama queen, I'll humor you, but I really think it's a concussion talking'?"

He grins, leaning over to kiss me instead of expanding on his answer. "Okay, as in okay."

There will be plenty of time to decide how much I want to convince him, or whether I even should. For now, we are quiet. No talk of the past or of prom. No revisiting our argument. Just boyfriends enjoying a silence, trusting each other enough to not fill the air with chatter. We are lying on our backs, looking at the heavens. I don't know what he sees, but my eyes are on the Big Dipper.

His head rests on my shoulder, and we're breathing, soft and slow, as one.

The night, the sky, the universe—it's all ours.

Prom

I DECIDED TO RECLAIM prom night from its past horror by replicating the Duckie outfit I never got to dance in, with a few significant twists: the same style jacket, but now in a really hot shade of fuchsia with a flawless DeLorean pin at my collar. At the formal wear shop, I convinced Cheng to rent a tux in tangerine, he calls it orange, which I let slide, so together we're like a walking sunset. And my god, he's so gorgeous, I could jump him right here on the school lawn where everyone is taking photos.

We're posing, at my insistence, in front of the amazing (and new-to-me) "Wilson-Gale Center for the Arts." Improved in every way from the arts building of my original timeline, this one boasts a plaque in Chaz's honor, thanking him and his husband Ernie for funding the project. Cheng thinks it's the wrong spot for photos; there's a tree up front that's prettier. But I remind him that I saved their lives and, in turn, he and I get to go to prom together.

His response? "Okay."

Whatever he thinks of my time traveling, he looks gorgeous tonight as Mrs. Somboon-Fox herself takes our prom photo. She has heard our exchange and chortles. "Are you on that story again? You're hilarious." Days ago, I tried to talk to her about what happened, thinking she was like Mom and Ms. Silverthorn, a witness who'd back me up. But it was as if the decades had erased the memory that we'd ever met.

I try again now. "It's not just a 'story,' and you should know because you were *there!*"

She pats my arm, quoting the *Wizard of Oz*. "And *YOU* were there, Scarecrow!" I start to argue, but she won't hear it. "I didn't even *GO* to this school. I was on campus three or four times, always delivering flowers."

"I know. I've seen the van!"

She moves on to take pictures of Bryce and his date, a starry-eyed freshman, chuckling. "You kids are so *WACK!*" Ugh. In any timeline, her 2020s self *always* knows just the wrong word.

What's wild is that everyone thinks that an inclusive prom was her idea. She has a reputation for being nearly as accepting as Ms. Silverthorn, and no one has a clue that her openness was made possible by two boys being true to themselves in 1985. She can't really picture how much the truth once cost. A week ago, you could've said the same about me.

Prom flies by too fast. I built up this night for years, *years*, and it only lasts a few hours. But *what* hours!

The art kids made a Takashi Murakami–style rainbow arch—a massive, glossy thing in eye-popping colors—for photos. Our theme has led to a lot of kids wearing bright tuxes and dresses, and the decorating committee has made the entire place shimmer. Kids who didn't really like each other in my original timeline are praising each other's outfits, and people dance unselfconsciously, as if they know our youth won't last.

I can't help but think that Leeza would love this—I wish she'd gotten to go to this version of our school. I promise myself to google her tomorrow. She can't be that hard to find, and won't she be surprised if I do.

When Yasmin mounts the stage and takes the microphone, a rhinestone-studded crown in hand, I have a brief flutter of hope: Is she going to call my name? But that's the old me talking. The new me has learned that the school no longer indulges in gendered prom kings and queens. And since I spent the last two weeks campaigning for someone else who is even more deserving, I'd bet good money that my best friend is about to have the night of their life.

"The Antic Springs Academy Prom Royal is . . ." Yasmin has barely formed an *N* before the whole room is chanting, "Nix! Nix! Nix!"

Nix's look has a lot going on: a cropped velvet tux jacket and a tulle skirt over expensive athletic pants. But they're just *slaying.* When they take the mic and ask the whole class to be their date, it's like a massive Billie Eilish mosh pit.

Cheng whispers in my ear, the sort of sweet nothing an athlete is prone to. "I'm starving. Let's ditch and beat the rush at Popeye's."

Okay, I know the biscuits at Popeye's are butter-porn, but still. "We're not done yet, babe."

He does the "hungry eyes" thing—puppy dog eyes with a subtitle that reads "feed me"—but keeps dancing anyway.

I scan the banquet hall: Mom, having snagged herself a chaperone spot, is talking to Shreya, perhaps asking how she has gotten her strapless dress to stay up this long; Ms. Silverthorn and Mrs. Somboon-Fox are flanking Bryce, whose red Solo cup the principal is sniffing; Nix is dancing in the middle of a crowd of kids who came without dates, looking for all the world like their guru. It's everything I could hope for.

With only a few minutes left, the DJ announces a special request for a "blast from the past, from Luis to Cheng." Cheng doesn't blush—he's way too chill for that. But my heart races a little faster.

"What did you do?" he whispers, looking pleased and nervous all at once.

Our classmates have instinctively made space in the center

of the dance floor for us. Everyone's expecting a ballad—including Cheng, who *hates* slow songs but likes being good to me. He's gearing up to endure a cliché prom climax just to make me happy.

But I have something else in mind. "You Spin Me Round" fills the air and, after a moment to adjust, everyone's bopping to a song our parents would've danced to. The DJ cranks it.

Cheng just shakes his head, grinning and obviously relieved. But I know he doesn't quite get it. He leans close, almost shouting to be heard over the booming beat.

"Why this song?"

After everything I experienced, I could answer that I *had* to bring a little 1985 with me to prom. But instead, I tell him the truth.

"I just wanted to let you know how you make me feel."

He stops dancing and pulls me close, resting his forehead against mine. "I know. *I know.*"

If I were ever to be trapped in time, I would pick this moment.

I could stay here forever.

A Note from the Author

When I was a kid, I read a lot. I mean, A LOT. My small-town library had a six-books-a-week rule, but a half-dozen books never lasted me a week, so sometimes the librarian let me cheat the system by also taking out books under my brother's name. Hundreds of books a year (the best ones twice!) and never once, not a single time, did I read a book with a Cuban character, much less one who was my age. And gay? Not in that library. My story didn't seem to exist.

My daughter, who is of African American descent, is growing up in a very different time than I did, but she, too, has experienced the comparative scarcity of characters of color, especially in the books chosen as required reading in school.

She noticed early on how often the kids of color who do make it into a story are the sidekicks to the hero, not the stars of the show.

When I started *Spin Me Right Round*, I knew that kids of color had to be at the heart of the action, not just spectators. I knew I wanted a story whose hero is a queer kid—and that he wouldn't be the only one. And I wanted it to be fun, the kind of book I'd have checked out of that tiny library more than once. It's a thrill that I got to write the book I wanted to read as a kid, a book for me and my daughter and all of us hungry to see our stories filling the shelves.

Thanks for reading,

Acknowledgments

A few summers back, when my daughter, Lily, and I got sucked into the *Stranger Things* universe, it was fascinating for me to see her reactions to some of the more mundane oddities of the '80s, which I remember so well. The hair, the clothes, the rotary phones—every episode was a little bit like time travel for me.

I went to a religious boarding school in upstate New York in those years and I borrowed some of the campus to use here. The students in this book are all fictional creations and the situations are too, but there are glimmers of my time at school: My principal, though definitely an inspiration for Luis's, was more of a hero to me (and he never played the villain role in my life). My school was even more conservative than Luis's: there was no prom, only a dinner called "reception." The dorms and the sidewalks alike were segregated by gender. There were definitely a few guys in my school who seemingly had my number and did occasionally torment me; I have stolen some of their lines for Gordo.

Even so, the other kids made the place magical. My high school besties (Becky, Dave, Lance, Debbie, Jennie, Lisa, Deanna) were such bright lights in my life. They didn't know I was gay at the time, and I wouldn't have dared tell them (seeing how the only kid who was outed got kicked out on the spot). But all of my crew were unwavering in their love when (years later, on my own terms) I came out myself.

I didn't have a Ms. Silverthorn of my own until college, when I had several: Mary Norcliffe, who felt like a friend, and Karen Guthrie, who helped me appreciate how members of the gay community were watching out for each other during the AIDS crisis (literally the first positive thing I ever heard anyone in a school setting say about gay people).

At college, just as in high school, being outed meant an end to belonging. Delmis, Mary, Joe, and Lynn were windows into self-acceptance for me and none of them made it to graduation. I wish that was fiction. (Note to the universe: Wherever Lynn McGee is, call me.)

Happily, those experiences have led to this one, the creation of *Spin Me Right Round*. Writing this book was a joyful kind of work, and I am grateful to my "coworkers" who made sure it got to readers, especially Annie Bomke, my agent, who took the tale from first draft to submission and sale in a matter of months, and Allison Moore, who read and reread it, bringing a sharp and enthusiastic editorial eye to the manuscript.

It's been a two-year span of time from first writing to publication date and, along the way, a pandemic happened. It could have been a blue time, deprived as I was of hugs and travel and the chance to gather people at my table, but I am blessed with a constellation of friends so stellar that even Luis would be envious. Thanks to Ashley, Stacey, Jen, Amy, LeeAnna, and Kristin, who kept my heart singing. And, speaking of my heart, I am so grateful for Sari: Yay!

Above all, I am thankful that I have had the fantastical journey of raising my daughter. Being a single parent (like Ma Elena and my own mom) can be a lot of work and worry, but it's made easier when your kid is a gem. Lily has been a pretty swell companion during the pandemic, and the rest of the time, too. I'm thrilled to have written a book she'll dig at least half as much as she likes *Stranger Things*.

About the Author

David Valdes is the lauded author of memoirs *Homo Domesticus*, *A Little Fruitcake*, *The Rhinestone Sisterhood* and more than a dozen produced plays. A former *Boston Globe* columnist and HuffPost blogger whose posts have received over a million hits, he has also written an advice column for Medium, and was recently featured in the *New York Times*'s Modern Love column. He teaches writing at Boston Conservatory and Tufts. David lives in the Boston area, USA, with his daughter.

davidvaldeswrites.com
Twitter: @dvaldestweets
Instagram: @davidvaldeswrites
Facebook: davidvaldeswriter